SUSAN VALLES

ZIMRAH

DREAM WALKER

SUSAN VALLES

ZIMRAH
DREAM WALKER

Published by Place of Rest Music, Raleigh, NC

ISBN 978-0-9969050-2-2
Library of Congress No. 2018946344

Zimrah Dream Walker is a work of fiction. Where real people, events, establishments, organizations, or locals appear, they are used fictitiously. All other elements of the novel are drawn from the authors imagination.

Edited by Yvonne Perry Consulting Services, LLC, Raleigh, NC
and Erynn Newman, A Little Red Ink

Cover design by Damonza.com

This book is dedicated to my beloved husband ANTONIO VALLES for tangibly teaching me of the healing love of Yeshua.

Contents

Foreword

We need more stories like Zimrah Dream Walker, because we need more Zimrahs in the world today. Women & men who are sold out to our Lord Jesus Christ and who want everything our loving Heavenly Father has in store. People who pursue intimacy with God not just as something they need, but really desperately want. We need more children of God who walk in His love and fear, completely dependent on the Holy Spirit to guide them in every circumstance. This book will inspire you to be just that.

A good story has multiple facets about it that appeals to different aspects of the reader's disposition. Some people enjoy the revelation of things unknown – perhaps even a nudge to think beyond the current boundaries of what we have been taught, or what we have chosen to accept as our limits. Others enjoy an unfolding of characters and events in a new, yet somewhat familiar way that incites a variety of emotions. Regardless of your inclination, *Zimrah, Dream Walker* will draw you in with its simplicity, while elucidating often ignored spiritual lessons in a boldly creative manner.

Oscar Wilde, in his play *A Woman of No Importance* - the title being ironically antithetical to the character of the book you are about to read - writes that every saint has a past, and every sinner has a future. Many of you will closely identify with Zimrah's intense desire to know where she came from. I, in particular, was extremely delighted by her origin story – but you will need to read it for yourself to figure out why! All of you will most certainly identify with the expectant hope Zimrah has about her future as she grows in her relationship with the One True God.

This story, however, is not just about Zimrah. It's about the people around her. The ones that love her, those that despise her, and even those that sought to destroy her. They are all part of what makes this book special. The author does a wonderful job weaving in recognizable characters into key situations while keeping the integrity of known and documented history. But mostly, this story is about a loving Heavenly Father who comes to us when we call upon His Name – and if I may speak from experience, especially when we don't know Him yet!

The songs that arise from Zimrah's soul are sweet and profound. Make up your own tunes and sing them aloud – at least that's what I did. Some of the songs have been recorded and sung by the author in her latest music CD "When Selah Runs". Go and download it from your favorite digital store and be doubly blessed.

The best part about this book is that the author has experienced the love of the eternal and gracious God that is so beautifully expressed through Zimrah's adventure. Having known Susan and her lovely family for over a decade, I have personally seen how the Lord has drawn her into deeper waters and matured her in the areas of true worship, prayer, spiritual warfare, and the prophetic. Its one thing to write a good story, it's totally another when you live it out well.

As you read through this book, keep an open mind, and an open heart. Be prepared for a multi-faceted adventure full of hope, joy, action, romance – and moments of revelation that will truly delight you.

Sumit Deshpande
Founder of The Dyfference, award-winning author of "The Ballad of the Traveller"

PART ONE
LINEAGE

Prologue

The One who was the Lamb stood alone on the terrace of His dwelling, which overlooked the circle of the blue earth. His hands rested lightly on the rail. He surveyed the oceans and land below Him amidst pockets of swirling white clouds. Eyes blazing like fire, He turned His attention to the billions of tiny sparks of light, like beacons, which drew Him to those distant shores.

Lightning flared on the slip of land connecting two continents, where His primary interest lay—the Holy Land, His predestined birthplace. As the rotation of the earth brought it more fully into view, a sliver of anxiety rose in His heart. But it was instantly overcome by a wave of love, deeper than any ocean He made. The Holy Land. The greatest concentration of sparks was there. They were waiting.

"The time draws nigh," the King declared, materializing at the speed of thought in response to the sliver that had risen in the heart of His Beloved Son.

The King fixed His attention on the myriad of stars in the first heaven. He read in them the giant cosmic clockwork that

He had created from the beginning to display His seasons of time.

"I know," the Lamb whispered. "I hear their songs."

The sparks of light on the earth joined with the twinkling lights above in one joyous melody.

> Glory to God in the highest heights.
> Glory to the One who was and is and is to come.
> Blessing to the One who reigns forever and ever.
> Honor and power to the Lamb who was slain.
> The One who has authority to proclaim,
> "It is finished. It is done."

Instantly, the Spirit was there beside the Lamb, adding the comfort of His presence and kindling to the fire that burned in Them All. The flame was the fire of love, love for the world They had spoken into existence. As the fire blazed brighter with the combined passion of The Three, a rumbling trembled in the heavens and the earth.

"I will go!" the Lamb declared with a sudden and decisive shout.

"I will go as well," the Spirit proclaimed like a mighty rushing wind.

"Let Us go and bring them back to Ourselves." The King's cry resounded in a glad wave that rippled the waters above and below. The morning stars sang together, and the Sons of God shouted for joy.

Chapter 1

A PROPHESY AND A SONG

Zimrah was a married woman now. It was hard to believe. She kept closing her eyes and opening them again, just to delight in the sight of her husband. Theophilus lay peacefully in the grass on the bank of the Leontes with his strong arms behind his head and his long, lean legs stretching in front of him. He was beautiful under the shade of a wild almond tree.

He had the body of the soldier he had been, wrapped around a heart full of warmth and understanding. The years of service in the Roman army had only served to deepen his compassion and kindness.

As he looked at Zimrah, his brown eyes were bright and intense. "I love you."

The full force of his love thrilled her. It used to scare her, but now she was warmed by it. She had never felt so cherished and protected. As she brushed a lock of his cattail-colored hair behind his ear, love for him filled her heart.

"I love you too." She tucked her head in the crook of his shoulder and sighed a deep sigh of contentment.

Zimrah wished this day would never end. This complete happiness was a feeling she was discovering could be normal, in contrast to the sadness and despair of her earlier years. They had been apart for the last two of them. They were hard years, years spent battling doubt and growing in faith. Yahweh promised she would be his wife, and He had proved Himself faithful. Being married and in love still felt a little like a dream.

She brought her left hand up to lay against his chest and admired her new betrothal rings. Theophilus had presented the delicately crafted gold rings to her at the conclusion of the wedding feast only days before. His mother, Vita Servillian, had worn them until her death. It was Vita's express desire that Zimrah should have them. She was glad to be accepted by the woman who had raised such a wonderful man, even as it saddened her that they would never meet. She breathed deeply, blinking the sorrow away. Another mother lost to her.

Theophilus spoke above the almost musical sound the wind made as it blew through the leaves above them. "Tell me, Zimrah. I would know your thoughts."

The low timbre of his voice vibrated against her cheek. The sensation brought a smile to her face, but she could not speak yet. Her emotions were too strong.

He put his arm around her and kissed the top of her head as if his lips could battle whatever dark thought had assailed her.

"I was just reflecting on everything that led me to being here with you right now." Sharing what had truly saddened her would do the same to him, and she did not wish to spread her sorrow.

"Hmm. My mother warned me that the thoughts of women were sometimes kept behind many secret veils. Very well, keep your secret." Theophilus rubbed her hand with the tips of his fingers. "It has been a journey, but we're together now, and will never have to be apart again."

"For you, it was a journey indeed." She laced her fingers with his—the contrast of her amber skin next to his light bronze complexion was lovely—and lightly ran her thumb along the lines of his palm.

"Yes, but I think you have traveled farther than I." He drew his arms around her a little tighter.

They were lying on the green bank of the Leontes, gazing up at the house of Jesse and the city wall of Chasah. It was a city on a hill. The house of Jesse the Merchant—the last remaining Jewish house in a city established by Jews—where she had spent her childhood as Jesse's slave. Chasah was five miles inland from the port city of Tyre and the city where she had been brought by a caravan of traders as a baby. She had never been more than five miles from its walls.

Zimrah had traveled a hard road. She crossed from slavery to freedom, from despair to joy, from the loneliness and rejection of being an orphan to accepting the love of a father and a husband. She had traveled the road from despair over the past to hope for the future.

"And we still have a journey ahead of us."

His words surprised her. Was he reading her thoughts, or had he simply followed the path her thoughts had taken? Then she recalled they had been discussing the topic of journeys a few moments before.

By the sound of his voice, he was close to drifting off to sleep there in the shade with the sun peeking through the leaves and the sound of the Leontes flowing merrily over the rocks. She did not blame him for dozing.

"It's so peaceful here." Theophilus yawned and stretched his arms up behind his head. "It will be hard to leave this for the dusty road in two days."

"Do you think we will have any trouble at the temple without my father there?"

"We have Jesse's document of adoption. It's sealed with his signet and written up properly. Everything is in order. I don't see why they wouldn't accept it. They may charge us twice the usual rate though."

"Would they do that?" Zimrah could lay still no longer. She sat up and hugged her knees to her chest.

"They may, especially since we're not Jews ourselves." He rubbed her back. "At any rate, Jesse has given us enough to pay whatever fee they decide is fair. We would've travelled too far not too."

"It is far, but I'm excited to travel with you, alone, without my father." Zimrah turned so she could see his eyes.

"As am I."

She was destined to take this trip. Everything in her believed that on it, she would discover the truth about her parents. Although the reason for her belief made hardly any sense, Zimrah knew it was true. She *hoped* it was true.

Regardless of the lack of logic, the mystery surrounding her birth would be solved in Jerusalem. Nina, Jesse's servant and the woman who had raised her, would say her hope was faith and needed little explanation.

A song drifted to the forefront of her mind. It was a song she had heard Yahweh singing over her ever since she had learned to recognize His voice. The first time she had heard it was in a dream, sung by a young man beside a river. She dreamt of this man often, yet his face she could never see. She looked out over the water and sang.

"Daughter Mine,
Fair and fine,
Light in the morning sun.
Follow the river, come.
Come to Me,
Sing to Me,
Before the day is done."

"We can follow the river." Theophilus picked up a stone and tossed it into the water.

"What do you mean?" she asked.

"From the song. 'Follow the river.' The Leontes flows mostly east to west. Except for a curve to the north into the mountains further west from here. The river could guide us. If we follow its course and continue west when it turns north, we'll run into another river. The Jordan."

"The Jordan River runs south and empties into the Dead Sea, just west of Jerusalem. Doesn't it?" She turned her body to face him and sat up straighter. "Are you saying the rivers can take us to Jerusalem?"

"Following the two rivers isn't the most direct route. It'll take us off the safety of the Roman roads, and the terrain will be more difficult to travel." Theophilus sat up as well. "But, if we follow the rivers as your song says, we will reach Jerusalem."

"Yahweh's been showing us the way." She wasn't sure if it was a question or a statement. She lay back in the grass and gazed through the leaves up into the blue sky. "He's been singing that song to me my whole life, Theophilus."

"I know. And you sang it to me the day I asked you to marry me. Perhaps through the song, Yahweh's been showing us which path to take."

"I believe He has." Zimrah's hope solidified firmly into faith. They would follow the rivers to Jerusalem.

Chapter 2

RETURN OF AN OLD FOE

That night Zimrah lay with Theophilus beside her in the ancient watchtower that was her room in the house of Jesse. A familiar sensation wrapped around her chest and legs so tightly that she could not breathe. Zimrah lay paralyzed, unable to move, or cry out.

By the light of the moon, she could see her chamber and even Theophilus as he lay sleeping beside her. He may as well have been miles away. She tried with all her might to call out to him, but she could not reach him.

The Tormentors had returned.

Yahweh, preserve me. Her lips were moving, but no sound came. It had been years since she had been attacked in this way.

In that moment, Zimrah was a little girl again, trapped within herself, alone and afraid. All the victory from fear, all the progress she had made was a hollow triumph. For here she was again, just as powerless as she had ever been against the unseen forces that stalked her. She lay in despair until she

7

remembered the truth. The Tormentors *were* stronger. She had not a shred of power to free herself. She never did. The power came from the Most High God.

"Rest."

Yahweh spoke to her in her mind as He had always done. The single word was her first and greatest weapon against the Tormentors that had plagued her nights since she was too young to remember. Yahweh had given her many other tools for this kind of warfare. He had left weapons hidden in His word. But it was still up to her to use them.

She *had* been using them, so the only conclusion she could make was that the Tormentors had returned to test her. Calming herself and willing all the muscles in her body to relax, Zimrah did what Yahweh instructed. It was the exact opposite of what her body, aching for the pressure on her chest to release, wanted to do.

When the Tormentors first began to attack her, she fought them the only way she knew how. She struggled in panic and fear, but that only gave them greater strength. Yahweh helped her to see the truth. The Tormentors never had any real power over her, except that which she fed them by believing what they wanted her to believe.

She was powerless.

She was weak.

She would never be free.

She would die alone and afraid.

Zimrah willed her body and mind to relax. She turned all her attention from the Tormentors and fixed her thoughts on the only One who had any real power. She turned her attention to Yahweh, singing to Him in the battlefield of her mind.

The Lord is my light
and my salvation.
So why should I fear?
The Lord is my fortress,
protecting me from danger.
So why should I fear?

Yahweh's calming presence covered her like a warm blanket. Her forehead tingled as it always did when her attention turned to Him. This time though, the tightness around her chest and limbs remained. *Abba?* A little of the panic returned. *What did I do wrong? I know You are here. I feel You with me. Why is the Tormentor not gone?*

She opened her eyes to Theophilus sitting up in the bed. His face was turned to the window and the night sky.

"The morning sun has come," he said.

Zimrah awoke with a start to Theophilus's concerned face leaning over her. "Are you alright, Zimrah? You were struggling in your sleep."

It was a dream.

"What did you say?" She rubbed her eyes, unsure if she was still dreaming or if she was truly awake.

"I asked if you were alright. Did you have a nightmare?"

"No, before that, you said something about the morning sun?" Zimrah sat up, trying to shake the disorientation that clung to her like a wet robe in the darkness.

"What? I said nothing about the sun."

Even in the dim light of the crescent moon shining through the window, she could see the concern darkening his features. "It felt so real. I must have dreamed it. I saw you sit up in bed and look out the window a moment before I woke up. I thought you said, 'The morning sun has come.'"

Theophilus continued to gaze at her with his forehead furrowed into little triangles. "Zimrah, before I met you, when you were just stories that Jesse told me on the *Cygnus*, I loved you."

Not for the first time, she pictured Theophilus and Jesse on the deck of a wave-tossed merchant vessel. What stories had Jesse told him?

"I wanted to protect you even then." He ran a hand through his hair and took her hand. "When you agreed to marry me, my feelings only grew. Now you're my wife, and the desire to keep you safe is even greater. We're going on this journey together, and I'm aware that the route we've chosen will probably be dangerous. I am fully prepared to do what I must to protect you. But I am also aware that there are things you battle, against which all my training is useless. How can I protect you from these things? I cannot fight what I cannot see. In truth, I think if I did have to fight the battles you do, I would not have remained as strong as you have for so long."

"Theophilus—"

He put a finger to her lips. "Remember *your* training. I don't know much yet about this God you love. I do know enough to know that even though Yahweh allows these

Tormentors to plague your nights, He is good. He has trained you to fight. He has not left you defenseless."

Her husband's admonition sounded like the voice of Yahweh to her ears. His words raised the hairs on her arms.

"Use your weapons," Yahweh whispered in her mind. *"The morning sun has come."*

The morning sun. The words were from the song Yahweh sang to her all her life.

Daughter mine
Fair and fine
Light in the morning sun

Why was He repeating them now? As she settled into Theophilus's arms, the loving hand of Yahweh caused her forehead to tingle. His touch reminded her that He was there. She had nothing to fear. Yahweh's song floated through her mind as she fell into a deep, torment-free sleep.

***

Theophilus lay beside Zimrah. She slept peacefully in his arms, but try as he might, he could not find peace. She had tried to explain to him about the Tormentors. Just hearing about them caused his hardened soldier's heart to quake. He was used to battles he could win with the sword and with cunning. He had not the training for battling spirits and demons.

He looked around the room. Every shadow seemed ominous, every sound the approach of an unseen foe. Then his mind filled with doubts. They were leaving in the morning. Was he right to suggest they follow the rivers? It was not the wisest route. What if he couldn't protect her? What if she was lost to him again?

Stop it, Theo! Pull it together. He took a deep breath and slid from Zimrah's side. Donning his tunic in the dark, he padded on bare feet from the room and to the courtyard below.

It felt good to be in the open air.

Theophilus took up the sword he had left in its scabbard leaning against the courtyard wall and belted it on his right hip. He put his left foot and hip forward, bent his knee, and drew the gladius with his right hand. Combat stance.

One, two, three, four.

He ran the forms slowly at first. His muscles moving perfectly without much conscious thought.

Cut, thrust, block, thrust.

Half an hour later, he was drenched in sweat, but his mind was clear. He washed, climbed the stairs, and lay down beside his wife. In less than a minute, just as the sun was lightening the eastern sky, he fell asleep.

***

Zimrah awoke when Theophilus returned to bed, but only for a moment. She settled into his arms and let herself drift back to sleep.

She was standing beside the sparkling clear water of a river. Before her there were stairs, skillfully cut from single large stones and placed into the side of a hill long, long ago. They looked like they had always been there, the rock worn smooth by time and many sandaled feet. She climbed them—they must have been made for giants—and counted as she climbed. There were twelve.

At the top there was an ornately decorated archway whose scale matched the steps. It stood by itself with no wall attached, as if it had crumbled with the passing of years beyond count, leaving only the archway as a single testament to some forgotten city. The gate remained, shut with a heavy wooden door. Reaching up for the latch, she pushed, but the door was locked.

Then she heard the familiar voice of a young man.

"I Am the key."

Zimrah awoke.

***

In Heaven's Courtroom, the beast ground his teeth and tried hard to keep them from showing. The Almighty was sitting on the throne made of twelve precious stones. Court was now in session. The Herald's trumpet ended its resounding against the marble floor and columns. All waited in anticipation for the hearing to begin.

Warriors sat at the table with The One, outside of time, and the beast sat in his place on the left of the throne.

"Where have you come from?" the Almighty asked as if He did not already know.

"I was roaming the earth, going back and forth on it." The beast's reply was the same every time. His words dripped like honey.

"Have you considered my servant Zimrah? She loves Me and shuns evil. She is walking in My ways as I have instructed her."

This rankled the hairs on the beast's head, and the Almighty knew it! It seemed to bring Him such pleasure to remind the beast of His faithful ones. Zimrah had won the victory against Fear—that worm that dared call himself a dark one. The beast remembered it well enough, reminders or no. He could foresee where her obedience was leading and desired to thwart it if he could.

"Does she love You for no reason?" The beast took only a moment to think. "You have protected her on the battlefield with these warriors." He gestured to the table on his right. "Remove them, and we will see how strong she is without Your swords fighting for her."

"Very well. They will not lift a finger against you unless she herself gives them command."

The beast left Court with a satisfied grin. He rubbed his hands together in glee, recalling the warriors, straight-backed and composed, their swords and armor disappearing from their bodies. Finally, a win! Zimrah possessed little knowledge of her authority, much less the wherewithal to command angels! This was going to be too easy.

The One and the Father shared a knowing look as the Spirit danced around them. Zimrah's training had only just begun.

Chapter 3

A SECRET AND A BLESSING

Zimrah sat on colorful cushions at the low table surrounded by columns and arches. Under the arches and built into the walls were niches filled with pottery jars of flour and olive oil and stacks of platters, bowls, and cups. There were bags of spices and colorful fruits and vegetables of every kind. Bunches of herbs hung in every corner of the room and in many of the archways, lending their sweet aromas to the air. Theophilus and the two people who were the only family she had ever known sat with her.

Jesse's brown eyes were moist. Nina smiled bravely, causing the wrinkles around her eyes to bunch together. They were mother and father to her, having raised Zimrah from infancy to adulthood. They had sheltered and protected her—teaching her not only the things she needed to know for daily life, but also how to read and to write. This was far beyond what was acceptable, or even legal, for the slave girl she had been.

Zimrah was leaving them for the first time. Their bags were packed and this was their last meal together before she and Theophilus began their journey south.

"I will not be gone that long." The promise was for her own benefit as much as theirs.

"I will bring her back safely." Theophilus nodded solemnly at Jesse and gave Nina a wink from across the table.

"I know you will, Theophilus. I have entrusted my daughter well." Jesse took her hand and held it for a moment before letting her go. "We're going to miss you, Zimrah."

Jesse seemed to be holding back his emotions, but she could see his heart was breaking. Was it sadness or regret? She was the daughter he had always longed for. Now she was grown, and the time had come for her to leave. Was he thinking of all the wasted time as she was?

"Remember, Abba, the reason we are leaving is to make my adoption legal. When I return, I'll officially be your daughter. We can make up for lost time then."

"I wish I could make the trip with you, but that incident a few weeks ago has caused some conflict in the trade routes out of Tyre. I need to stay and keep an eye on my ships."

"This house won't be the same, Zimrah," Nina said. "What will I do without you? Who will I have to talk to?" She gave Jesse an exaggerated glare.

"Talk to her, Abba. *Please!*" Zimrah said dramatically.

"Will she leave me any choice?" Jesse asked.

Nina slapped him on the arm. An outsider may have found this behavior between master and servant strange, but Jesse's household had never been typical. Zimrah cherished the tender moment before returning to her plate of food.

Breakfast was simple—olives, cucumber, and tomato, cut small and mixed together with olive oil, warm flatbread, and tea made with herbs from Nina's garden.

After a moment of comfortable silence, Zimrah's thoughts returned to the journey ahead. "I cannot wait to see Jerusalem. Oh, and the Temple!" She put her cup down to grasp Jesse's shoulder. "I have longed to be there, where the presence of Yahweh dwells. I have read about it over and over in the scrolls, to walk where they walked! Imagine, Abba! King David and King Solomon! I think it will feel like a dream when I see it for the first time with my own eyes."

"It is not the same Temple that Solomon built." The corner of Jesse's mouth tipped up at her excitement. "It's been destroyed and rebuilt twice since then. Herod's temple is a marvel though. You will be able to see it from a great distance. It sits on the highest point of Mount Moriah." His smile grew forced. "I pray you will find what you're looking for."

"I feel such expectation, like all my questions will be answered there." Zimrah was unused to sharing her deepest feelings. Her next words came out with some hesitation. "I know it makes little sense. Yet, I believe I'll discover the mystery of where I came from and who my parents were."

"It doesn't have to make sense, Zimrah," Nina said. "Faith is often unexplainable. What does it hurt to believe?"

Zimrah leaned over the table to squeeze Nina's hand. Jesse's expression changed though, when she spoke of her questions being answered. He seemed lost in thought. His brows drew close together, and there was moisture in his eyes when he looked at her again. He gripped her wrist.

"What is it, Jesse?" Theophilus asked.

"Zimrah, there is a story I have waited a very long time to tell you." His expression was grave. His eyes pleaded for mercy before his story even began.

"When you were little, I thought you were too young to have to bear the burden." His words came out in a flood, and his grip on her wrist tightened. "As you grew, I simply did not have the heart to tell you the truth. Please forgive me for keeping this from you. I wanted to tell you so many times."

The intensity of his request sent Zimrah's stomach flipping. "Whatever it is, Abba, of course I forgive you. I know you have only done what you thought was best for me."

Jesse took a deep breath. "It concerns a part of the story of how I found you. I've never spoken of it to anyone. I want you to know it now, before you begin this journey."

The room was so silent, she could hear the birds singing outside the open door. All waited expectantly for what Jesse had to say.

Zimrah's thoughts swirled in expectation. There was a time, not so long ago, when she was tempted to believe she was Jesse's illegitimate daughter. Everyone else in Chasah seemed to believe so. He treated her better than any master was expected to treat a slave, and Zimrah's features were unlike anything anyone had ever seen. Everyone assumed she must be the offspring of some foreign woman Jesse had met on one of his trading voyages.

He adamantly assured her, and everyone else, that he had indeed bought her from traders. Zimrah had believed him. Although now, as she sat waiting for whatever truth he had kept from her, she braced herself for the possibility that the rumors were true after all.

"I've told you many times about that day I found you," Jesse said. "How I followed the caravan all the way to the center of the city. The part I have not spoken to a soul until now was that when I picked you up and saw how young you were, I asked the traders how you came to be in their possession without your mother. How had you survived so long without her?"

Nina gasped and then covered her mouth with her hand. Water clouded Zimrah's vision. Tightness gripped her throat and chest as the full import of what he was saying struck her.

"The traders told of their trip on the road between Tyre and Caesarea," Jesse said. "They turned north on the road to Chasah and had to halt their trek because of a sick slave. While they were stopped, they let their donkeys loose to graze, and one of them disturbed a snake hidden in the tall grass. The donkey bolted off the road and into the trees."

Jesse paused to take a breath. Zimrah could not tell whether he did so for dramatic effect—he was a wonderful storyteller— or because he was anxious over what he was about to reveal.

"The man who went after the frightened animal found a beautiful woman lying in a glen about a hundred paces from the road. He described her as a foreign woman, the like of which he had never seen, with dark skin and straight, black hair. He thought her an apparition or a vision from the gods until he heard the distinct cries of the newborn in her arms. When he ventured closer, he saw that she had given birth some days before, and the birth did not go well. By the look of her face, he knew the truth. The woman was dying.

"The man imagined she had used all her strength to keep the baby alive. How long she had lain there and how the wild animals had not found her, he did not know. When he knelt beside her, the trader thought she might have already died, until she opened her eyes and grabbed his arm. With her last breath she said only, 'Her name is Zimrah.'"

Theophilus put a comforting hand on her back as tears streamed from Zimrah's eyes. Doubt over rumors forgotten, all she could think of in that moment was that her name had come from her mother. Zimrah now had some knowledge of the woman whose blood she shared, where she had nothing a few moments before.

Her mother had given her a name.

"Oh Zimrah, I am so sorry to have kept this from you. You struggled with so much when you were younger, I didn't have the heart to add this burden to your shoulders. I was away so much, and when I was home, it never felt like the right time." Jesse bowed his head in remorse. "I wanted to tell you so many times. I almost did the day when the elders of Chasah rejected your adoption."

Jesse covered the top of his head with his hand. "Almighty God, forgive me! I love you Zimrah, as much as I would if you *were* my own flesh. I'm sorry I have not always shown you the love you deserve. I hope you can forgive me. Can you forgive me for what I've done?"

"Forgive you? Abba, I want to thank you!" Zimrah took his hand in both of hers, smiling through her tears. "I always thought that *you* named me. How wonderful to know that my name came from my mother! Whenever I wondered about her before, thought of who she was or what she was like, there was only empty space. I had no base for even the slightest imaginings. Now I have something. Someone saw her! She was dark like me. She loved me and gave her life to save mine. She didn't give me up or throw me away or sell me. She loved me!"

Zimrah broke into sobs, unsure whether they were from joy in the truth that her mother had loved her or the crushing grief over her loss.

In a heartbeat, Nina was up and encircling Zimrah in a teary embrace. Theophilus held them both.

"I feel horrible. How could I have been so selfish?" Jesse, still holding Zimrah's hands across the table, let his tears flow unchecked into his beard. "You thought your mother didn't want you? That she sold you? I feel worse now. I thought you would be angry, disappointed in me for withholding this from you, but you're happy?"

"No, Abba. I am grateful." When Nina and Theophilus released her enough to do so, she reached up, put a hand on his cheek, and wiped his tears.

"I understand why you didn't tell me. You know the pain of death. I know you still feel it deeply. You could not save your own daughter from dying, so you saved me. You desired only to protect me for as long as possible from suffering the same heartache you had. You've known all along that we had this one thing in common. You lost your wife, and I lost my mother. But you gained a daughter, and I a father. Yahweh is merciful. His unfailing love continues to every generation."

Zimrah moved from her seat to take Jesse in her arms. Compassion and love overwhelmed her heart. "I love you, Abba."

"Listen to me, Daughter. Listen to the father who loves you." He pulled away to hold her at arm's reach. "You are the child who was promised to me, the one chosen by God." He began with such great solemnity that Theophilus and Nina sat back on their cushions.

"Zimrah, my daughter, you are wise beyond your years. Like a lioness, you crouch in the tall grass, waiting to surprise all who have overlooked you. You've been taught compassion, patience, and love by adversity's hand. It has not broken you but made you strong. You are safe in the hands of Yahweh. Your voice is His bow, His words the arrow that will pierce the heart of your enemies. The morning sun is rising, and you will bask in its warmth. There will be a time of mourning. Yet after the day of darkness, you will sing."

"May the Lord bless you and keep you. The Lord make His face to shine on you and be gracious to you. May the Lord turn His face toward you and give you peace." Jesse spoke the Father's blessing in Hebrew, taking her face in his hands and kissing the tears from one of her cheeks and then the other. She couldn't think any other more appropriate goodbye.

Chapter 4

AN UNSETTLING BEGINNING

Zimrah and Theophilus left the ancient city of Kadesh, a trading outpost, in the predawn hours. Picking their way along the trail in the gray light turned out to be not as easy as they hoped. The river would be their guide for the rest of the journey south to Jerusalem, but first they had to get there without tripping on an exposed root or turning an ankle on a loose stone.

"Let's stop here and wait." Theophilus scratched at the back of his neck. "Whose idea was it to set out *this* early?"

"I believe your words were, 'We'll make great time.'" Zimrah was going to nudge his side with her elbow, but he grabbed it before she had the chance. Leaves rustled in the trees in front of them.

"Theo—"

"It's alright."

The morning sun slipped above the horizon as four hooded men stepped onto the gravel path, blocking their way.

Zimrah stood against her husband's side. His muscles tensed, and his sword arm moved slowly to the belt under his brown cloak.

"Bandits," Theophilus muttered under his breath. "Stay behind me."

Nausea curled through Zimrah's stomach.

The robbers glanced at each other, broad, confident smiles on thickly bearded faces, but the fourth man seemed unsure. He looked at the forest around them as if expecting the trees themselves to be watching with disapproving eyes. "I don't like this."

"There are four of us, Nathanael, and only one of him," the one who stood slightly in front of the others said. He was the tallest of the four, although the top of his head barely reached Theophilus's chin.

"He is big, grant you. But look at them! Their robes alone will sell for a fortune!" The second man raked the couple up and down with his eyes. His gaze came to rest on the gold betrothal rings on the fourth finger of Zimrah's left hand.

The third man leered at her from under thick brows. "It's the reward *under* the lady's robes I'm looking forward to."

His words tied Zimrah's stomach into knots. She dug her nails into Theophilus's shoulder. In all her years of slavery, Yahweh had protected her from the kind of "rewards" the robber intended. *Preserve me now, Oh Lord!*

***

Theophilus's jaw tightened, and he gave the one who had spoken such an intense glare that the bandit's leering smile disappeared. He took an unsteady step back.

"You would have to remove our robes before you receive any reward, and you may not like the one I have planned for you." Theophilus shifted his stance to block more of his wife's body with his. He'd sworn to protect her, knowing the path they had chosen could hold many dangers. Bandits were one of them.

The interchange only made the fourth man, the one the leader called Nathanael, look more nervous. "There's something unsettling about him." He gestured to Theophilus. "He stands like a legionnaire."

"Officer really. I command the legionnaire, but I wouldn't expect you to know the difference." Theophilus smirked.

Nathanael shook his head. "Stealing from travelers on the road is not how I anticipated funding our rebellion against the Roman Empire. Look at them! It's obvious they're Roman citizens. You hear his accent as well as I. And a legionnaire? Assaulting a member of the army is beyond foolhardy. We'll all find ourselves stripped naked with our hands and feet nailed to a tree! I don't know how I let myself get mixed up with you fools. Just let them be on their way before there's even more trouble."

"You should listen to your friend Nathanael," Theophilus raised his voice just a little as he inched to his left, forcing them to circle him and create a path to the river for Zimrah. "He seems to be the only one among you with any sense."

When her path was clear, Theophilus shrugged off his cloak and packs and drew his sword in one swift motion. The metal caught the edge of the scabbard and rang like a bell in the morning air.

Nathanael pointed a trembling finger in the direction of Theophilus's sword. "See? *See!* He carries a gladius! Didn't I tell you he was a legionnaire? And now he knows my name!" He ran off to the right into a thicket of trees.

"Officer!" Theophilus called after him.

The three remaining bandits lost their smiles and their confidence in the face of his gladius. It was a weapon designed for close combat—short, sharp, and deadly. The wise knew to fear it. The robbers glanced at each other, shifting from foot to foot, but stood their ground, drawing their own swords. Fools. They should've taken to the trees with their friend.

Theophilus bent his knees slightly, prepared for battle. He whispered to Zimrah, "Run to the river and wait for me there."

***

The Jordan River lay about a hundred feet to the left of where Zimrah stood. Now that it was light, she could make out its slowly moving currents. The water held a feeling of safety below the grove of rocks and trees.

"Theophilus—"

"Go, Zimrah." He took his eyes from the men for the first time to offer her a wink and an upturn of his lips. "I will join you shortly."

Theophilus's mischievousness disappeared as the men advanced toward them. "Go now!"

Zimrah ran as fast as she could down the steep slope, keeping her eyes on the ground in front of her.

"Yahweh! Preserve us!" she fervently prayed between ragged breaths.

The sound of grunts and clashing metal chased after her. She fought the urge to look back. How had their peaceful journey so quickly turned into a fight for their lives? How had they gotten to this place, when just the day before they had left Chasah with such joy and excitement?

Chapter 5

LIGHT IN THE MORNING SUN

Tears flowed onto Zimrah's cheeks as she reached the banks of the Jordan River. She never imagined this would be the circumstance in which she first reached them. She could no longer hear Theophilus fighting with the robbers behind her. Somehow, not hearing them was far worse than hearing them. At least then she knew Theophilus was still alive.

She sank to her knees on the sandy bank, trying to shake the images from her mind of Theophilus's body, stripped and bleeding in the middle of the gravel path. Imagining the footsteps of three men coming up behind her, Zimrah squeezed her eyes shut and grasped for the words that had always been her comfort, Yahweh's words.

There were none! In her distress, her mind could not recall any words at all. There was only the fear. She couldn't settle her mind enough to find Yahweh or His comfort. Her face fell into her hands, and she sobbed. *I knew it was all too good to be true. What if I am cursed to be alone forever? Just when I have found love and happiness, could it all be stripped away so easily?*

Zimrah may have gone on like that for many more minutes. But only one minute passed before a sound broke through the wild jumble of raw emotion flooding her mind. The most beautiful voice she had ever heard began to sing softly.

"Those who live in the shelter of the Most High God
will find rest in the shadow of the Almighty.
For this I declare of the Lord,
You alone are our refuge,
our place of safety.
You are my God,
And I trust in You.

"I know you are always with me.
I will not be shaken, for You are right beside me."

When Zimrah had no strength to sing, someone else had done so for her. Still kneeling, she raised her head from her hands. Her eyes were closed, and the first rays of the sun shone on her upturned face. The warmth of the sun had always reminded her of Yahweh's love. Just like the sun, Father Yahweh was ever there, faithful to rise each morning and dispel the darkness.

A shadow blocked the light, and she opened her eyes. Standing before her was a stranger in simple leather sandals and a sand-colored linen robe belted at the waist. By the way he was clothed, she knew he was Hebrew. The light was so brilliant behind him that she could not see the details of his face.

"Do not be afraid." His gentle tone felt familiar. "All is well."

"Was that you singing?" She was still taken with the beauty of the voice she had heard. "It was so beautiful."

The stranger did not answer. Instead, he reached down a hand to help her off her knees. Only a moment passed before Zimrah recovered enough to remember the reason she was kneeling by the river in the first place.

"Please help us. There were men in the road—bandits! My husband was fighting with them."

"I know. He is coming."

As she stood, her vision was no longer limited by the sun, and Zimrah could see his face. She had never seen him before, yet his eyes were not those of a stranger. Both his hair and beard were brown and trimmed short. His eyes were also brown, and he wore the deep complexion of one used to the rays of the sun. His smile was warm and genuine. Even though she was a woman alone in the wilderness, Zimrah was not afraid.

He had no beauty or attractiveness to draw her to him. There was only the strength in his arm as he helped her up, the compassion in his eyes, and the memory of the majestic voice that had sung for her when she could not. His song held ancient words that she recognized as King David's.

"Zimrah!" Theophilus came out of the trees a little upriver from where they stood.

"Theophilus." Zimrah breathed his name in a flood of relief. He was alive, just as the stranger said.

Zimrah ran into his arms, but he winced at her touch.

"Oh, Theophilus, you're hurt." She pulled away to see a rip in his tunic and enough blood that the fabric clung to his skin.

"Come. I have a fire." The stranger gestured to a sheltered place under the branches of a low hanging tree. "We will see to his wounds."

Theophilus glanced at the stranger and looked as if he might object, but he sucked his teeth and gripped his side instead. The pain seemed to change his mind.

Zimrah had moved under his left arm—his wounded side—to help support him, when she remembered the bandits. "What happened to the robbers?" She looked behind them as she tried to help Theophilus walk.

"They'll not be robbing anyone else anytime soon." Theophilus grimaced. His face was beginning to pale as they made their way to the fire. "I may have a few broken ribs, but you should have seen what *they* looked like."

"Did you...?" She worried for the men suddenly. It was true that there had been three of them, but Theophilus was a warrior. He was trained by the most fearsome army to ever walk the earth. Somehow, she had not remembered that before when she was so afraid for him that she couldn't even sing.

"So, the tears that mark your fair cheeks are for the bandits?" Theophilus raised his eyebrow, and his eyes twinkled with the familiar mischief despite his pain.

"Of course not." Zimrah wiped her cheeks with the corner of her headscarf and replied with some mischief of her own.

"However, now that I see you are relatively unscathed, my lord, your past occupation came to mind, and my concern shifted to the bandits."

Their banter relieved some of her fear. Her heart was only now beginning to slow to a more normal pace.

"Well, be at ease. They're breathing still." Theophilus leaned his weight a little more heavily onto her shoulder. "How unscathed I am though, is yet to be seen. The robbers may need a bit more than the convenient fire of a stranger by which to regain their strength."

He turned to the man in the tan robes. "Thank you for your hospitality."

The stranger nodded and helped Zimrah lower Theophilus to the cloak he had laid over the sand and small rocks along the Jordan.

Theophilus winced when the shorter man touched him and then groaned. "We may need the fire to close this wound." He took a deep breath, and his brow knitted together in a frown.

Zimrah cringed as understanding dawned. They were going to have to use the heated tip of his gladius to sear his torn flesh back together.

"It's not a task I'm looking forward to," Theophilus said.

"I have some supplies with me. Nina thought we might need them." Zimrah was grateful for Nina's forethought.

Theophilus removed his bloody toga to assess the damage and cursed under his breath. "I'm paying the price for neglecting my forms since we left Chasah. My muscles were stiff. I overextended a stroke and left my side undefended."

Using a clean section of the cloth, he wiped the blood from his skin and from around the wound.

"How is it? Is it bad? I have some honey and linen strips in my pack." She had been reaching for them when she stopped. "What is it?"

Theophilus was staring in confusion at his ribs. "Nothing." He looked up at her in wonder. After all the blood was wiped away, it was clear to see there was indeed no real damage done. "The pain was almost unbearable just a moment ago. Now it's gone. There's hardly a scratch. I suppose it felt worse than it was."

"How can that be? There was so much blood." Zimrah was relieved and confused at the same time. She had seen the pain in his eyes.

"I don't know. Perhaps the blood was from one of the men who attacked me." Theophilus looked from Zimrah to the man who was with them as if really seeing him for the first time and smiled. "I'm glad—relieved really, you have no idea how relieved—that we won't be needing your fire after all." He stood and extended his hand. "Forgive me. I've not even introduced myself. I'm Theophilus of Rome, and this is my wife Zimrah of Chasah."

The stranger stood with the morning sun behind him once more. As he did so, something stirred within Zimrah's heart.

"It is good to meet you as well, Theophilus and Zimrah." His smile was broad and wonderful. "I'm Yeshua, from Nazareth."

***

Rebecca stood in the heavenly courtroom with eyes only for her King. He sat, majestic beyond what her words could describe, on His throne to preside in righteousness and justice. She and Garbar, angels of the warrior class, assigned to accompany, defend, and preserve Zimrah in all her ways on the earth, stood side by side before Him.

Here in the heavens, they were allowed their armor, and the onyx and obsidian shone like liquid metal. Rebecca's diamond sword reflected the glory that came from the throne, throwing rainbow colors over the marble floor and the twelve pure white marble columns encircling the court.

The Archangel Phanuel was also in attendance to these proceedings. He stood behind her and Garbar, dwarfing them in both height and width. He shone with his own measure of glory as did the angels who were behind the throne. With all the beauty of those in attendance though, all else paled in comparison to the majesty of her beloved King.

The Herald blew the trumpet signifying Court was now in session. A hush fell over the room. All were listening for the word of the King.

"I am preparing a place for Zimrah to walk here among Us."

As the King spoke, a chair appeared in the court before them.

"I will call to her, and she will hear Me. She will obey the word of my Mouth and come up here! She will sit beside Us in these heavenly places."

The King's command rang forth in visible sound waves that flowed from heaven to earth and back to Himself at the speed *of light. When His declaration returned, a shining scroll appeared, and an unseen hand upon it wrote His words. It was the command of the Most High. His will would be done.*

The scroll then rolled itself up and floated into Rebecca's waiting hands. The warriors and archangel nodded to each other. They now had their orders.

Chapter 6

WELCOMED IN

Zimrah and Theophilus stayed with Yeshua of Nazareth for a little more than an hour before continuing on their way. They offered him a meal from the supplies they had with them, but he gracefully declined. He was there in the wilderness for a time of fasting and would not be dissuaded by food or drink.

During the time by the fire, while the men spoke of the conditions of the road ahead, Zimrah dozed on Yeshua's cloak and had a dream.

She was standing beside the sparkling clear water of a river. Before her there were stairs cut into the side of a hill. The setting was so familiar, reminding her of the back stairs of Jesse's house where she used to fetch water from the Leontes. The bend of the river, the shape of the hill, all of it was reminiscent of the only home she had known. There was, however, one slight difference. The stairs were huge, as if made for a giant. Suddenly, Zimrah remembered why it felt so familiar. She had been there before—in another dream.

Climbing the steps one-by-one brought her to the top of the hill. From there she could see the beauty of the river below, water reflecting a red sky. Dark clouds veiled the sun, but yellow, gold, and orange rays revealed its location in the eastern sky. In the other direction, an ornately decorated archway, shut with a heavy gate stood alone on the hillside. Disappointment bowed her head. In the other dream, the door had been locked.

Didn't someone say there was a key? Thinking of Jesse and a dream *he* once had, her hand went to her collarbone and felt a chain resting there. It must have been there the whole time. She hadn't noticed it under her tunic and outer cloak. She pulled on the chain and there, at the end of it, was a gold key.

Zimrah unlocked the door with hurried hands. When the gate swung open, she understood why her heart had been so thrilled.

The gate led to a vast and wonderful courtyard. Enclosed on four sides by twelve towering white columns—three on each side—the courtyard was canopied by countless stars in the velvet sky. The floor was also white and looked to be made of the same iridescent material as the columns.

What drew her attention most of all was the majestic throne set in the very middle of the courtyard. It was so monumental that, like the stairs, she wondered at the size of whoever had the authority to sit there. Whoever it was must be a king. It was not just covered in precious stones—it appeared to be made of them.

A quiet solemnity pervaded the court and all its grand splendor. Whatever proceedings took place here, they were of great importance.

Zimrah had thought the courtyard empty until she noticed a female form to her right. A woman stood peacefully beside one of the columns with her arms at her sides. A thick red braid rested over her left shoulder and fell to her waist. She wore a lovely, long blue tunic and stood as if waiting to be noticed. Zimrah was drawn to her. Perhaps it was the familiar warmth shining in her eyes.

"Shalom." Her voice was low and richly timbered. "You are welcome here."

***

Zimrah opened her eyes to see water flowing steadily a few feet away. Was she still beside the Jordan River with Theophilus and Yeshua? The dream had been so vivid, she put a hand to her collar to check for a chain and key. There were none. It took her a few moments to reorient herself to her surroundings.

The river. The bandits. Theophilus's wound that was not a wound. The events of the morning came back to her, and she sat up.

Yeshua was looking at her, the warmth in his eyes reminding her of the woman she had just seen in her dream.

"You had some rest," he said.

"Yes, it must have been all the excitement." Zimrah rubbed her face with her hands. "I dreamed…"

It was on her tongue to tell them about it, yet something held her back. The wonders of the dream still lingered.

Her words could never convey the beauty of that place. Speaking of it would diminish it somehow. Walking there felt so real, so intimate. She wasn't ready to let it go. She looked at Yeshua, and he nodded as if he knew exactly what she was thinking and held no grudge against her for not wanting to speak about her dream.

"Well, we should be off. We have much ground to cover, and the day is already half gone." Theophilus stood and pulled her up to stand beside him.

He had changed from the bloody, sword-torn toga he had been wearing into the longer tunic and mantle Jesse had given him.

Zimrah was grateful for Jesse's wisdom. As they had seen with the road robbers, perhaps it wasn't a good idea for Theophilus to wear anything that suggested his origin or occupation. His accent would still give him away, but at least with his new clothing, he wouldn't immediately be recognized as Roman.

Zimrah sighed. It probably made little difference what he wore. He couldn't change the way he walked or stood. They were as much a part of him as his roasted almond colored hair.

Theophilus stood more than a head taller than the average man, and his chest was twice as broad. Her own height—she looked the average man in the forehead—as well as her dark skin, gray eyes, and foreign features drew just as much attention as his stature and bearing. Theophilus once said they made a compelling pair. Indeed, they did. They were bound to stand out in any crowd.

"Thank you, once again," Theophilus said to Yeshua, bringing her back to the moment. "We're grateful for your assistance. Are you sure we can't give you anything for your trouble?"

"It was a pleasure meeting you. I am glad your wound was not more severe." Yeshua changed the subject with an upturn of his lips.

"As am I." A slight furrowing of Theophilus's brow revealed that his mind was still not settled about the result of his encounter with the bandits.

"If you are heading south to Jerusalem, you will come across a man named John," Yeshua said. "You will not miss him as he is gathering great crowds with his teaching. Tell him you saw me and that I am well."

"We will give him the message." Theophilus gathered his packs and hoisted them over his shoulder.

Zimrah picked up hers and wondered at the name Yeshua mentioned. It was not an uncommon name, just significant. It was part of a story that Nina told along with a prophecy. They had begun to walk away when she recalled her confidence that she would learn more of her origins.

On impulse she turned back to Yeshua. "Excuse me for asking, but is this John, by chance, the son of Zechariah the priest?"

"Indeed, he is. You have heard of him?" Yeshua smiled, raising his voice a little to cover the widening distance between them.

"Yes, I have! Shalom." She spoke the Jewish farewell with excitement bubbling within her.

Seven years before she was born, the priest Zechariah—whose wife bore him a son named John—spoke a prophesy to Jesse and his wife Aliza. They had no children, and the prophesy spoke of a daughter who was to come. Zimrah was that daughter.

Yeshua stood on the bank of the Jordan and waved. "Shalom! Peace be to you as well, my friends! I hope we will meet again."

Chapter 7
BESIDE QUIET WATERS

Zimrah's heart was racing, and she breathed a silent prayer of thanksgiving. *Thank you, Yahweh. You are guiding our steps.*

They followed the river south, obeying the instructions Yahweh had been singing to her since she was only a girl. When the bandits crossed their path, she'd been terrified. She thought they'd stepped outside of Yahweh's protection. How could bandits be part of His will? But they were part of His plan all along. The bandits had led them to Yeshua. Without them, they might have walked right by him. They may not have spoken to him at all.

Yeshua knew John, the son of Zechariah the priest. He had even told them how to find him. Right here, at the beginning of their journey, Yahweh was extending His kindness. He was showing her that she was exactly where she was supposed to be, exactly when she was supposed to be there.

Through the song and now the prophecy, Yahweh was speaking. Her faith bolstered, Zimrah took these sign posts as a clear indication that Yahweh was with her just as He promised. She was on her way to Jerusalem, the Holy City, for much more than formalizing her adoption. They were in Yahweh's hands, and her heart was glad!

Zimrah found this and many other reasons for praise around every bend of the river. The beauty of Jehovah was all around her. It swayed in the trees and shouted from the rocks and hills. She couldn't help but sing. Her voice echoed off stone and boulder, water, and sometimes close valley walls. A song came to her as they walked.

> "You are leading me somewhere,
> to places I'd never go.
> You are preparing a place for me,
> a place that I can call home.
>
> "You lead me beside quiet waters.
> You lead me to quiet streams.
> You guide me along the right pathway for my life,
> to strength and rest.
>
> "Those who wait upon the Lord
> will renew their strength.
> We will soar
> on eagles' wings.
> We will run and not grow weary.
> We will walk and not faint.

"You lead me beside quiet waters.
You lead me to quiet streams.
You guide me along the right pathway for my life,
to strength and rest.

"I will fly, fly, fly.
Fly away home."

The Jordan River Valley was breathtaking. Well below sea level, the river collected all the water of the region into itself. Its headwaters stemmed from three springs that emerged from the feet of Mount Hermon. Zimrah turned to the north and saw the great snow topped mountain, like an old companion that had been there her whole life. It was a comforting presence at her back as they travelled though unfamiliar territory.

The river appeared to be collecting not only water, but also every shade of green imaginable. There was the deep evergreen of pines and fir trees, the lighter green of olive and poplar, and the bright, almost yellow shades of maples and willow. New shoots of green reed grasses and the brown fuzzy heads of cattails waved to them as they passed by. These and many other kinds of plants grew along the Jordan's well-watered banks.

The river exploded with life among the camel-colored sands, copper boulders, and charcoal mountain ridges of the much more arid Jordanian highlands. Birds of every hue added splashes of color to the dance of beauty. Splendor moved with the melody of wind and water in the sunlight.

"It is very beautiful here," Theophilus said.

A particularly lovely bend of the Jordan created a crescent shaped pool that reflected the sunlight in a million diamond sparks of light. The hills rose up in tans and browns behind the pool of green and blue.

His eyes moved from the landscape to his wife, and he paused to take her in his arms. "And the river too." He breathed in her ear, causing shivers to run down her back.

She pulled away to see the sparkle in his brown eyes. "I love you, Theophilus. I *was* afraid, you know, when those men attacked. When I saw all that blood..."

She cut off the words before they could be spoken and searched his handsome face instead. "Were you afraid?"

"I *was* afraid." He matched her tone. Did he need her reassurances as much as she needed his?

"Every time I draw my sword, I'm afraid, Zimrah. I fear not for myself. War trained that kind of reaction from me. I fear for what I might do to others." His voice was low and full of emotion. His expression was grave. "I entered the army at fifteen. My father thought it would be good for me. In truth, I was excited. I was grateful to be away from home and all the silence there."

A redheaded duck flew from the water into the sky. He followed it with his eyes. "During my training, I learned well and moved up through the ranks quickly. I was good with a sword and bow, kept my head. I was just as good on a horse and could lead men. It meant I was often sent to quell skirmishes in the borderlands. I've seen enough death, and too much by my own hand. If I was not a patrician's son, and my father had not the means to pay Emperor Tiberius, he would not have released me until I'd given all my youth and strength to the empire. I would be there still."

Zimrah held him tighter, wishing her love could undo the sorrow in his eyes. He rarely spoke of his time in the army and what he had experienced during his commission. That he was doing so now was precious to her. With all he had seen and done, she had often wondered how he had remained so full of optimism and love.

"I love you." She lowered her cheek to rest on his chest. His heart beat a deep bass rhythm in her ear. Zimrah closed her eyes, relishing the feel of his arms. *Thank you, Yahweh, for blessing me with such a husband as this.*

"I was afraid for you too, you know. It was why I sent you to the river. I feared for your safety. More than that, though, I feared what you would see. Men fighting other men, the blood and the violence...Watching that changes you." He sighed deeply.

"Here in Judea, people lead simple lives away from the endless thirst for entertainment, away from the Colosseum and all that comes with it. Wine, physical pleasures, comforts, and social status—it all means nothing here. There is purity in your innocence, Zimrah. I would not want to see you lose that." He let go of her to pace the grassy riverbank.

"Romans. We grow up in the shade of the Colosseum. The gladiator fights began long ago as part of funeral ceremonies. We believed the blood appeased our gods, helped to repay the debt one owed. Now, they are only spectacles to appease the mob."

***

Theophilus was no longer standing beside the Jordan River. He was a child of eight years, visiting the Colosseum for the first time. Back on the day his innocence was lost. He smelled again the mix of cooking meat and spices sold by vendors outside. He saw the women crowded around stalls selling jewelry dipped in gladiator blood.

Inside was worse. He willed away the memories of what he had seen that day. No matter how tightly he shut his eyes, the images remained. He recalled the faces of the condemned slaves ripped apart by ravenous dogs. The color of the sand that soaked up their blood was etched in his memory, just as how the final gladiator match was won. One of the gladiators had stabbed the other in the neck and through the collarbones with a long-sword. He had heard the dying man's gurgled screams for weeks in his dreams.

"Violence seems to be bred into our bones." He let the river, the trees, and the hills beyond root him in the serenity of the present again. "The crowds scream for it, and there's never enough. My soul finds rest in this land—in Yahweh's land, and with you."

Theophilus closed the distance between them and held his wife close. They stood that way for a moment with only the sound of the birds and the river in their ears.

"I'm aware that I have little control over what may come for us on this journey. If we find ourselves in another dangerous situation and you cannot flee, close your eyes. Shut them tight. Do you hear?"

Theophilus held her by the shoulders with such intensity, Zimrah answered right away, "Yes, my lord. I will. I promise."

At her assurance, his tension disappeared. His brow smoothed, and he loosened the grip on her shoulders. He brought his forehead down to touch hers and breathed in her scent. Despite the days' travel, she still smelled of lavender and almond oil, grown and processed in the courtyard of her home. Theophilus let the scent wash his soul clean.

Chapter 8

SEATED IN HEAVENLY PLACES

As they continued on their way, Zimrah thought about what Theophilus said about his past. She could not help but be grateful for everything Yahweh had done to rescue her from hers. She could have easily ended up in Rome or anywhere else. Instead she had been raised in Chasah, a City of Refuge. She had been isolated and protected from things that other slaves had not. The hand of Yahweh in her simple life did not escape her notice.

Even though living in Chasah had sometimes been hard, and she had daydreamed of the outside world, she had been kept safe from much of its ugliness. Even as Jesse's slave, Zimrah had been treated as a daughter and kept pure for her husband—for Theophilus, the man she loved.

Thank You, Abba. She prayed as a steep section of bank forced them to wade in the shallow water. She removed her sandals first to not soften the leather. *Allow Theophilus to hear Your voice speaking through this land and its people so he can know beyond all doubt that he belongs to You. Heal him of his past, and give him hope for the future.*

Among all the life and beauty around them, people were few until they reached the more populated region around the Sea of Galilee. There were many towns and cities gathered on the hilltops around its fresh waters. Chorazin, Capernaum, and Magdala hugged the western side of the sea while Bethsaida and Gennesaret ringed the eastern side.

Just as Yeshua said, along the Jordan River near the northernmost tip of the Sea of Galilee, they began to hear talk of John. Many were calling him The Baptist. He was not hard to find as indeed, many crowds of Jews gathered to him to repent and return to the God of their ancestors.

Theophilus and Zimrah joined the tail end of a group of people going to hear him. As soon as they topped the ridge of the hill they were climbing, Zimrah was confronted with a view that took her breath away.

There below them, ringed in mountains, shined the Sea of Galilee. It was beautiful and huge! Larger than she had imagined. Mount Arbel, with its sharp face, stood tall and proud beside them. Like the commander of an ancient procession, Mount Arbel led the other mountains in an eternal march around the sea.

A flock of birds flew noisily overhead, and the clouds floated white and fluffy in the clear, blue sky. The water reflected the sky in miles of unbroken beauty.

On a grassy slope overlooking the Sea of Galilee below, many people had gathered to listen to what John was saying. People from every walk of life were present. There were men in fancy black robes, simple white robes, and hardly in any robes at all. There were families, women with children, and women without children. Young girls huddled in groups while boys chased each other up and down the slope before being called to obedience by their mothers.

Zimrah's heart beat faster. There were so many people! She *had* grown up in a small city. The only other time she had been surrounded by this many people was on the streets of Tyre. She had been small enough then for Jesse to catch her up in his arms. She remembered burying her face in his robes. Zimrah moved closer to Theophilus and wished to be that small again.

"Are you alright?"

"I had no idea there would be this many people."

Theophilus moved her to stand in front of him and smiled as she leaned back, gaining comfort from his presence behind her. "Fear of large crowds isn't uncommon. My mother also feared the mob, and with good reason. I comforted her the same way, letting her feel something familiar at her back. Close your eyes. It'll pass."

"I'll be fine as long as we stay here, behind everyone." Zimrah's chest felt tight as she thought about being in the middle of that crowd. Just the thought of the suffocating crush of all those bodies pushing against her made her heart race. Her palms began to sweat, and dampness moistened her hairline. She fought the urge to turn around and hide her face in Theophilus's chest.

The sudden fear had taken her by surprise. Anxiety was an emotion Zimrah had been accustomed to in her earlier years. There was a time when something as simple as the setting sun would cause it. The Tormentors would come during the night hours, when all was quiet, and she was alone. Whispering with their accusing voices, their cold breath on her skin. Until Yahweh came and saved her.

At the sound of His voice, the Tormentors disappeared quickly. With His own voice, He had taught Zimrah to sing His praises. When she did, all her fears disappeared. It had been years since fear like this had gripped her so strongly.

"You do not have to be afraid even now, Child. I Am with you." Yahweh broke through the fear as He had always done.

Zimrah closed her eyes, and a smile curved her lips. *Yes. Abba, You are with me right now.* She took a few deep breaths and willed her heart to still its racing.

"You know the way to My Shelter."

Her mind was filled with an image of stairs cut into a hill beside a river.

Yes. She knew the way.

"Come up here!"

Tipping her face to the sun's warmth, with eyes still closed, she climbed the stairs in her imagination. Zimrah saw the gate, found the key on its chain around her neck, and unlocked it just as she had done in her dream.

Inside the courtyard, she marveled again at the beauty of the court. There was the throne, surrounded by three beings shining in light. Zimrah could not have explained how, yet in that moment, she knew they were angels. One was quite larger than the others, and one of the smaller two was female. They stood as if to direct her attention to the throne and what was beside it.

A chair. The chair was much smaller than the throne, yet beautiful and ornate, decorated with gold inlays and purple amethyst stones.

"You may sit."

What she was seeing began with her imagination, but it quickly turned into a vision. One not directed by her, but by Yahweh. The Almighty had taken what she gave Him—her willingness to be with Him—and given her more. By the time Zimrah opened her eyes, the beating of her heart had slowed to its normal rhythm. She was at peace.

***

Theophilus could feel Zimrah's body relax and her breathing slow. Her eyes were closed, and her lips were slightly upturned. What was she seeing? Yahweh spoke to Zimrah often, and hearing His voice always calmed her.

Theophilus's brow furrowed with the turmoil of his own thoughts. Would Yahweh ever choose to speak to him? Would he ever hear the loving voice his wife described? She was good and kind. She'd never hurt anyone in her life. With all the blood Theophilus had shed, all the brutality he had witnessed, he feared he was unworthy of hearing the voice of God.

He rubbed her shoulders. "Better? Did He speak to you?"

"Yes, Yahweh spoke. He reminded me that He is with us. We have nothing to fear." Zimrah's face was radiant with a smile that made him catch his breath.

The love in her eyes did not escape his heart, even if his mind did not yet fully understand. She said Yahweh was with them. Both of them. Could this mean he had nothing to fear either?

"What does He sound like? Yahweh, I mean," he asked. "I've asked you before, but I don't know if I understand any better now than I did then."

People around them were beginning to sit. Zimrah followed their example, and he sat with her. "I once asked Nina almost the same thing. He sounds like your own voice, like your own thoughts inside your mind."

"Well, how do you know it's Him? How do you *really* know?"

"I don't." The wind blew her headscarf, and she adjusted it, throwing the end over her shoulder. "I suppose over time, I've learned to recognize what He sounds like, separate from my own voice, because I know Him. You know Him too."

Theophilus had to think for a moment. "When I left Rome, I was caught in a storm in the middle of the Mediterranean. I vowed then that if Yahweh would keep me alive and allow me to reach you, I would serve Him only. He heard me and answered my prayer. He proved the truth of His existence. None of the gods I knew in Rome had ever done such a thing.

He picked a red flower from the grass and brought it to his nose. "Before I met you, I thought the gods vile and vindictive. Yahweh is nothing like the myriad of gods my people bow to— Jupiter, Pluto, Mars, and the rest. In all the legends and stories, they are faithless and corruptible, made in the image of men. Yahweh is different, higher. He created men in His image and desires for us to be like Him—loving and kind. I do know *that* much."

"You know more than you think you do. Yahweh will show you the rest." She reached up to put a hand on his chest. "I think this journey is part of that."

Theophilus tucked the flower behind her ear. "I've heard it said that Yahweh's home is in the temple in Jerusalem. I've set my mind to the goal of getting you there. I will see the document we carry registered. Perhaps in doing so—along with loving and protecting you along the way—I can show Yahweh my devotion. I can make right all the wrongs I've done and prove myself worthy."

Zimrah opened her mouth to speak but was interrupted by a loud voice that boomed from the bottom of the hill. The noise of the crowd dimmed to silence, and everyone rose to their feet as John began to speak.

"Repent of your sins, and turn to God, for the Kingdom of Heaven has come." John's voice swept up the hill like a wave and crashed over them.

John the Baptizer was a wild man with a roll of dark hair piled on the top of his head. He was dressed in a strange, tan tunic of some kind—too bulky to be cloth—that was held in place with a belt of leather. His beard fell almost to his belt. Had the people come to see the spectacle of the man himself, or had they come to hear what he had to say?

People began to call out in response to his plea. "John, what should we do?" a male voice shouted from the middle of the throng.

"Tell us!" A female voice rose up from the front.

"How do we enter the Kingdom of Heaven?" A man standing next to Theophilus surprised him by shouting the question.

"Prove by the way you live that you have turned away from your sins. If you have two tunics, give one to the poor. If you have food, share it with those who are hungry."

The common people called out in response.

"Yes!"

"I will!"

But not everyone in the assembly accepted John's words. At the front of the crowd, there was a sound of disapproval coming from a group of men. Looking like a flock of crows in their black robes, they stood huddled together with scowls on their faces. They wore their beards long and covered their heads with white scarves fringed with horizontal black stripes. Many tassels hung from the scarves.

John heard the murmuring and turned to face them. "You brood of snakes! Who warned you to flee the coming wrath? Don't just say to each other, 'We're safe, for we are descendants of Abraham.' That means nothing, for I tell you, God can create children of Abraham from these very stones!"

At this, Theophilus's blood pounded in his ears. This wild man in the wilderness was piercing his very soul. John's words stirred his heart and his imagination. Kingdom of Heaven? Repent? God's coming wrath? What were these? What was he saying? What quickened Theophilus's spirit the most was what John said about God creating children of Abraham from stones.

This meant there was a chance for Theophilus. The Almighty God was indeed The Creator. If He could raise up children from the very stones around them, then He could create a child of God from Theophilus's own stony heart! He heard nothing more of what John said until he called to the crowd once more.

"Come! I baptize with water those who repent of their sins and turn to God. For there is one coming, indeed who is already here, who is greater than I am—so much greater that I am not worthy even to be his slave and carry his sandals. He will baptize you in the Holy Spirit and in fire!"

Theophilus was elated! This John also thought himself unworthy. Perhaps there was hope after all!

***

Zimrah's blood galloped through her veins. What was the Baptizer talking about? Who was coming? Who would baptize in the Holy Spirit?

She had studied the scrolls and texts of Scripture. There was a Spirit of God. David himself had begged of Yahweh, "Do not banish me from Your presence, and do not take Your Holy Spirit from me!"

This Spirit would come upon people—Sampson, Samuel, David, Elisha—all these performed mighty acts of God when the Spirit rested upon them. If there was one who could baptize her in the Spirit of Yahweh, she wanted to find him! John knew of such a man. She had to reach him, to ask him where he could be found.

People throughout the crowd were moving to follow John as he made the climb down to the Jordan River. The only problem was the crushing crowd of people between them. Fear rolled in her belly just thinking of wading through that crowd. *Yahweh preserve me!*

Then, to her amazement, Theophilus said, "I want to go down and be baptized." There was moisture in his eyes. "I want to be a Child of Yahweh. I want to know Him as you do and hear His voice. But, I don't know how to repent as John asks."

"Oh, Theophilus!" Her fear forgotten for the moment, Zimrah reached a hand to his cheek. "You already are, my love! You already have. You hear Him because He speaks to us all. Every time you choose to love, to do what you know to be right, it is His voice inside you that you are obeying."

Tears streamed unchecked down her face. "You have repented. The day you vowed to follow Yahweh, you changed. You decided to turn from your old gods and choose to worship Him alone. Right then, you became His Child, and He became your Father. Immersion in the Jordan is like our mikveh at home. It is a symbol of a cleansing that's already happened in you."

As Zimrah was speaking, the desire for a new beginning rose up in her as well. Was that not one of the reasons for this journey, to finally put to rest the questions of her past and discover the plan Yahweh had for their future? She would not allow the fear that had always tried to keep her from the purposes of God to stop her now that she was this close.

"Come. Let's go together to be baptized. We have to give John Yeshua's message anyway." She wiped the tears from her cheeks with the hem of her headscarf and smiled.

"Zimrah, you are amazing." Theophilus took her in his arms.

His actions drew a few stares from the people around them. "What about the crowd?"

Zimrah looked down at all the people, and the dark forms of the Tormentors that she could sense around them. They taunted her, baiting her to walk into their midst so they could pounce on her as they had before. She turned to face them and leaned into Theophilus's comforting presence at her back.

She remembered what Yahweh had taught her. Closing her eyes, she calmed herself and chose to rest. She sat in the chair she had seen in her vision. When she did, the fear lost its hold and retreated.

Opening her eyes, she saw the crowd again. "I am afraid. But we will go anyway. Yahweh is with us, remember?"

Zimrah was so filled with joy, she almost didn't notice a black robed man—one of the ones John had called a snake—following them with narrow eyes. He was just one of many the Tormentors swirled heavily around, but it wasn't enough to dampen her joy.

***

"Did you hear him?"

"We are sons of Abraham! That means *nothing?*"

"How dare he?"

Unlike the others, Saul of Tarsus was unaffected by the Baptizer's rebuke. In fact, he had barely been listening.

"What do you think should be done, Saul?" One of his companions gestured rudely in the Baptizer's direction. "What would the brothers in *Tarsus* do about one such as this?"

Saul looked the other way. The question did not warrant a response. He was new to Judea, and the gibe was intended to raise his ire. Letting it would be foolhardy.

He had come all this way from Jerusalem for what? To hear the ravings of a lunatic dressed in camel skin? To be belittled by a simpleton?

What a complete waste of time.

He shook his robes, giving the scene up for lost, until the tall Gentile woman caught his gaze. Was she going down to be baptized?

"The Baptizer is immersing Gentiles?" He grabbed the sleeve of one of his fellows and pointed down the hill.

"Looks like it."

Now, that may be a cause worthy of the trip to Galilee. Saul would see what the Sanhedrin thought of that.

***

Rebecca stood on the slope with Garbar and Phanuel. The color emanating from Zimrah's spark meant that the Spirit was resting upon her. The Spirit created a bubble of light around her and Theophilus. It was the shield of faith! Dark spirits scurried like rats among the people. They either voluntarily retreated or were involuntarily thrown back when they hit the shield.

The Spirit was doing the angels' job for them. Rebecca shared a look with her companions. They minded not in the least that they could do nothing in this moment. They rejoiced, for they knew that if the Spirit was present, something of great significance was about to happen. It didn't matter that they were forbidden their swords and shields. Zimrah was using the weapon of rest. She was sitting in the chair the Father had prepared for her in the heavenly court.

The three warriors nodded at each other and moved as one into the light of the Spirit. They soaked in the strength of His glory. Rebecca had a feeling they were going to need it for what lay ahead.

A tendril of blue light, alive and obeying the will of its Master, shot out from Zimrah's spark and came to rest in Phanuel's open hand. By this, he knew what was required. He drew in close behind Zimrah and spread his mighty wings around her.

Matching her steps, he began to sing.

Chapter 9

JOY IN THE JORDAN

Zimrah raised a hand to block the glare of the sun. It hung just above the mountains in the western sky, drenching everything in gold light and long shadows, when she and Theophilus reached the water where John stood. They were the last of those who had waited faithfully for their turn to be immersed in the flowing river. They left their packs on the rocks at the river's bank and waded into the sluggish water.

John spoke to Theophilus first, and then Theophilus bent down into the water and back up again with a smile on his face. He waded back to help as Zimrah made her way across the invisible pebbles underfoot to the waist high water where John waited.

"I baptize you in water," John said.

As Zimrah immersed herself in the frigid water, the familiar tingling on her forehead told her Yahweh was with her. She held her breath and closed her eyes. As the water covered her head, she had another vision, like a waking dream.

She was in the courtyard with its white marble columns and floor. There was One standing before the throne. It was the young man she had seen often in her times with Yahweh. Light shone so brightly around him that she could not see the details of his face. Then, in his place, a lamb appeared. It had a wound on its neck, like an animal given for sacrifice.

When her head emerged from the water and she opened her eyes, the tingling on her head burned like fire. She stood and released the flame dancing within. She sang, and her voice echoed back to them off the rocks of the river valley.

> Worthy is the Lamb who was slain—
> To receive power and riches
> And wisdom and strength
> And honor and glory and blessing!

A tremor went through Zimrah's body, and she was filled with joy to the point of laughter. She did not understand what she had seen while under the water or the song given to her by Yahweh. All she knew was that she had faced her fear and acted in obedience.

The baptism was more than a symbol. She was new! Every part of her being was alive with new life. John, still supporting her with a hand on her back, laughed as well. Drops of water sparkled like diamonds on his hair and beard.

Theophilus tipped his head back and shouted to the heavens. His voice sounded like a war cry. John's disciples in the river and on the bank splashed water and danced. They were rejoicing together in the presence and love of the Almighty.

Zimrah felt such an intense sense of belonging that tears joined the river water wetting her cheeks.

Looking around at all who were gathered here, her heart was overwhelmed with gratefulness. Her eyes locked with Theophilus's. They were together in this gathering of followers, and Yahweh was with them just as He promised.

After the tears and laughter passed, John's face was still bright with joy. "What did you see while under the water?"

"How did you know?" She took the hand he offered.

"I heard the Spirit in your song." He said it like it was the most natural thing in the world.

Theophilus joined them, and she traded John's hand for his. The three waded out of the water together. It gave Zimrah time to gather her thoughts before she answered.

"I saw a courtyard where there is a large throne. I'd been there before in my dreams." She looked up at Theophilus, guilt for not sharing this with him before making her cheeks burn hot. "Standing before the throne, I saw a young man circled in light like the sun, and then a lamb given in sacrifice."

They stepped up onto the rocky bank where John's disciples waited with dry cloaks in their hands. The sun had set, and Zimrah smiled her thanks to the woman who covered her against the evening chill.

"Do you know what it means? And who is the one you spoke of who will baptize in the Holy Spirit?" she blurted, not wanting to forget the question that compelled her to the river in the first place.

John was silent for a moment, stroking his long beard. "The Lord will reveal all in His timing. I have no doubt your paths will cross soon."

Zimrah was disappointed by John's response. Although, she understood from experience that Yahweh sometimes withheld His answers for a time. He seemed to take great pleasure in revealing them in ever more inventive and exciting ways. Zimrah resigned herself to wait until understanding came. The ways of the Almighty were worth it.

"We have a message for you." Theophilus gathered their packs from where they had left them on the river bank. "On our way here, we came across a man by the river. He asked us to look for you and to let you know that he is well. His name is Yeshua of Nazareth."

"So, you have crossed paths with him already." John's answer confused her even more. "He is the very one of whom I spoke!"

John must have seen the questions burning in their eyes. He chuckled before speaking again. "Go, dry off, and then come and eat with us. Andrew here made a good catch of fish today."

He pounded the back of the man standing beside him. "We will make our camp up on the hill where we gathered this afternoon. Come and join us for the night. We will speak more then."

Chapter 10

ALL IN HIS TIMING

Zimrah and Theophilus camped that night under the stars with John and his disciples. Zimrah's forehead tingled as they shared a meal and the circumstances by which they had come to meet Yeshua. She told John of his father Zechariah's prophesy thirty years ago and the song that had them following the Jordan River.

The night was cold and she was glad for the fire and Theophilus's warm side. They sat together under a lean-to they had made with two olive branches and Theophilus's outer cloak. John sat across the fire, and the heat of it radiated between them. He did not speak until Zimrah came to the end of her tale.

"Have you noticed that both the prophecy and the song have themes of the sun?"

Zimrah and Theophilus could only stare at him blankly.

"Obviously not." John chuckled. "Recite them again if you would?"

Theophilus spoke the prophecy from memory.

"In the despair of night,
a daughter will shine like the dawn
who will lead you by the light of the sun.
Through whom you least expect,
salvation will come."

And Zimrah sang quietly.

"Daughter Mine,
fair and fine,
light in the morning sun.
Follow the river, come.
Come to Me,
sing to Me,
before the day is done.

"At the setting of the sun,
My heart is drawn by the one
who is waiting for Me.
In the safety of our secret place, she sings."

John stroked his beard again. "What if, through both the song and the prophecy, God is revealing more to you than you realize?"

The small fire crackled between them and made his face shine with a golden light. They held their breaths until he spoke again.

"I believe you have been thinking God was speaking figuratively about the sun in the sky." John gestured to the expanse of stars for emphasis. "What if He is speaking literally?"

"I do not understand." Zimrah's brow furrowed in concentration.

"You have been thinking of S-U-N, the sun in the sky, but what if it were S-O-N?"

John paused to study their faces.

"What if the emphasis was different in the prophecy my father spoke,

'A daughter will shine like the dawn.
Who will lead you?
By the light of the Son,
through whom you least expect,
salvation will come.'"

Zimrah's head was hurting. Understanding was so close, yet she could not wrap her mind around what John was saying. Which son? Whose son could Yahweh be referring to? It was a riddle she could not yet work out. And when they asked him to explain what he meant, he responded as he had before.

"The Lord will reveal all in His timing."

Later, before sleep came, they lay wrapped in Zimrah's cloak against the cool of night. Theophilus absently twisted a ringlet of Zimrah's hair between his fingers. "Did you understand any of what John was saying?" he whispered.

"No, not really." Zimrah spoke just as quietly, so her voice would not disturb the others sleeping around them. "That is often the case, I think. The prophets of old were misunderstood in their times and killed because of it. Did you see how upset those men in dark robes were today at John's teaching?"

"Yes." Theophilus pulled his wife closer. "If we come across them again, we should keep our distance. Those men—with their sweeping gestures and air of superiority—they remind me of the priests in the temples in Rome. Their religious zeal is a façade. Most crave the position only for the power it gives them over the people. I wonder if these men are like that. If so, they could be dangerous. They take advantage of the fears of those who they are supposed to serve and fiercely attack any who question their authority."

After a few moments of silence, she said, "We may not understand what John is saying now, but I believe we will later. Yahweh will reveal it to us in His time."

If Theophilus had more thoughts on the subject, he did not share them. He twisted locks of her hair until she fell into an exhausted sleep.

***

The next morning, she dreamt she was by the river again. The giant steps loomed in front of her, and this time, Zimrah did not hesitate. Not wanting to waste any of the precious time she had, she ran up the stairs, unlocked the door with the gold key, and opened the gate. There was the courtyard just as she had seen it before, its white columns and floor reflecting the glory of the throne. The chair she had sat in before was gone.

"You came back," a familiar female voice said from her right.

Zimrah turned in that direction and saw the woman in blue patiently waiting, as if in expectation of Zimrah's return.

"It is good to see you." She was beautiful, with full, upturned lips.

"It is good to see you, too." Zimrah felt just as much joy as the woman expressed. It didn't seem like she was meeting a stranger. Instead, she gazed into the eyes of an old friend.

So many questions were burning in Zimrah's heart. Which should she ask first? Urgency beat a quickening rhythm in the back of her mind.

"Please, what is this place? Why do I keep coming here? Do you know who sits on the throne? Who is the young man whose face I can never see? And what is the lamb that I saw? What does it mean?" Her words were rushed and bunched together. Time was short.

The woman laughed, like the ringing of many tiny bells. "So many questions, Little Zimrah."

Zimrah remembered Silas, her old tutor who used to say the same thing.

"You already know the answers."

"I do?" Zimrah did not believe she *did* know. There was so much truth in the woman's eyes though, she didn't think to argue with her.

"The answers don't matter as much as you think. Come with me. There is much the King would like for you to see. You are very precious to Him." She held out a hand.

Zimrah took it, surprised by the gentleness of her touch. The woman was tall and muscular, yet graceful and tender at the same time.

Suddenly, they were no longer in the court but in a field of green. A river ran beside them as they walked a worn path. The sky above was a beautiful blue, with puffy clouds floating along on a gentle breeze.

"I've been here before," Zimrah said.

"Yes, you have, and many times. This is where you first heard the Master's song, wasn't it?"

"Yes, sung by the young man! Is he here? Is he Yahweh?"

There was the ringing of tiny bells again. The woman's laughter held no scorn or arrogance. It welled up from the overflow of joy that she carried with her. "That is a question even we who dwell here do not fully understand. The answer is both yes and no."

Zimrah thought for a moment. "They are very much alike. I have seen them both here before. Sometimes I would be speaking with an older man who looks like my father Jesse, with gray in His beard, and then He would appear as the young man and answer."

"See? You know more than you think you do." Folds of the woman's dress blew like wings in the wind behind her. "The King has revealed much of Himself already. He appears in many forms to those who have learned to see."

"*Learned* to see?"

"What do you think is the purpose for the gift of imagination? Definitely not what most squander it on, the lust of the eyes and of the flesh." The woman's features darkened slightly for the first time.

She appeared to grow twice her size in a moment. For all her joy and kindness, she was not someone with whom one should trifle.

"I do not understand. Why do I come here? Is there something I must do?"

"No, Little Bird, not to do...but to *be*." The woman paused on the path to take Zimrah's hand. She was back to normal size. Her eyes were piercing, giving her words great importance.

Zimrah returned her gaze, wanting to burn whatever she would say next into her memory.

She paused only a moment. "You must go back now. All will be made clear, in His timing."

"No, wait!" The feeling of urgency came back, and Zimrah's heart beat faster. "Who are you? What is your name? Will I see you again?"

"You *will* see me again. You only have to call." She smiled. "My name is Rebecca."

Chapter 11
SURPRISED BY AN OLD FRIEND

Zimrah awoke from her dream with a start and the kiss of the morning sun on her cheeks. Theophilus stirred next to her.

"Are you alright?"

"Yes. Just a dream." Zimrah almost told him about it, yet once more, something held her back. The dream had been so real, the images so clear, she wanted to be back there. But it was a new day. Every new day brought them that much closer to Jerusalem.

After a reluctant farewell to John and his disciples, they made their way down to the glassy Sea of Galilee. The morning sun reflected off its waters and made the last of the boats—coming in from a night of fishing—harder to see. Fishermen tended their nets or hauled in the load they had caught in the dark of the predawn hours. Women washing clothes along the shore paused from their work to gaze at Zimrah and

Theophilus with quizzical expressions. They were not a sight often seen on a morning at the sea.

They were traveling on the Roman Road now and shortly came upon a city nestled snugly on the seashore. Black, volcanic stone, called basalt, formed protective walls that hedged in its buildings, including a beautiful new synagogue. It was the city of Capernaum.

Date palm, walnut, fig, and olive trees grew lush and abundant both inside and outside of the city. In many places, grape vines twisted and clung to the black walls, so thick that the stones were completely hidden beneath large, heart-shaped leaves. They walked under a shady canopy, among houses and small shops, and smiled at shopkeepers calling their wares.

"Fresh bread!"

"Date honey!"

"String of beads for your beautiful neck, daughter?"

"Wool! No better wool in all of Galilee!"

Zimrah breathed in the smell of warm flatbread and roasted fish. Her mouth watered thinking of bread dipped in spiced oil as she watched a couple of bearded men pressing olives in the square. A donkey, led by one of the men, pushed a heavy, basalt circle around and around in the press, crushing the olives beneath the stone.

***

It was not the food that caught Theophilus's attention, but the groups of soldiers. One group of young cavalrymen in particular, whose uniforms lay draped haphazardly on a nearby bush, paid more attention to the women who passed than to the horses they were supposed to be grooming. When Zimrah walked by them, they sniggered and gestured crudely behind her back.

Theophilus, following a few paces behind, half wished for his old position. Those men would learn a lesson not soon forgotten about respect. Instead, he whistled sharply between his teeth and quickly brought their attention to the gladius under his robe. The metal and the giant before them were enough to keep the young men's eyes in their heads and their minds on the task at hand.

Zimrah and Theophilus feasted on a midday meal of dates, sweet as honey, and fresh fish roasted on hot coals. They wandered in and out of brightly colored booths buying supplies for the next few days of their journey south.

"You haven't opened that pack since we left home, Theophilus," Zimrah said. "You've been carrying two, but I've only seen you storing our supplies in one. What are you carrying in this one?"

She reached for the neglected pack. He blocked her hand and planted a peck on her forehead in one smooth motion.

"Nothing with which you need concern yourself, woman. See to your own affairs." He shouldered the pack in question away and out of her reach.

A young vendor woman, who Theophilus had just given a bronze coin for a cluster of red grapes, smiled at their playfulness.

"Alright, keep your secret. I'll learn of it eventually." Zimrah turned to appreciate the sights and smells around her. "It is so beautiful here. I wish we could stay longer."

"Not if you wish to reach Jerusalem before Sabbath."

Theophilus followed her lead, enjoying the peace of everyday life in this city. A group of boys were playing with a ball in a grassy open space along the road. Mothers chatted in groups, carrying baskets or young ones in their arms. Old men told stories in doorways, and young men studied from scrolls. Staying a little longer in this city may not have been such a bad idea. Theophilus smiled at his wife, hooking his thumbs into the strap of his leather satchel. His shoulders relaxed and there was a lightness in his step until he noticed a large man behind her, walking purposefully toward them. His guard went up for a moment, before he realized he knew the man.

"Domitian!" Theophilus was beyond pleased to see his old friend. He clasped first his arm and then his shoulder, giving them both a hearty shake.

***

Zimrah stowed the cluster of grapes Theophilus had handed her and regarded the man he greeted so warmly. A wide grin stretched across Domitian's beardless face. He was dressed in a belted toga and leather sandals—in the Roman style—and wore a Judean cloak over his shoulders. His dark hair, which was gray at the temples, was cropped short. A few age lines bunched around his eyes.

He wore confidence as easily as the clothes on his muscular frame. His straight back, powerful shoulders, and square chin only added to the air of strength he carried. By the way he smiled, and the softness in his eyes when he looked at Theophilus, the genuine affection he had for Zimrah's husband was obvious. She liked him immediately.

"I heard talk of a Roman dressed in Hebrew robes wandering the city and terrorizing the men. I never imagined it would be you, Theo! What in heaven are you doing here in Capernaum?" Domitian asked in Greek, he and Theophilus's native tongue.

"I could ask the same of you!" Theophilus pounded his shoulder a final time before letting him go.

"Emperor Tiberius finally gave me leave to retire." Domitian grinned. "I was centurion over this backwater corner of the empire for so long, I couldn't help but come back. I suppose I've grown accustomed to the Judean air." He gestured to the view of the sea and the mountains beyond.

Centurion. Zimrah now understood the confidence and strength he carried. It was authority.

"I know the feeling, my friend." Theophilus turned to introduce her. "Domitian, this is my wife, Zimrah, daughter of Jesse the merchant of Chasah." He brought her to stand in front of him as he spoke and rested his hands on her shoulders.

"It is a pleasure to meet you, Zimrah," he said, switching to Aramaic.

Domitian's tone when he spoke to her was very different than the one he used when addressing Theophilus. His voice lowered, and there was an appreciative, fatherly smile in his eyes. Zimrah wondered if he spoke Aramaic for her benefit, assuming she did not speak his native language.

"As it is to meet you," she replied in perfect Greek.

Domitian's eyes widened, and his smile grew.

"From Chasah? I didn't know they spoke Greek in Chasah."

"They do not, my lord. They speak Aramaic as they do here. The old ones sometimes still speak Phoenician to each other when they don't wish to be generally understood. Although, it is enough like Hebrew that I can usually follow the conversation."

Domitian's mouth tipped up on the left side, and his eyes grew bigger still, moving from her smiling face to give Theophilus a questioning look.

"You have no idea." Theophilus beamed, kissing the top of her head. "Not only can she speak all those languages, she can read and write them as well. And I won't allow her to sing for you lest she steal your heart with her voice and lyre as she stole mine."

At such praise, Zimrah turned to look up into Theophilus's gaze and smiled at him in a way that made his eyes take on a look she was growing to know and adore. Complete love.

"Well," Domitian said with a chuckle. He continued to address Zimrah in Greek and held out his arm for her to take. "You must grace my home with your intelligence and beauty. I doubt this one will have any to offer it." He gestured in Theophilus's direction.

"Come, Theophilus. I see the hand of the Almighty in our meeting today. I would like to hear of your travels and how you came to be in Capernaum." Domitian then turned his attention back to her. "I was Theophilus's commanding officer when he first enlisted in the army. Did he tell you that? I'm used to giving him orders, and he, my dear, is used to obeying them."

Zimrah gave Theophilus a backward glance and a smile that suggested, *I suppose we will not reach Jerusalem before Sabbath after all.*

Theophilus shrugged and followed as the centurion spoke excitedly.

"He was as stubborn as an ox to train at first." Domitian led them through the market, nodding or smiling greetings to almost everyone they passed. It was easy to see how well loved he was in the city.

They walked the tree-lined streets of Capernaum, past the synagogue, and on to the houses beyond. "At fifteen, he was already bigger than most. He had too much of the high-born in him though. It was nothing a year or two of sweat and discipline could not remedy, mind you."

"Sweat? Is that what that was?" Theophilus raked a hand through his hair. He was now flanking Zimrah on the left. "All this time, I thought it was tears."

"Don't interrupt, Theo. Let me tell your lovely wife my story." Domitian patted her hand in the crook of his arm. "*Sweat* and discipline. I had to beat the patrician out of him to find the soldier. Once I did though, he moved through the ranks quickly. He soon had many soldiers under his command and led them with honor and good judgment. The men loved him. Perhaps it was his knack for breaking every rule I ever taught him."

"I know that knack well." Zimrah gave Theophilus a nudge with her elbow.

Without that disregard for breaking the rules, he never would have pursued his interest in her. At the time of their meeting, she was still a slave.

"He never lost a man under his command though, and they followed him into many daring adventures. Do you recall, Theophilus, that time in Britannia? You charged your mount straight through the rebel lines on The Devil's Highway. Your men gave it not a second thought. They charged in like fools right behind you."

"I recall you thought we should hold and wait for reinforcements." Theophilus's face left no room for doubt. "The men would *not* have lasted through another snow storm."

"You should know this, Zimrah." Domitian patted her hand again. "Your husband is not very fond of snow."

The men laughed, and Zimrah smiled with them as they reminisced over more than this story. They had years of shared memories making strong the bond between them.

When they arrived at Domitian's home, she found it to be simple and comfortable. There were minimal furnishings and strong doric columns holding up the high ceilings. Domitian walked them through to a modest courtyard.

A young, dark haired manservant waited to greet them. "Welcome back, my lord."

"Thank you, Caius. Tell Felix we have guests, if you please." Domitian removed his outer cloak and handed it to Caius, then gestured for his guests to do the same.

"Welcome, my lord." Caius took them with a slight bow to Theophilus and a nod at Zimrah. "My lady."

He then hurried off to another part of the house. Zimrah couldn't help but feel welcomed by Caius's warmth. He held no fear in his eyes while his master was present. This only strengthened her growing fondness for Domitian.

About a fourth of the courtyard was a covered atrium, and Domitian led them there, inviting his guests to recline on the cushioned benches. As if on cue, Caius came back in with a pitcher and cups filled with watered wine.

While the men brought up stories of old times, Zimrah soaked in the look and feel of the house. It was the first time she had ever been in the home of a Roman. A small pool of water reflected the clouds in the center of the courtyard, and colorful wall paintings depicted landscapes of green hills and expansive skies. She especially liked the flowering clematis vines that stretched across the slats of wood crisscrossing the atrium overhead. The vines muted the sunlight and offered a pleasant aroma from little purple and white flowers. Zimrah was about to comment on the loveliness of his home when Domitian spoke first.

"So Zimrah, your father is a merchant, did you say? I have never been to Chasah myself. Are there many Easterners living there?"

Zimrah tilted her head and pulled her eyebrows together. "Easterners, my lord?"

"Your features are decidedly eastern—your high cheekbones and tone of skin. I would say one or both of your parents are of eastern origin. I find the many varied and beautiful peoples of the world intriguing. Yahweh did not have to make us so. He has made us all for His good pleasure."

Domitian sighed and sipped his wine. "We have begun to trade more heavily in the east as the water route through the Red Sea has become more utilized. Additional legions have been assigned to make sure merchants will trust this new way to their wares. That route is definitely a more convenient option than the Silk Road. I did not realize there were any Easterners living this far north though."

Domitian introduced them to Felix, the servant who had brought a plate of cheese and grapes while he was speaking.

"I've never seen any with such lightly colored eyes as yours, Zimrah." He turned to Theophilus. "Very becoming. Your wife speaks Aramaic, Greek, Phoenician, and Hebrew? It is clear to see she's been educated well, rare for a woman. She is intelligent, beautiful, and has a peaceful spirit. That is an unusual combination. Invaluable. You have done well, old friend."

Zimrah was too full of excitement to respond. She had never had anyone look at her and see anything other than a foreigner. No one could ever tell her from what foreign land her features had come. It was another piece of the mystery Yahweh was unfolding on this journey and another sign she was exactly where she should be.

Before she could gather herself enough to ask the questions that tripped over the excitement in her heart, Theophilus responded for her.

"Zimrah's father is Hebrew. She was recently adopted into his house. It is the reason we are on our way to Jerusalem, to register her adoption formally at the temple. Traders found her as a baby in the arms of her mother, who died before revealing anything but her name."

"Ah, I am sorry about your mother. But now you have two stories to tell me." Domitian's eyes were bright.

He sat enraptured as they told him Zimrah's story. Theophilus told of their meeting and betrothal, of his mother's death, and of his harrowing journey on the Mediterranean. Domitian rejoiced with them as he listened to their testimony of love and how Yahweh had shown Himself faithful time and again.

"Domitian is a God-fearing man." Caius walked in with a fresh pitcher of watered wine. "He has spent enough time in Judea to experience the God of the Hebrews for himself. The citizens and priests alike love him as he has given some of his portion, allotted by the emperor when he retired, to help build the new synagogue here in Capernaum."

Zimrah's hand went to her heart. Domitian was living proof of God's promises that Gentiles would come to know the Almighty as their own and give of their wealth to serve His people.

"I'm also a military man." Domitian took the cup Caius offered him with a nod of thanks. "I'm particularly interested in the bandits you encountered on the road between Kadesh and the Jordan. You say there were three of them?"

"Well, four." Theophilus smirked. "One retreated into the trees when he saw my gladius."

"Smart man. Only three untrained men, and you were injured? You're neglecting your forms again. You left your side undefended." Domitian teased.

Zimrah smiled. How did Domitian know?

"Have you forgotten everything I have taught you, Theo?"

"No, sir." Theophilus's smirk turned into a frown. "I *thought* I was injured. It turned out to be no more than a scratch."

"I see uncertainty in your eyes. It leads me to believe there's more to this injury than you're telling me." He let the matter fall with no further inquiry. "The Roman roads are patrolled. We don't have the manpower to deter such actions on all the outlying byways though."

Zimrah shuddered as images of what could have happened when the bandits attacked flashed through her mind. She put them aside, choosing to focus on the conversation instead.

Domitian's brow furrowed. "I cannot entirely say that I blame these bandits. Taxes grow higher and higher each year, and the people have nothing left to feed their families. What does Tiberius expect will be the result? And all to keep the voting populous of Rome pacified with gifts of grain and sand enough to cover the blood spilled in the Colosseum. *Pax Romana* indeed. It is no wonder the Jews await their Messiah with such fervor."

Domitian clapped Theophilus's shoulder, none too gently. "Forgive me, Theo. I was once idealistic about the empire to which I've given my life in service. Do not mistake me. It has brought order to a chaotic world. This old commander has just seen too much. The Empire could do better—should do better." He paused to chew a grape. "Then there is John the Baptizer preaching in the wilderness that the Messiah has come, is here now, living among us. It is no wonder the rebels are growing increasingly bold. I fear there will be consequences."

"We heard his teaching, Domitian." Theophilus filled the silence that Domitian's sobering words left in the air around them. "John's, I mean. We were even baptized by him in the Jordan."

"We heard him say nothing of the Messiah though," Zimrah said.

Messiah. It meant Savior. Deliverer. The Anointed One who would come like King David, unify the Jews and set them free forever. She had heard of his coming all her life. It was said that his kingdom would never end. "But he did speak of one who would baptize in the Holy Spirit and in fire. Everything he said was of a personal nature. He spoke nothing that would incite people to rebellion against Rome."

"Unfortunately, history has shown that our beloved Jews need little coaxing for rebellion. They expect Messiah to come and free them from oppression. They think he will arise and unite a great army and throw Rome's sandals from their necks." Domitian's face was grave. "Yet I have heard the prophecies read in the synagogue, and I wonder if when Messiah does come, he will be who they expect."

The hairs stood on the back of Zimrah's neck, and words floated to the forefront of her thoughts.

Through who you least expect,
salvation will come.

She thought on all that Yahweh had been showing her since she first began to hear His voice—the songs, dreams, prophesies, and visions. Somehow, they all fit together like pieces of a puzzle. She knew, as John suggested, that the picture they were forming was bigger than she could yet see. He was leading her somewhere.

Like the song she sang by the river, He was leading her where she would never go on her own. It was a place where all she was, all she had gone through, would make sense. All the lessons she had learned in overcoming fear, doubt, and shame, all the spiritual weapons she was still learning how to wield, were tools on her belt. They were for a purpose and not just for herself.

I do not understand, Yahweh. The men continued speaking of other things while she prayed. *Please help me to see.*

The words Rebecca spoke in her dream came back to her, that she must *learn* to see.

"All will be made clear," Yahweh whispered, bringing peace to her troubled mind. *"Do not be afraid. I Am with you."*

Domitian insisted they stay the night, and the next morning Zimrah awoke before dawn. She was sure she had been dreaming, but when she tried to recall what she dreamed, the images slipped away. What remained was the desire to be out by the shores of the Sea of Galilee. The coming dawn was drawing her there.

Slipping out of bed into the morning chill, she felt her way in the dark to her tunic and shawl. Zimrah lit the lamp beside the bed and used it to move through Domitian's house as quietly as she could. Felix was already up, preparing the morning meal.

"If I'm not back before Theophilus wakes, will you tell him I've gone to the sea?" Zimrah whispered as he helped her with her outer cloak.

"Of course, my lady."

The Sea of Galilee stretched before her like a huge, gray blanket in the predawn light. She stood on the seawall that separated its waters from the city, still cloaked in mist and quietly slumbering behind her. Gentle waves lapped the wall, and a slight breeze teased tendrils of hair from her shawl. She pulled the fabric closer and flung the edge over her shoulder absently.

The promise of the sun's warmth lay beyond the far mountains. Her body began to tremble in the cold. She wrapped her cloak tighter and listened to the voices of fishermen calling to each other from boats out on the water. Birds bobbed in the gentle swells and flew gracefully overhead, adding their songs to the coming day. All else was still.

Am I here to see Your beauty, Abba? The sky was dark blue over her head and dotted with only a few of the brightest twinkling stars. The coming dawn brightened a band of yellow in the east, causing the distant gray humps that were the mountains on the horizon to stand out in stark relief.

"There is something else I want you to see." The words rose slowly from the back of her mind. *"Watch and wait."*

Zimrah didn't have to wait very long. Her forehead tingled as the band of yellow grew brighter and brighter and then erupted with a sliver of blinding light over the tip of the mountains. Inch by inch, the sliver grew until a burning circle of white shot streaks across the now light blue sky. Obeying the command by which its course first began, the sun rose with enough promise for a new day. Warmth from its radiance kissed Zimrah's cheeks. Within its light was power enough to sustain hers as well as all life on earth.

"Do you see?"

"Yes, Lord. I see." Zimrah's heart was filled with gratitude. He always knew just how to teach her. "You are wonderful in all Your ways. You are a Mighty God! Before the sun came, there was cold and darkness. All was gray. I felt alone. When the sun rose, it brought light and beauty."

Zimrah tipped her face to receive its brilliance and closed her eyes. She did not understand fully, yet she knew Yahweh was revealing something of great significance. She was grateful for the lesson and the reminder of the warmth of His love.

"It is so beautiful here," Zimrah said, her heart overwhelmed with joy.

"This is what your heart looks like to Me right now, when you are at rest, fully trusting in Me."

The words of the Almighty brought tears to her eyes. It felt like He was standing right beside her, enjoying the beauty of all He had created.

"I have waited since eternity to be here with you in this moment, Daughter Mine."

She could do nothing but let His words wash over her and sob into her scarf. She stood watching the course of the sun until words floated from her lips.

"The sun of righteousness is rising,
rising with healing,
rising with healing.
Rising with healing in its wings."

Full of joy, Zimrah quietly sang the words of the prophet Malachi through the streets of the city all the way back to the centurion's home.

Chapter 12

TROUBLE HIDING IN THE ROCKS

After sharing a morning meal, Zimrah and Theophilus bid farewell to Domitian. He made them promise to pass his way again on their return trip. Zimrah embraced Felix and Caius in turn with pledges to stay longer next time.

"We've been so warmly welcomed and cared for." Zimrah stayed in Domitian's embrace a moment longer, holding on to his forearms. "I'm looking forward to our return. It feels wonderful to now have friends in such a beautiful city."

The couple joined a caravan of traders traveling south, leading their donkeys piled with woven rugs and thick tent cloth. The river road was patrolled, though like Domitian had said, there were not enough soldiers to deter attacks. They were still common enough that Theophilus thought it wiser to increase their numbers. The caravan they joined skirted the Sea of Galilee, bypassing the Jewish city of Magdala and the Roman city of Tiberius, built on its hill by the sea. Bypassing the cities allowed them to move quickly, and soon they were following the waters of the Jordan south once again.

They spent joyous nights out in the open with the merchants and other travelers who had joined the caravan. Men and women naturally separated, and new friends were made around bright fires. When the other women discovered they had a newly-wed among them, they were happy to fill Zimrah's ears with wise advice and funny stories of their own experiences with their husbands.

"Only listen to half of what he has to say," one of the women said.

"If he is doing most of the talking during an argument, you know he's done something wrong." another said.

"Claim a headache."

Zimrah laughed more than she could ever remember. Stories, songs, and dancing went on well into the night.

More often than not, the music was started by the women, but the men needed little coaxing. One by one, they joined the circle of dancing. The children clapped and watched their parents with wide, smiling eyes.

Zimrah missed her lyre until she discovered she was rather adept at playing a borrowed tambourine. The circlet of wood, covered tightly by animal skin on one side, was like a simple handheld drum. She had a wonderful time learning to master its rhythms.

"Try this one." A young woman beat an intricate pattern on her tambourine. Her fingers and palm were moving so fast, Zimrah was going to ask her to show her more slowly. She never got the chance.

An old trader grabbed her by the arm and pulled her into the dancing—tambourine and all—making a lighthearted game of "stealing" her from Theophilus.

Stepping to the rhythm of the hand drums, he traded her to another right before Theophilus could swoop in and come to her rescue. The game went on until Zimrah was breathless and dizzy. Hearty laughter rang in the hills.

After traveling hard all day, she looked forward to the evenings shared with new friends.

The road was not easy, filled with countless hills and valleys in a constant downward slope. The days ran into each other, one day much like the next until the road turned west and upward again after they passed the city of Jericho. Here it became much more difficult. They stopped many times on the steep road for the burdened donkeys to rest. She was very grateful for the donkeys.

"My legs are on fire." Zimrah stood at the top of a windblown hill and filled her lungs with blessed air.

"These mountains are like nothing I've ever seen." Theophilus was beside her taking in the view. "It's beautiful, but my legs are feeling every mile as well."

She gave him a nudge. "You only say that to make me feel better."

Jesse had said Jerusalem was built on a mountain, and now she saw what he meant. Nearby, a couple of young shepherd boys led their flock on the side of the hill. If not for their black heads, she might have mistaken the round sheep for stones strewn on the hillside. They had no difficulty. Four legs seemed to be much better suited for this rough terrain than two.

***

Theophilus used the rest times to note with unease the growing frequency of crags and outcrops along the road. They were perfect hiding places for robbers. Even less helpful were the ravines that had been formed by rushing rainwater coming off the highlands on which Jerusalem was built centuries before. All the waters of the Jordan and the rain of that region rushed to the Dead Sea. All this water had carved a million different places deep enough for entire legions to hide in wait. This was the most dangerous part of their journey, and all five of Theophilus's senses were on high alert.

The stretch of road from Jericho to Jerusalem was notorious for attacks. There was too much road and not enough patrols to cover it. When they entered a section with high walls on either side, the caravan stopped, and a stillness fell over the road. The hairs on the back of Theophilus's neck stood on end. No bird sang, and even the wind stopped blowing. Time seemed to slow, and he could hear the blood pulsing in his ears. It was still enough to hear pebbles shifting from their place above.

The last pebble had not stopped rolling before Theophilus bolted into action. Pushing over the burden of the donkey closest to him and startling both the animals and people in the process, he created a mass of wood and heavy tent cloth. It was a meager shield for Zimrah and the other women and children to hide behind, but at least it was something.

"Over here, get down!" The women—all except Zimrah he was proud to note—saw the reason for his actions and began to panic. A group of raiders hiding in the crags shouted a battle cry and dropped onto the road like vultures on a carcass.

The cry sent his heart racing. Heat charged into his limbs. Zimrah had time enough only for a furtive grip of his hand before the echo bounced its last.

"Keep your heads down!" Theophilus raised his voice to be heard over the women's wailing. They ran to huddle with Zimrah behind the shelter, a couple of them pulling screaming children in tow.

"It will be alright. Don't be afraid." Zimrah gathered the children close to her, rubbing a few of their backs. "Yahweh will protect us."

Fierce determination and anger swept over Theophilus in response to the children's fear. Unaccustomed to the restrictive Hebrew tunic he wore, he grabbed the hem and hiked it up into his belt. The mantle he let drop to his left arm, quickly twisting it around and around until a thick wad of cloth covered his forearm as a shield. Only then did he release his gladius from its scabbard.

Theophilus's actions were clear, smooth, and concise. Step. Turn. Strike. Stab. Not a muscle moved in excess. Not an ounce of energy was wasted, not even to bellow his own war cry. It was ingrained. The Roman legionnaires were trained to fight in silence, to unnerve their foes all the more. The affect was clear. Fear widened the eyes of every man who faced him.

Theophilus didn't think. He didn't have to. His years of training took control. Every form and set of motions practiced and calculated to produce the desired effect, to thwart the enemy and be victorious. He put everything else out of his mind. Fear, doubt, regret, concern for Zimrah—these thoughts were peripheral, insignificant to the battle at hand.

Fight. Win. Succeed. These were the only words he let into his mind. His muscles remembered well.

The other men in their party followed his lead. The traders had swords of their own and were used to the dangers of the road. The other men traveling with them had only their staffs or sections of wood to use as clubs. Even the young boys picked up stones and threw with excellent aim. The men were not defenseless, just outnumbered almost three to one. Theophilus was on the way to evening the odds.

***

"Yahweh, preserve us!" They were hopelessly outnumbered. Zimrah squeezed her eyes shut as she promised and prayed that any blood shed would not be from the man she loved or any in their party. Fear for Theophilus tempted her to watch, but she fought it and kept her eyes closed tight. Hot tears tracked lines down her cheeks.

Amidst the sound of battle and the screams of the other women, Zimrah heard a voice she knew well. Like a gentle hand on her head, it warmed the cold of fear that gripped her.

"Do not fear. I Am with you, Beloved. Remember your weapons."

With her eyes still closed, she moved to her knees, took a deep breath, and opened her mouth to sing. She had no idea *what* she would sing, but the words just came out of her.

"Fear cannot stand
in the face of Your love,
in the face of Your love.

"Through the wind and stormy sea,
You are with us.
Through the fire and deep water,
You are with us.
We will overcome.

"Fear cannot stand
in the face of Your love,
in the face of Your love."

***

The beast saw his opportunity coming and seized it. He had a contingent of dark spirits assigned to orchestrate the attack and another waiting to pounce when it began. His spirits of fear had instigated thoughts of terror among the travelers, and now the road's notorious reputation worked in his favor. The human's imaginings of doom created a wall of protection for his demons, and from there they attacked.

The beast observed the scene with glee from his throne in the air as the angelic warriors seethed, unable to do anything but watch. Even the Archangel stood immobilized. The Word of the King held them bound. They could do nothing to help, and the beast's demons knew it. They taunted the stone-faced angels just as much as they did the humans.

When Zimrah began to sing, he clenched his jaw, balled his fists, and forced a string of curses through his teeth. At every turn, this Child of God grew more and more adept at frustrating his plans. His fury burned hot as her song created an impenetrable wall of light that enlarged in pulsing waves from her heart. It demolished the walls the humans' fear had erected! Even the children ceased their delicious negative thinking to listen to the song.

The wall of light grew until it encompassed the women and children with her. Then, it circled the hated Roman and the men fighting with him. The circles of light grew in intensity and power with every note she sang, until they merged into one. Nothing could harm them now!

"Ggrraaahhh!" The beast growled in disgust. She was using the weapon of rest. He thought he had her beaten when he disarmed her angelic protection. He should have known the "Almighty" would simply change the rules. He was the biggest cheater of them all!

The beast wrinkled his nose and muttered another string of curses. If cheating was the game they were playing, he could cheat like no other. There was more than one way to get a thing done. He signaled the biggest of his demons to take command of one of the raiders and silence her song.

***

The men who attacked were not interested in the caravan's goods. They were slave traders. After their thwarted initial attack, every raider Theophilus faced kept shifting his eyes to the huddling group of women and children. He cursed under his breath. He'd unknowingly gathered them all in one place.

Zimrah.

All the thoughts Theophilus had shoved to the background came rushing back. Flashes of Zimrah smiling and laughing, images of the way her eyes changed color in the firelight, her smell, her touch—all this filled his mind. It overtook him, disrupting his battle focus. Another wave of anger rose in its place.

He slashed the man who leaped down at him with such force that two parts of him fell to the road instead of one. Remorse would come later. His eyes searched for Zimrah among the other women and found her safe for the moment. Kneeling the way she was though, her head and torso were above the barrier. She was completely exposed! The next moment Theophilus saw something else, and his heart stopped.

The biggest of the raiders had a bow with an arrow notched at the ready. The arrow was aimed straight at Zimrah's throat.

"No!"

The roar of outrage and denial erupted from his chest, echoing in the enclosed space like thunder.

***

Zimrah's eyes may have been closed, but her heart was wide open. As she sang, her body trembled in the presence of the Living God. With the eyes of her imagination, she saw a scene entirely different than the one surrounding her. She sat in the chair beside the throne in the marble courtyard. All was dark except for the light that shone from within the One who sat on the throne.

He turned her around to look out across the heavenly court, and something like a window opened up before her eyes. Through it she saw the narrow space of road where her body knelt, still within the barrier of wool. She could see Theophilus and the battle. Forces swirled around them like whirlwinds of black smoke and fire.

Suddenly, a sound filled her ears. The One who sat on the throne began to sing.

"Fear cannot stand
in the face of My love.
In My love,
you will overcome!"

The voice of The One sang behind her. The warmth of His breath filled her with sensation she could only describe as love made manifest. It melted into the skin of her back and burned like fire in her bones.

The song changed, and new words flowed from her lips.

"You have overcome!
You have overcome!
And so shall we,
Overcome!"

The images in the window began to ripple and flow too quickly for her mind to grasp. Sights, sounds, melody, and words all merged together, threatening to overwhelm her senses. She was seeing through an expanse of time. Her mind could hold on to only two things. She saw herself, an old woman in the house of Jesse, and she and Theophilus were there together.

Zimrah was so entrenched in the reality unfolding within her that she was totally unaware of anything going on around her.

***

At Theophilus's shout, the bowman's arrow slipped from his fingers and flew. Theophilus didn't think. He reacted. His gladius tore from his hands and into the chest of the bowman five yards away. He was hit and thrown back into the rocks behind him. Bone connected with stone. There was a terrible sound as his skull cracked. The man was dead, but his arrow could not be stopped.

Theophilus followed the course of the arrow with his entire being. Time itself slowed down.

No! Yahweh, please!

He did not breathe until the arrow struck the pile of wool instead of Zimrah's flesh. If it was meant to silence her singing, its purpose failed.

After seeing what happened to the bowman, the slavers—those who were left alive—lost heart and scurried back up into their warrens within the rocks. The cheers of the victorious followed them.

Zimrah stopped singing and opened her eyes. They widened at the sight of the arrow quivering in the barrier next to her and Theophilus's gladius protruding from the chest of a man nearby. Covering her mouth with her hands, she shut her eyes tight again.

Theophilus could not get to her fast enough. In a heartbeat he was at her side. He lifted her out from the barrier, breathing hard. He crushed her in a fierce embrace and breathed deep in the crook of her neck, as if her smell alone could wash away the thought of what had almost happened. If the arrow had struck a foot higher, she would have died.

"I'm sorry, Zimrah." His voice was hoarse with emotion. "I'm so sorry you had to see that. You're safe. You're safe now." He was unsure if his reassurances were for her benefit or his own. "I thought—I thought I was going to lose you too." His voice came out in a rush and broke at the end.

"I'm fine. There was nothing to fear." Zimrah was breathless. "Yahweh was here. *He* saved us! I saw our whole lives. We were together, Theophilus. We will grow old together." She held onto him just as tightly as he held her.

Theophilus did not understand what she said or what she had experienced. In that moment, the only thing that mattered to him was in his arms. She was alive.

Chapter 13

RECOGNIZED IN THE CROWD

Zimrah and a couple of the other women tended to the wounded—Nina's honey and linen strips came in handy after all—while the men pushed dead raiders into a deep ravine beside the road. Zimrah kept her eyes on her work and mourned. Raiders or no, they were still men.

The caravan continued on and reached the small town of Bethany just before sundown marked the Sabbath. Theophilus arranged a room for two nights in Bethany's only inn. Many of the priests in black robes were also taking their Sabbath there and seemed none too pleased to have to share their lodging. She was glad the Pharisees gave them a wide berth.

Most of the others they had been traveling with were people of modest means and camped outside the city with the caravan. Zimrah missed their company but was grateful for the real bed before they began their final ascent up the bustling road to Jerusalem.

A few hours past noon on the day after Sabbath, with burning legs and lungs, they climbed to the top of the backside of the Mount of Olives. Just as Jesse said, there lay Jerusalem with the temple reflecting the glory of the sun. The Holy City in all its splendor. Jerusalem, the perfection of beauty indeed.

"There it is, Theo!" Zimrah gripped his shoulder and pointed across the Kidron Valley. She was having a hard time not jumping up and down. She recited all the facts she'd studied about the city. "Did you know it was an ancient city when King David established his capital here over a thousand years ago? It was not David, but his son Solomon, who built the first, most majestic of temples. Solomon built it right here on Mount Moriah, following his father's explicit instructions."

"Why here?" Theophilus stepped out of the way as the last of their companions continued on. "Why Mount Moriah?"

"This is the mountain where Abraham was directed to sacrifice his son, Isaac, but God stopped him and gave him another sacrifice. It's where Yahweh spoke the promise to Abraham that his descendants would be as numerous as sand on the seashore, and through him all the nations of the world would be blessed. Is it not the joy of the whole earth?" Zimrah's smile was radiant.

Theophilus gathered her in his arms.

"We made it!" Her breath came heavy from the climb and from excitement. "We followed the rivers, and Yahweh brought us here safely."

"Yes, He did. It was worth every step just to see that smile." Theophilus kissed her with such passion, Zimrah was grateful the rest of their group had continued on the road. Without the others there to watch—or tease her later—she gave herself fully to his embrace.

When they parted, her heart beat wild from more than just the incline. Zimrah was intoxicated by the way he smelled, like honey and spiced milk. Their eyes locked, wordlessly making promises to be fulfilled at a later time.

Parting company with the caravan was a teary business. Her traveling companions had become friends. They had been through much together. Some of the women gave Theophilus gifts of bread, fruit, or skins of wine in thanks for saving them from the slavers. Zimrah held the children, spoiling them with coins in their hands and kisses on their cheeks. She hugged the married women she had spent most of her evenings with and promised to remember their advice.

Speaking shalom blessings where the road split at the bottom of the Kidron Valley, they took the steep, switch-backing road up and entered the Temple Mount through the Golden Gate.

The whole of the rectangular temple courtyard was built in grand scale. All of Zimrah's imaginings fell short of its actual size. Built to accommodate tens of thousands who gathered to worship, Herod had spared no expense. In scale and majesty, the temple itself rose above them, a wonder and testament to the glory of Jerusalem.

Zimrah and Theophilus made their way past Solomon's Portico and into the Court of Gentiles. This was as far as Theophilus could go into the temple grounds. From there they found the office of records and paid the fee. Jesse had done all the work for them. He'd made sure the document was prepared properly, signed, sealed, and in order, so all they had to do was hand it over to be registered by the proper official. They did so with relative ease.

It was done. Zimrah was now legally a daughter of the house of Jesse! She watched as her name was written into the genealogical scrolls. No words could describe her joy. It could only have been greater if Jesse was there to celebrate with her.

The sun was setting the western sky ablaze by the time the couple, along with a host of others, spilled from the temple grounds onto the streets of Jerusalem. The city had been much more beautiful from a distance. Hundreds of people packed narrow thoroughfares on their way out of or back into the city before nightfall. The press of bodies caused fear to flutter in Zimrah's middle, and she tightened her grip on Theophilus's arm.

"We should find lodging and get you out of these crowds. It will be dark soon." His concern for her was evident on his face. "You're not used to such hard travel, and we were longer in the temple than I expected. I'm trying to remember anything I've heard about where to find lodging in Jerusalem. I should've questioned Domitian before we left Capernaum."

Theophilus's head easily reached above the crowds of people. "I can just make out the top of the barracks of Antonia Fortress from here. It's where the Roman battalion is stationed. If I were alone, the fortress would be my destination, but I would never bring you there."

His gaze swept the street-side vendors as if considering which to ask where they might find a room for the night, when a female voice behind them called out. "Zimrah! Zimrah!"

It took her a moment to register that the name being called was her own. Her mind reacted slowly from exhaustion. Did she know anyone in this city?

A woman, veiled in blue, pushed her way through a group of chatty young women and stopped, breathless, right in front of Zimrah. She lifted a trembling hand to touch her cheek.

Zimrah stood confused and glanced at Theophilus, who looked just as confused as she. With the veil covering the lower half of the woman's face, she could tell only that she was about her own height and build. The skin of her uncovered hands and arms was smooth and a deeper brown than Zimrah's. Her almond shaped eyes were outlined in kohl and looked almost black in the fading evening light. She was clothed from head to foot in layers of blue cloth embroidered in gold, and her feet were shod in leather sandals. The sweet fragrance of balsam oil floated around her, and several silver bracelets jingled at each wrist.

"It *is* you," she whispered in a lightly accented Aramaic. "I knew it the moment I saw you."

"Forgive me, my lady," Zimrah replied in the same tongue. "How do you know my name?"

"You would not know me. Yet I know you." Her words caught in her throat, and tears flowed freely from her eyes.

"I know your name because I was there when your parents named you. I dreamed of this day for so long. I imagined what it would be like over and over." She raised a hand to brush tendrils of hair from Zimrah's cheek.

"With each passing year, I felt it more strongly, and the day has finally come. I knew you survived. Almighty God be praised! He has heard my prayers. I walked the streets of Jerusalem hoping, praying one day I would find you, and here you are!" Her bracelets jingled as she took Zimrah's hands. "No, you do not know me, but I would know you anywhere. You have her face."

The woman's words caused the hairs to stand on Zimrah's arms and a tingle to flutter at the nape of her neck.

"And mine." She dropped Zimrah's hands to slowly pull her veil away.

Zimrah gasped, and tears came unbidden into her eyes as well. She stared at the woman standing before her in open-mouthed wonder. Never before had she looked into another face so much like her own.

"My name is Sanya." She took Zimrah's hands again with great solemnity. "Your mother's name was Sejal. I am her twin sister."

Chapter 14

HALVES THAT MAKE A WHOLE

Zimrah had been wearied from the road, but now she was wide awake. Fire danced and crackled in the brazier and lit the faces of the three surrounding it. Zimrah and Theophilus had left the busy streets for richly adorned rooms above a perfume shop in Jerusalem's upper city. The pleasant aromas of cinnamon, cardamom, and myrrh permeated the air, mixing to awaken her senses.

Sanya sat close to her and held her hand, as if the physical touch assured her that Zimrah was really there. "Forgive me. I've waited so long. I don't want to let you go now that I've finally found you."

Zimrah was just as affected. Her vision blurred, and she wiped her eyes with the hem of her scarf. If she tried to speak, her heart might spill out of her chest onto the Persian rugged floor. She pressed her lips tight together and held on to Sanya's hand instead, unable to keep the tears from her eyes.

Theophilus watched them in the firelight. "How amazing are the ways of this God? What kind of God is Yahweh, who cares so much for his children as to bring you two together? But I suppose He has done no less when He brought Zimrah and I together."

Zimrah smiled at her husband, grateful he was filling the space with words when she could not.

"I have to admit, it is strange, looking at you, Sanya. I know we just met, but you look so much like my wife. The shape of your hands, the curve of your mouth and cheekbones are so familiar. But you don't share Zimrah's gray eyes."

"No, she inherited those from her father," Sanya said.

At the mention of her father, Zimrah was able to unclench her jaw enough to speak. "I have so many questions."

"As do I." Sanya finally let go of her to put water on for tea. "I knew the moment Sejal passed from this world. Those born together in the same womb sometimes share a bond, as she and I did. I felt her pain in birthing you, Zimrah, and two days later, I felt her die. I also felt her joy at the end. I knew the joy could have been for no other reason than that you had lived."

When Sanya sat down again, she let her hand run lightly over the long curls of Zimrah's hair. "Before you were born, Sejal dreamed of you many times. She knew you. Perhaps Yahweh granted her those dreams because He knew she would never live to see you grow. In her dreams, she saw you as an infant and grown into a woman as you are now. You are just as she described you to me—beautiful, with a gentle spirit."

"My mother was a dreamer? So am I." Zimrah was overcome. The familiar ache in her heart this time for the woman who bore her.

"I lost my mother recently. I miss her every day. I can't imagine never having known who she was or what she was like." Theophilus stared down at his folded hands.

"I wish I could have known her." Zimrah's voice came out in a whisper forced through the ball in her throat. "Until I met you tonight, Sanya, I had never seen anyone who looked like me. I know nothing of where my mother came from. Who was she? Who is my father? Is he still alive?" Hope stirred her to sit up straighter and take Sanya's hand.

Perhaps her father *was* alive. Perhaps he was here in Jerusalem, and Sanya could take her to him. Her hope, however, was cut short by Sanya's eyes.

"No, Zimrah. I'm so sorry. He isn't."

Zimrah couldn't hold it together any longer. She sobbed into her hands. Her whole body shook with the power of her loss.

Sanya moved close enough to put her arm around her, her body trembling as well. Her breath heaved as she stroked Zimrah's back.

When the sorrow passed, Sanya wiped her face with her scarf and gave Zimrah the other end to use as well. "I can think of no other way to ease your pain. But I can tell you about them. It's a tale I feel I was born to tell. Praise be to the Almighty God that He has given me life and breath to tell it."

"I would love that." Zimrah looked up, her belly fluttering like a caged bird.

"To the southeast, there is another great sea. East of that sea, there is a land. It is the land of the Pandyas."

Zimrah smiled at the cadence of Sanya's voice. She had been trained in storytelling, and her voice took on the cadence and tone of those skilled in the craft.

"That is where Sejal and I were born. At a very young age, we were taken from our village and groomed for the courts of kings. Sejal was taught to sing and play instruments, and I to dance. It suited us. Sejal had a calm, quiet spirit, like you Zimrah. I, well, I was much more fiery." Sanya smiled a half smile and gazed into the flames of the brazier.

"Just before the age when girls become women, we were carried away on a long voyage and given as gifts to Pharaoh. There we continued our training and grew both in skill and beauty. One day, we were noticed by an Egyptian nobleman who, for his own ambition, sought the favor of king Herod. This nobleman bribed Pharaoh with gifts of gold and promises of favors to purchase us and bring us to Herod. Pharaoh acquiesced, and the nobleman brought us north, across the desert, to Jerusalem."

Sejal poured three cups of hot water and spooned in a paste of herbs and spices infused with honey from a small ceramic bowl. "Herod saw the benefit of adding such foreign beauty to his court. He took pride that none of his guests had ever been entertained by such as we. So, I know what it is like to be alone in a strange land, Zimrah."

After handing a cup to Theophilus and then Zimrah, she sat back on the cushions and sighed deeply. "Do you know what I remember most about my homeland? I remember that we were storytellers."

"Zimrah tells wonderful stories." Theophilus grinned. "And this tea is amazing!"

Sanya took a moment to smile back at him. "I was taught many of the secrets of my people before leaving my homeland. I learned well. It is what affords me to live as I do here in the Upper City." Sanya gestured to the luxurious room around them. "And storytelling is in her blood." Sanya patted Zimrah's knee. "I would love to tell you the story of your mother and father if you would allow me."

Zimrah leaned toward her aunt and gripped the hand that had been patting her knee. "I can think of nothing I've ever wanted more."

Chapter 15

JAAZIEL AND SEJAL

Zimrah settled into the cushions and tried to keep her legs from shaking. Was it apprehension, excitement, or joy that was causing her heart to race? She was in the sitting room of her mother's sister in Jerusalem, and all the questions she had asked herself for as long as she could remember were about to be answered. *Abba, who is like You?*

Sanya took a sip of tea and in smooth, rhythmic tones, began the story of her parents.

"During the last years of the reign of Herod, who some now call The Great, a star rose in the eastern night sky, brighter than any that had ever been seen or have been seen since. Magi from the east saw this star, and reading the signs in the heavens, knew it was the herald of the birth of a great king, the Jewish king of kings." Sanya looked up and spanned the heavens with her hand.

"They crossed oceans of sand to see him and to bring the gifts and homage due such a king. They went to Herod, told him of the star, and asked where this great king could be found so they might worship him.

"When Herod heard this, he was greatly distressed, and all of Jerusalem with him. Herod called a meeting of the leading priests and teachers who knew the prophecies and asked them where this king was to be born." She gestured to the south.

"In Bethlehem." Zimrah said under her breath, not wanting to interrupt the story.

"That's right. 'In Bethlehem,' was their answer. After meeting with king Herod, the priests went back to their homes, only to hear an astonishing tale of shepherds in Bethlehem who had witnessed a host of angels singing and praising the Lord, declaring good news.

"'Rejoice, rejoice O Israel! Unto us a child is born! The Messiah has come!'

"The priests held a meeting of their own and assigned a man from among them to look into these claims, to search for this child and report back to them all he found. The man they chose was highly respected among them. He was a man of wisdom and understanding. He was one whose unbroken bloodline went back to the time of Israel's Golden Age, when his forefathers, the Sons of Korah, served in the tabernacle of King David. This man was named Jaaziel."

Zimrah's heart raced like it had the morning she watched the sun rise on the Sea of Galilee. "Was he my father?"

Sanya nodded and stroked her cheek. "Jaaziel, a man of faith, was also a man with a curious mind, full of wisdom and understanding. He took his assignment seriously. He had happened upon the Magi while they were in Jerusalem. They pointed out the star to him, the convergence of Jupiter and Venus, and explained all that brought them from their distant eastern homeland.

"Jaaziel found the shepherds and heard their testimony firsthand. He spoke to a widow named Anna who heard the words of the elder Simeon, who declared the child would be a light to reveal God to the nations. She had seen the child herself when he was brought to the temple for his dedication.

"Then Jaaziel traveled south to Bethlehem to try to find the child. Fatefully, Herod, in his arrogance, had slaughtered all the male children born within the given time, and Jaaziel could not find him there. If the infant king was born in Bethlehem, he was either killed or had been taken somewhere else."

"I remember my father speaking of this. They had heard of it even in Rome. When Herod killed the babies, I mean." Theophilus sat up and shook his head. "Many in the senate wanted the emperor to have Herod deposed."

"It was a terrible time. We could hear the mother's wailing in the night. I will never forget that sound." Sanya closed her eyes, and the room fell into silence for a moment.

Zimrah had heard of the tragedy as well. It affected her differently now sitting with Sanya and hearing of it from someone who had lived through the sorrow.

When the moment passed, Sanya spoke again. "In disappointment, Jaaziel reported all he had found to the priests. They concluded that the child could not have been the promised Messiah if Herod's soldiers had killed him. To them, the matter was settled." Sanya brought her legs up and crossed them beneath her.

"Jaaziel was not so easily satisfied. It remained like an ember burning in his thoughts, and he never forgot all he had seen and heard.

"It was a year before he returned to the palace of king Herod. On this occasion, he heard something that stopped him. It was a pure, sweet sound. A woman was singing on one of the balconies overlooking the palace grounds. Being a Levite, whose fathers sang before the Ark of the Covenant in the Tent of David, Jaaziel was drawn by the melody. He stopped to rest against a fig tree and stared upward, transfixed by the woman he saw there. She was the most beautiful woman he had ever seen."

"I know the feeling," Theophilus said.

Zimrah waved her fingers in his direction. "Shh, Theo! Don't interrupt!"

"Sorry, Sanya. Please continue."

"When the woman finished her song, Jaaziel called to her.

"'Do you not know any Hebrew songs?' he asked with a wide grin on his bearded face.

"Looking down and seeing the tall, handsome man who had spoken, the beautiful maiden replied, 'Alas, I know only one, my lord. And it is a love song.'

"'Will you sing it for me?' he asked.

"She leaned over the rail, contemplating her answer. 'I will sing it for you.' She laughed before disappearing beyond his sight in a flutter of colorful cloth. 'When you return tomorrow!'

"Jaaziel was no fool. He returned the next day and found the lovely maiden waiting for him on the balcony. As soon as she saw him coming, she began to sing." Sanya's lovely, low-timbred voice permeated the air around them like sunlight peeking through the clouds after a storm.

"'Rise up, my darling!
Come away with me, my fair one!
Look, the winter is past,
And the rains are over and gone.
The flowers are springing up,
The season of singing has come.
Rise up, my darling!
Come away with me, my fair one!'

"And Jaaziel sang the song's response.

"'My dove is hiding behind the rocks,
Behind an outcrop on the cliff.
Let me see your face;
Let me hear your voice.
For your voice is pleasant,
And your face is lovely.'

"And then they sang together, their voices blending sweetly in the morning air.

"'Rise up, my darling!
Come away with me, my fair one!'

"'What is your name?' Jaaziel asked, delighted by the harmony of their voices when they sang together.

"'Sejal,' she replied. 'What's yours?'

"'Jaaziel.'

"He returned every morning until their love could no longer be contained within the distance between them. Their love grew perhaps stronger because it was forbidden. He was a Jewish priest and she a gentile slave within the house of a hated Hasmonean king.

"They married in secret, no one knowing of their hidden love but I, Sanya." She put a hand to her chest. "Sejal's sister.

"They lived apart in this way for many months, stealing time together whenever they could. They shared a passion for making music. Jaaziel was excited by the exotic rhythms and melodies with which Sejal was so proficient. Their voices were often heard joined together in perfect harmony.

"Do you remember any of those rhythms? Can you teach me?" Zimrah asked.

"Now who's interrupting?" Theophilus raised an eyebrow in her direction.

Zimrah clasped her hands in her lap. "Sorry."

"Yes, I can teach you. Sejal's execution was much better than mine, but I will do my best." Sanya smiled indulgently and returned to her story. "Later, as Jaaziel instructed her, they shared faith in Yahweh. Jaaziel confided in his wife all that he had researched surrounding the birth of the child the Magi had come to find. He also shared his growing frustration over the priestly community's refusal to accept the truth.

"'How could they not believe? The one we have awaited for generations is here somewhere, living among us!' Jaaziel gestured to the rocks and trees around them as he paced the secluded glen high on the Mount of Olives. The young couple stole away as many nights as they could, descending into the dark Kidron Valley and up again to meet together in secret.

"'I cannot believe that Yahweh would declare the birth of the Messiah in the very heavens and then allow him to be slaughtered by a madman!'

"Sejal lowered her head in despair. Herod was a vile and evil king. He was also her master. She had witnessed herself the soldiers he dispatched to Bethlehem as they left the palace in the dead of that fateful night. She saw the fires burning in the distance, smelled the burnt flesh of the children on the soldier's armored bodies when they returned through the palace gates. At the mention of the massacre, Sejal burned with helpless anger over what her master had done. Jaaziel came to her in her distress.

"'Forgive my harsh words, my love.' He stroked the silky smoothness of her hair. 'I should not speak so about the man Jehovah has seen fit to place as king over us.'

"'He *is* a madman, and one day we will be free of him!' Sejal smiled up at her husband and whispered, 'The Messiah is among us.'

"Jaaziel returned her smile and took her face in his hands to kiss her lips. At least there was one who believed his message. When they parted, he said, 'Yes. I believe that he is indeed Immanuel, God with Us. He *must* have escaped the slaughter.

One day, when he is grown, he will reveal himself, and the priests will have to accept the truth.'

"Jaaziel kept the fires of his conviction burning low until one afternoon, a year after the death of Herod The Great, a chance conversation rekindled the old ember within him." Sanya leaned in toward them, and Zimrah's forehead tingled. She was overwhelmed with a sense of the familiar, as if she had lived this moment before. Everything was as it had been—the lamplight, the fragrance of myrrh in the air, and the taste of tea on her lips. She could almost recall Sanya's next words, but when she tried, the sense of *knowing* slipped away.

"He was walking on the road from the Pool of Siloam up to the temple when Jaaziel overheard a conversation between two men a few paces ahead of him.

"'I only just arrived from Nazareth this morning,' the younger of the two said.

"'Did you visit with our cousin Joseph? I heard he was back from Egypt. It will be good to see him at Passover again this year,' the second man said. He was older by only a year or two.

"'Yes, of course, I saw him and Mary and their oldest son.'

"'He must be at least four or five years old by now,' the older man said. 'What a thing to escape! That child would have died with the rest for sure if Joseph had not slipped them out of Bethlehem when he did!'

"'He said an angel warned him in a dream to leave Bethlehem!' the younger one said.

"Jaaziel closed the distance between them in a stride. 'Excuse me. Did you say a child escaped the massacre in Bethlehem?'

"After convincing the two men he meant no harm, Jaaziel learned everything they knew of this child and where he could be found. He sent word to Sejal and was on the road north to Nazareth within the hour." Sanya gestured in that direction. "He found the child and his parents just where the young man told him they would be.

"Joseph and Mary shared freely with him everything that had taken place. Mary spoke of an angel who had visited her. She told of how the Spirit of the Lord came upon her when she was yet a virgin so that the child born would be called the Son of God. It happened just as the prophets foretold." Sanya leaned back again.

"Hold on. Which prophets?" Theophilus furrowed his brow and crossed his arms. "There are prophecies that the Messiah will be born of a virgin?"

Zimrah opened her mouth to speak, but Sanya answered first. "I had a hard time at first as well. Just listen. The story may answer your questions. When Jaaziel returned from Nazareth, the ember had become a flame. He shared his findings with those who had originally sent him in search of the Messiah. Just as before, they would not listen. For three years, he searched the Scriptures and tried to convince the other priests that the one of whom the prophets had spoken had come. He showed them the ancient texts from the prophet Micah.

"'And you, O Bethlehem in the land of Judah, are not least among the rulers of Judah, for a ruler will come from you who will be a shepherd for my people Israel.'

"And about the slaughtered children. 'A cry was heard in Ramah—weeping and great mourning. Rachel weeps for her children, refusing to be comforted, for they are all dead.'

"And the virgin birth. 'Look! The virgin will conceive a child! She will give birth to a son, and they will call him Immanuel, which means 'God is with us.'"

Zimrah could hardly keep still. She had studied all of those scriptures herself but had not understood them until now. She stood up, too excited to sit any longer. "It's all about him...Messiah. Isaiah was speaking of this day...and my father was there? He met the virgin? He saw the Son who was to be the ruler of Israel like the scriptures foretold?"

Her forehead was not only tingling, it was on fire, and the heat was moving to cover her whole body. Her excitement was tempered only by Theophilus's reaction. He sat with his arms still folded and a scowl on his face.

"I understand your doubt, Theophilus." Sanya rose to stand next to him and place a hand on his shoulder. "It was at the point of the virgin birth that Jaaziel lost the priests as well.

"'What else could it be?' I appeal to you as He appealed to them. 'It has all happened just as the prophets foretold. What more proof do you need?'

"They shook their heads and turned away, pulling their black robes around them. Jaaziel still had friends among the priests who told him what the others were saying behind closed doors.

"'Something must be done.'

"'He will not keep quiet.'

"'Herod will hear of it.'

"'And there is a prefect from Rome over us now.'

"'Why do you think they have seen fit to appoint him?'

"'Why now?'

"'Perhaps they have already heard that rebellion is stirring.'

"'What if it is not only to us that Jaaziel has been spouting his lies?'

"'The people will believe anything!'

"'We must put a stop to this before he ruins things for us all!'

"'Something must be done!'

"Jaaziel paid little attention to their secret meetings, for he shortly had another concern pressing for his attention. Sejal, still a slave within the palace of Herod—owned now by Herod the Great's son Herod Antipas—was with child."

"Was it me?" Zimrah sat hard on the cushions.

"It *was* you, Zimrah." Sanya sat by her side again. "Only three people knew of the secret marriage, and about you—the child that was its result. We met by night in a deserted palace storage chamber to discuss the matter.

"'What will we do?' Sejal whispered with tears of panic wetting her cheeks. 'I will not be able to hide this for much longer.' She pulled the fabric of her tunic to expose her swollen middle. 'What a fool I have been. I knew we could not keep our marriage a secret forever. Did I not think eventually there would be a child? Herod will kill us all!'

"'Stop it, Sejal!' Jaaziel took her in his arms and held her close enough to rest a hand on her swollen belly. 'You've not been foolish. Our child is not a mistake. This is a joyous time. Children are a blessing from Yahweh. He will protect us.'

"'We have enough gold for one of us.' I whispered feverishly. Both Sejal and Jaaziel turned to meet my gaze. 'We will offer it to Herod for your freedom.'

"'No Sanya! How could I leave you here alone? Besides the fact that our master would never let only one of us go. We are the Pandyan Sisters—the *two* of us. All of Jerusalem knows us. Herod would never let either of us go!' Sejal said in exasperation.

"The fact was true. We were a novelty highly regarded in the city. It was said by many a government official and foreign dignitary that we were one of only a few reasons for visiting Jerusalem. Like his father before him, Herod boasted that he had kept us pure and untouched by all but the gods. Our purity increased our value. Both Herod's reputation and his word would be ruined if it were known that one of us was with child.

"'If Herod finds out about this, he will have me hanging from the palace walls!' Sejal wailed in despair.

"'That will not happen.' Jaaziel grew suddenly intense. He took one of our hands in each of his and said, 'Listen carefully. There is a city far to the north called Chasah. It is what my father and grandfather called a City of Refuge, a city where, in times of old, my people were kept safe. Not many even know of it anymore.'

"'There is a house there, a fortified house that contains a secret way of escape to the north and out of Judea. We can go there. We can leave this city and find a place where it does not matter whose slave you are. We can go somewhere beyond Herod's reach! You will be free, and we will be together. We can make a home for our child.'"

When Sanya mentioned Chasah, Zimrah had gasped and covered her mouth with her hand. Her eyes were still wide, and her pulse was racing. Sanya raised an eyebrow at her reaction but continued.

"'Our daughter,' Sejal said with conviction.

"'Yes, our daughter.' Jaaziel took his wife in his arms. 'We will name her Zimrah. It means to play upon an instrument in praise to Yahweh. She will be His instrument of praise!'

"We began to hear stirring in the palace around us then. Dawn was near, and time was short.

"'Listen to me, Sejal,' Jaaziel held her at arm's length and gripped her shoulders. 'I have heard rumors. The other priests are complaining about me. They believe I am stirring up too much trouble with my talk of Messiah. I will make preparations for us to leave within the week. If anything happens to me, you two must go.'

"'No! You will be with us Jaaziel!' Tears flowed freely onto Sejal's cheeks once more.

"'Shh! Listen,' he said. 'There is no time! Follow the river.'"

It was Theophilus who gasped this time.

"'The Jordan will take you north. It is a much harder route, and Herod will never suspect that you have gone that way. Follow it past the Sea of Galilee and Lake Huleh. Then go northwest toward the Mediterranean until you reach another river. It is the Leontes. You will find Chasah along that river. The fortified house is built into the southeast corner of the city wall. You cannot miss it. You will be safe there.'

"The sound of voices was louder now, coming from farther down the corridor.

"'I must go.' Jaaziel said, kissing his wife and squeezing my hand in reassurance.

"Take this." He pulled a scroll from his satchel and gave it to me. "It is everything I have researched about the birth of the Messiah. I fear it is no longer safe with me."

"'Jaaziel, wait!' Sejal gripped his arm before he could leave the room. 'I'm afraid.'

"'Do not fear,' he whispered, holding his beloved for the last time. 'Yahweh is with us.'"

***

Theophilus leaned back on the cushions and released the breath he had been holding.

"We never saw Jaaziel again." Sanya filled their cups with more tea. "They said he was killed by bandits on the road between Jerusalem and Jericho, but we knew the truth. The priests had silenced him. Sejal and I made plans to escape the very night we heard of Jaaziel's death."

"But you did not go with her?" Theophilus asked.

"No." Sanya sighed a deep sigh. "Just as the sun was setting that night, Herod called for us. We feared he knew the truth, that perhaps one of the other slaves discovered our plans and betrayed us. That was when an idea came to me that saved your life, Zimrah."

Sanya put her cup on the table and took Zimrah's hand again. "I made the decision to stay behind and pretend to be both of us. Sejal would not agree at first. But her belly was growing larger by the day. What other choice did we have?"

Zimrah wiped a tear that had been rolling down her cheek. "You mean you played the role of both yourself and my mother?"

"I do not understand." Theophilus rubbed the hairs on his chin.

"That night when Herod summoned both of us, I told him Sejal was not well and could not come. The next time he called, I came before him as Sejal and said that Sanya was not well. I knew our ruse could not work for long. We'd done it before as children. We drove our tutors mad."

Sanya gave a nostalgic half smile. "By the time Herod figured out what had happened, Sejal had enough of a lead that the palace guards did not find her. And Just as Jaaziel predicted, they looked for her along the Roman Road, never imagining she would take any other route."

"But what happened to *you?* There must have been consequences." A knot had begun to grow in Theophilus's middle.

"Yes. There were." Her expression was grave.

Sanya stood and turned her back to them. With the slow and graceful movements of the dancer she was, she removed the layers of cloth from around her shoulders and back. The morning sun, just rising to shine through the windows, revealed lines upon lines of pale, ragged scars upon her dark skin.

Zimrah gasped.

"Herod caned me himself. Then he waited until I healed and caned me again in Sejal's stead."

Theophilus, who had witnessed many such beatings, shot to his feet and began to pace the small room. He fought to keep his mind free of the memories, of blood and skin torn from flesh until the ribs were exposed. That Sanya was so much like Zimrah in form and build made the images in his mind that much harder to bear.

With just as much grace and dignity, Sanya layered the cloth over herself again. "By the time I was healed enough for him to scourge me the second time, I knew my sister was dead. I felt the moment of her passing, and a part of me died with her. The pain of the beating was only a distraction from the pain in my heart. It was worse than death. With Sejal gone, I was alone for the first time. I prayed that Herod's cane would kill me so I could be with her. I lived in despair. Until hope found me. I realized that somewhere out there, a part of Sejal still remained. You, Zimrah!

"I had nothing to base my hopes on except a feeling. I *knew* you had survived." Sanya sat next to Zimrah again and rubbed her back. "I had no idea where you were or how to find you. Had Sejal reached the City of Refuge? Had she died somewhere before she reached it? I had only my prayers that the God Sejal and Jaaziel believed in would protect you and send you back to me. Now He has. Only the Almighty God could have done such a thing." Sejal stroked Zimrah's hair.

Theophilus stilled his pacing. "How did you escape Herod?"

"Just as Sejal predicted, the novelty was gone. Herod's guests were not interested in only one Pandyan Sister, especially scarred as I am now. Beating me must have satisfied his anger. He accepted the gold I offered for my freedom and let me go. We still had many friends among the other slaves in the palace who mourned Sejal as I did. They gave up their gold to help me open this shop where I mix perfumes and oils for Jerusalem's aristocracy. I have done well and paid them all back the money they loaned me. It was here that I met Maarku."

"Maarku?" Zimrah asked.

"My husband. He, too, is a former slave, the guardian for the daughter of a wealthy landowner. Her name was Sasha. It was on an errand to my shop for her that we met. The following year, Sasha married, and Maarku's master gave him the freedom he promised for once saving his daughter's life. Now we run the shop together. He sometimes travels to Egypt for our oils and spices. He has been away on such a trip and is due back sometime today."

Sanya stood and stretched, then moved to the corner of the room to uncover a bowl of dough that had been silently rising through the night. Zimrah helped her roll and braid the dough for baking in her small brick oven.

"I know you're tired. I have kept you up all night with my stories. You must tell me, though. Do you know what happened to my sister? How did she die? How did you survive? You must have been very young. I felt the pain of her passing only a week and a day after she left. Where have you been? Who dressed and fed you? Who held you and wiped your tears when you were hurt? You married this handsome Roman." Sanya gestured to Theophilus, who had settled himself once more against the cushions.

He raised an eyebrow and put on his most dashing smile.

The corner of Sanya's mouth tipped up before turning back to Zimrah. "So, you must have been cared for. Where have you been all this time?"

***

"We were so amazed when you spoke of Chasah because that is where I was raised." Zimrah gripped Sanya's shoulder.

They had eaten and the morning was half gone before she finished telling her side of the tale. As Theophilus dozed on the cushions, she told Sanya what Jesse told her of what happened to Sejal and how traders had found her just short of her destination. How she had been purchased, raised, and protected in the very City of Refuge to which Sejal was headed.

"Jesse adopted me into his house, the same house built into the southeast corner of the city wall that Jaaziel spoke of. Sanya, I am overwhelmed!" Zimrah took her aunt's hand. "The Almighty has been guiding my steps for much longer than I ever imagined. Jaaziel told Sejal to follow the river. Yahweh has been singing the same instructions to me all my life. I followed the river here, to you! There must be purpose in all this."

Zimrah laid a hand on Sanya's back and felt her scars. "You sacrificed so much for her, for *me!* Yahweh preserved you as well. Herod could have killed you, could have kept you for himself. I am thankful he did not."

A great weight had been lifted from Zimrah's shoulders. The weight of the all the questions, who she was, where she had come from, who her parents were—they now had answers. The details of her gifts and passions now made sense. Both her parents had been singers! Her father was not only Hebrew, he was a Levite and a priest, descended from the Sons of Korah!

"I longed all my life for answers. I could never have dreamed I would find them like this. Yahweh be praised!" Zimrah covered her face and cried into her hands. They were tears of joy.

"He has answered both our prayers in bringing us together." Sanya said.

Zimrah embraced her aunt. They held each other tight until a man coming through the door interrupted them. Zimrah stared at him in open-mouthed wonder. He was unlike any man she had ever seen.

Chapter 16

IN THE HEARTS OF MEN

Maarku!" Sanya rushed into the embrace of the man who had come in.

The sound roused Theophilus, and he stood.

Up until that point, Theophilus was the largest man Zimrah had ever seen. Maarku was taller by an inch or two at least, and his chest looked to be twice as broad. His shoulders and arms were bare, and his neck, like his arms, was thickly muscled. His hair, where not mixed with gray, was dark brown. Starting at the scalp, it was separated into many thick, ropelike sections that twisted around each other on the way to his shoulders. The skin of his face, scarred by a violent past, was the color of deep honey. Though the scars marked him, they did not mar his beauty.

Zimrah found Maarku, despite his age, to be decidedly handsome. By the loving way he looked at Sanya, he was a man unashamed to show his emotions.

"Maarku, you will never guess who I found wandering the streets yesterday! I knew her on sight." Sanya reached for Zimrah to stand beside her. "This is Sejal's daughter Zimrah. She's finally come home!"

Maarku took Zimrah's hands. His were large, yet gentle and warm. There was a softness in his eyes, like one looks at a baby in its mother's arms or a child taking its first steps. Zimrah understood instantly why this man had been trusted with the care and protection of his former master's daughter.

"I see why you recognized her," Maarku said to Sanya as he bent to kiss both Zimrah's cheeks. He spoke in Aramaic, yet with an accent Zimrah had never heard before.

"She looks just like you, Sanya."

"No, she looks like Sejal." Sanya rubbed Zimrah's hair.

"Well, whoever you look like, it is good to finally meet you, Zimrah." Maarku raised his eyebrows. "After all these years, the lost daughter has returned. I know how much Sanya still mourns for Sejal. She always believed her daughter lived. And here you are at last. There can be no doubt. Look at you!" He gripped her shoulders. "It's amazing. Sanya never stopped believing she would find you."

"There is a profound difference between us. Zimrah has her innocence and purity. I lost mine long ago. With all that I have suffered and lost, my innocence is now a part of a long-forgotten past."

"Well, wherever she has been these years, she has been favored." Maarku put a gentle hand to Zimrah's cheek. "I see it on her face, like the light of the gods shines on her."

"I have heard her story. You will not believe it, Maarku." Sanya turned to Theophilus. "And this is Zimrah's husband, Theophilus."

Zimrah sensed tension in Sanya's manner that wasn't there before. She had omitted Theophilus's origins from her introduction. When Theophilus spoke his greetings, and Maarku heard his accent, Zimrah understood why.

Immediately, something dark took over his features, and all the warmth drained from his eyes. The muscles in his arms clenched with the closing of his fists.

"Roman!" He seethed the word through clenched teeth. His tone and expression matched the anger, bitterness, and resentment written all over his face. Zimrah could feel it in the room like a tangible force.

His nose flared, his fists closed into tight balls, and he took a step toward Theophilus. Sanya stepped in front of him. "May I speak with you for a moment?"

Sanya led Maarku back out the door he had just come in, and they spoke in hushed tones. Zimrah and Theophilus could not see them but could not help but overhear what they were saying through the open door.

"I am accustomed to Romans," Maarku said. "They are everywhere in the streets—soldiers with their iron, bronze, and leather. Jerusalem, Egypt—their presence is felt in every city."

"I know." Sanya said.

"Out there I can put my head down and give them a wide berth. The past is kept at bay. But this one? This one cannot be avoided or ignored. He's here, a soldier—the stance and bearing

I'll never forget—masquerading in Hebrew robes and standing in my own home!"

"Shhh!"

Sanya and Maarku lowered their voices, and Zimrah looked at Theophilus. She could not read his face, so she closed her eyes instead.

Abba?

In a heartbeat, she was somewhere else. There was a burned village. She heard screams and smelled the burning of wood and flesh. The face of a dying man, covered in blood, tears, and soot, filled her vision.

I love you and will always be with you.

Understanding hit her like a flash of lightning in her mind. When Sanya and Maarku returned, she knew what to do.

"Go to him."

Zimrah did not think. She simply responded to the voice that had always proved true. She closed the distance between herself and this man she did not know, other than that he was joined to her mother's sister. She stood before him as he gazed down at her in confusion. Then slowly, Zimrah moved her arms around his waist and embraced him with her head against his chest.

"I sensed the battle you just waged, Maarku. It was not easy, but you won. You did well." Zimrah whispered for only him to hear. "Yahweh showed me what happened. He showed me the face of your father as he was dying. He loves you and will always be with you." Her words were not her own. Her whole body tingled with Yahweh's presence.

Maarku's breath caught within him. His arms came around her, and he bent to whisper just as quietly. "How did you know? You could not have known. Those were the last words that my father spoke to me. You are so young. And we've only just met, but somehow, you've seen beyond my anger and scarred face, just as Sanya did, and my beloved Sasha before her."

"I *didn't* know, but Yahweh does. He told me to come to you because He loves you, Maarku. He is the Father that will never leave. No matter what you have been through or what you have done."

Zimrah released him and turned to Theophilus. There was no malice in his face, no arrogance or hostility, not even a trace of fear. He smiled, open and receptive despite Maarku's reaction to him. He held a hand out to Maarku.

Maarku's wide eyes went from Theophilus to Zimrah to Sanya and back to Theophilus again before he took Theophilus's hand.

***

Zimrah helped Sanya close her shop for the day, and they spent the afternoon resting. Theophilus visited the public Gentile baths. Sanya warmed water for Zimrah to wash away her travel dust and weariness within the privacy of her home. She then spent time helping Maarku unload and categorize what he had brought back from Egypt.

The evening found them enjoying Sanya's table on the roof of her house. As the men ate and eyed each other with amicable caution, Zimrah sat with Sanya, their knees and heads together.

They were filling the holes in each other's hearts with words. Zimrah had a lifetime's worth of questions she wanted to ask.

"What was she like?" Zimrah looked across the table at the delicious meal Sanya had prepared. "What was her favorite food?"

Sanya's face transformed with the upturning of her lips. "Sejal liked anything made with honey. Honey cakes were her favorite."

"Mine too! I always thought it was because Nina made them so well. Perhaps it was something I got from my mother. And figs, I hate figs. Jesse and Nina thought it absurd."

Zimrah laughed while Sanya nodded "That was Jaaziel. He couldn't stand them."

They spoke like this until long after the sun went down and they had to light the table lamps to see each other's faces.

"I miss Sejal's voice the most." Sanya said as the sounds of the city died down below them. "She sang almost as much as she spoke. She awoke each morning with a song on her lips. My sister could transform the most mundane of tasks into a joy, creating a melody from the sound of the wind in the trees or the cook chopping vegetables in the kitchen."

"That sounds familiar." Theophilus walked into the circle of light holding the unopened pack he had brought with him—the one Zimrah had asked about in Capernaum. He held the pack out to her now and returned to his cushioned place opposite her at the table.

"What is it?" Zimrah asked, holding the heavy pack on her lap.

"You were so curious before. Open it and see." He offered a wink to Sanya's questioning glance.

Zimrah loosened the drawstring and pulled the fabric from around the wood. Before it was exposed, she knew what it was. She placed it on the table in front of her and brushed her fingers over the familiar carving etched into the wood—a meadow surrounded by lush trees on the side of a hill. Moisture gathered in the corners of her eyes at her husband's thoughtfulness. She had not realized how much she had missed what was inside.

Zimrah opened the case and pulled out her lyre.

"Sejal played as well." Sanya wiped tears of her own with the corner of her scarf. "I've not cried this much since my sister died."

"Thank you, Theophilus," Zimrah said.

"I thought you might want it before our trip was over." He took the case from her and placed it on the floor beside him.

Zimrah cradled the instrument with the wood against her heart. After tuning the strings, she began to entice a melody from them. The notes bounced off the floor and short walls of the roof before lifting off to be caught and taken by the wind. Zimrah began to sing the words to the song her parents sang.

"Winter is past and the rains are gone.
Flowers are blooming.
The birds are singing.
Winter is past and the rains are gone.

Flowers are blooming.

The time for singing has come.

"Weeping may last through the night.
Weeping may last through the night.
But joy comes, joy comes,
Joy comes in the morning."

Zimrah's attention kept being drawn to Maarku—reclining in the shadows—as she sang. It was as if the words were for him alone. She prayed that her song would be truth for him, that his sorrow would be gone like the winter rains and replaced with joy.

Something *was* happening. He put a hand to his cheek and seemed surprised to find tears there. After a moment he leaned back into the cushions and closed his eyes. The tension left his shoulders and he fell asleep.

Chapter 17

WHAT PLANS HE HAS PREPARED

Later that night, Zimrah and Theophilus lay together in the room Sanya reserved for guests. Zimrah was tired. She had not slept since they left Bethany two days ago, yet she could not force her heart to stop its wild beating. The cadence of Sanya's voice echoed still in her mind.

"It is amazing really. Your mother was a singer!" Theophilus whispered as one tends to do when speaking with another in a dark room. His comment revealed that Sanya's tale still echoed in his mind as well.

"I know, as was my father!" Zimrah was glad that Theophilus was awake. The experiences of the day were all the sweeter with her husband there to share them.

"And she played the lyre!" With all her excitement over discovering who her parents were, Zimrah was having a hard time keeping her voice low.

"Sanya said your father was a Levite, from the Sons of Korah. What does that mean?"

Zimrah stilled her racing heart to speak in even tones as she explained to him about the Twelve Tribes of Israel. As she spoke, she remembered her tutor Silas. She was very young when he taught her. The people and events were fascinating, but she had listened as one learning someone else's heritage. She had been sad that the stories she had grown to love and the land where they had taken place were the inheritance of a people she did not belong to. God created *all* people in His image, and that included her. Yet her heart still ached with the desire to belong.

Now, as she told the stories to Theophilus, of Moses and Aaron, and of Korah—who was swallowed by the earth for rebelling against Moses—a chill made the hairs on her arms stand up. She was born into the tribe of Levi as well!

"King David set up worship before the Ark of the Covenant, the vessel that carried the presence of God." Zimrah could no longer lie still. She sat up in the bed as she talked. "He hired thousands of musicians and singers, whose only task was to praise the Lord in His sanctuary. The Sons of Korah did not stand with their father in his rebellion. They were among those whose worship continued day and night in the Tent of David for thirty-three years! Only those from the tribe of Levi were allowed to serve the Lord in this way. Yahweh gave express instructions to Moses concerning this, and the law continues to this day. Only the descendants of Levi may enter the Most Holy Place."

Zimrah could not see Theophilus's face in the dark, but she could feel his question in the tension of his shoulders. "The Most Holy Place is the room where the presence of the Lord is said to dwell. It was where Nina said the angel appeared to Zechariah, John's father, to announce to him that he would have a son. The Ark has been lost, but the temple and the people who serve there remain."

"Your people."

"My people." Zimrah repeated in awe and wonder. Yahweh had led her to Jerusalem for this truth.

Oh, Abba. You are so amazing! You knew who I was all along! You have been guiding my steps, leading me into deeper understanding of who You are... and who I am. How can I express to You the joy in my heart? I used to wonder if either of my parents knew You. Was loving You in my blood? Now I know it is indeed! Both my parents loved You!

"This is just the beginning, Beloved. No eye has seen, no ear has heard, no mind has imagined what I have prepared for those who love Me. You are continuing the journey I began with them."

Zimrah did not fully understand, yet she cherished the words of the Lord.

"Can we stay in Jerusalem a little longer?" She could not imagine leaving this city so soon. There were so many more stories she needed to hear.

"Of course. We can stay as long as you wish."

***

Long after Zimrah fell asleep, Theophilus lay awake. He was happy for her. He could only imagine what meeting Sejal meant to her. She knew where she belonged now. She belonged right here in Jerusalem, here in this city, in this land. Yahweh was indeed her God, the God of her fathers.

He could see the hand of the Almighty in all they had experienced. It was clear that the path He was guiding her along was set before she was born! Every part of her—her faith, her dreams, and the songs she was given in them—was a reflection of her destiny. If where that destiny would lead was still unclear, she could rest assured. Yahweh would reveal it. Her purpose was as sure as her name. Zimrah, created in love to be an instrument, played by the hands of God!

Theophilus sighed, closed his eyes, and held her close. He *was* happy for her, yet a part of him could not help but wonder where he fit into Yahweh's plan.

Up to this point, he had always had a goal. His mission while in the army was unquestionable. There was the next assignment, the next battle to fight and to win. He had done his duty and done it well. When his time in the army was over, he fell in love with Zimrah.

During the two years they had been separated, his goal had been to get back to her. With Yahweh's help, he had done that. After, he vowed to help Zimrah reach Jerusalem and to protect her. He had done that as well. They were here, and her adoption was final.

He had hoped the journey would help him understand her God. Now that it was complete, he felt no closer to Yahweh than he did before. A tendril of jealousy and doubt, like a snake's forked tongue, invaded his thoughts.

What will I do now? Theophilus felt unstable without a goal to reach for. It was not a feeling he was used to. What was there for him to do with the rest of his life? His father, Lucius, would love for him to bring Zimrah home, take over the business, start a family. That path never appealed to Theophilus, and the idea of Zimrah in Rome was ridiculous. She would be as miserable there as he had always been, more so now that she knew she belonged here in Judea.

This was her home, and Yahweh was her God—and his. Theophilus was determined to keep his vow to worship the Almighty. Yet there, as before, was the nagging question like a sliver of wood under the skin.

What will I do with myself if we stay in Judea?

Into the jumble of his thoughts, there came a quiet answer.

"I Am a resting place for the weary. Let the weary find rest in Me."

The voice was so small and still to Theophilus's mind that it went mostly unnoticed. But underneath the reasoning and doubt, there was a part of his heart that leapt for joy at those words. It was the same part that decided to be immersed by John in the river Jordan.

Theophilus continued wrestling with the doubts and uncertainty for what seemed like hours before sleep took him.

Chapter 18

THE DANCE

All was dark, and Zimrah was flying over a battlefield. Bodies of the slain lay in heaps covered in mud. Enemy forces, dark twisted shapes that snarled and roared their battle cries, surrounded those who stood to fight.

A bow was in her hands, and she shot at the dark shapes with her arrows from above with uncanny aim. Every arrow hit its mark. Those on the field shot back at her, but she was unafraid. There was One flying beside her, and with Him she was completely safe.

Zimrah shot with her bronze bow until she saw the dark form of a man. He had another man with him. This man was different from any others on the battlefield. He shone with an internal light. The man of light was stripped and beaten until his face was no longer recognizable. Marred flesh and exposed bone showed the lines of the whip on his back. The dark man was preparing him for execution.

Flying low, Zimrah let loose her arrow and struck the dark man square in the chest. There was no effect! He brushed her arrow aside like one might a fly, giving her only the slightest glance. In the split second that his attention had turned to her, Zimrah saw his true form. Beneath his skin there was a second, leathery and lizard-like. He was not a man at all. He was a beast.

He raised his hand to signal the bowman under his command. The man of light had little time left.

"What do I do?" Zimrah asked the One who flew beside her. "How do I fight this beast? My arrows are not working like they did on the others."

"Dance."

"Dance, my Lord?" Zimrah had never danced on the battlefield before. The thought had never crossed her mind. Yet, she trusted the One who flew with her.

The bow gone from her hands, she flew down and stood between the dark man and the man of light. She stood boldly, her safety secure, and began to dance. Unused to the movements at first, she raised her arms and moved them in slow circles that cut and sculpted the air around her.

She closed her eyes and thought of her Lord. He was there. His unseen steps were guiding her. She began to move with Him more confidently, charging the air with particles of light. The light slid from her fingertips in circular waves.

Then the beast dropped his arm, and the bowman's arrow flew. It flew straight through her heart and into the man of light. His beaten body fell to the ground and died where he lay.

Zimrah did not stop her dancing, even when tears for the man's death wet the front of her tunic. She felt her Lord guiding her. She was only following in the dance He led.

Suddenly, something changed. Where there had been only darkness before, color formed on the battlefield. Light built within the translucent bubble of the presence of the One who was with her. Tension mounted in the air. Her movements continued, and the light grew brighter and brighter. The tension built until an explosion of light knocked her from her feet.

When Zimrah opened her eyes and stood, she found that the world was new. The battlefield was now bright in the light of day. The body of the man who was killed by the beast was gone, and the morning sun was bright in the east.

The next day Zimrah sent a letter to Jesse, letting him know all that happened. She wrote that they would be staying with Sanya in Jerusalem at least until the Festival of Lights. The dream stayed with her. Did it have something to do with the coming festival? She mulled it over all day, but it was not until the evening did she begin to understand its meaning. Both couples rested on the roof once more.

"Zimrah, will you play for me? I have not danced since the death of my sister. When I heard you playing the other night, it was like I had her back again. My feet ache for the feel of the ground beneath me."

"Of course, Sanya." The familiar tingle on her forehead as she retrieved the lyre told her there was something more happening than she could see.

What is it, my Lord? What would you have me play?

Zimrah heard no response. With the lyre against her heart, she paused, closed her eyes, and thought of her Lord. She waited until she felt His peace before beginning to play. As soon as her fingers touched the strings, a new melody emerged. She sang to its cadence and rhythm.

"Before I was born Oh Lord,
You called me Your servant
In whom You display Your glory.
You made me Yours,
Made me Yours.

"You made my mouth like a sharpened sword,
In the shadow of your hand, You hide me, Lord.
You made me Yours,
Made me Yours.

"To praise Your name,
Tehillah praise, tehillah praise.
Praise Your name,
Tehillah praise, tehillah praise.

"I write Your name on the palms of my hands.
Set my mind on the walls of Your land.
Take Your name as my own,
As my own.

And praise Your name,
Tehillah praise, tehillah praise.

"I want to drink from the cup of the Sons of Judah.
Take my place with the Sons of Korah,
Take Your name as my own.

"I will praise Your name.
Tehillah praise, tehillah praise."

Sanya danced as Zimrah sang. In graceful, flowing movements, Sanya's arms and hands sculpted the air. Her feet pointed, flexed, and leapt. The rhythm of the song beat through her legs into the floor of the roof, giving a heartbeat to Zimrah's melody. The light fabric of her clothing twisted and twirled, flowed and flew, offering its colors to the air like many feathered birds around a fountain. Her hands clapped, and her face expressed deep feeling.

Images from the dream filled Zimrah's mind as she sang. Except instead of a battlefield, they were within the vast heavenly court she'd dreamt of before. With her eyes closed, Zimrah saw the great jewel throne in the distance where Herod's temple actually stood.

There were twelve marble columns and a translucent floor under the starry sky. In her mind, Zimrah saw Sanya twirling and leaping around a flowing fountain. The One, whose face she could never see, danced with her. He was leading Sanya's steps. Light flowed from the tips of their fingers and brightened the air around them with each graceful movement.

Zimrah was overwhelmed with the feeling of significance. It was as if Sanya and Sejal, who had been groomed for the courts of earthly kings, now danced and sang in the court of the King of Kings. She was playing in her mother's stead. Yahweh Himself had prepared her for this moment.

She did not completely understand why, yet she was filled with the certainty that she had been led to Jerusalem for a great purpose. Not just for her adoption or solving the mystery of her past, but for *this* moment. She stopped singing and just played as Sanya danced, letting the music change and take all that was within her and give it sound.

Zimrah opened her eyes and looked beyond the roof to Herod's Temple high on its hill. It was glowing blood red with the colors of the setting sun. Deep within her, Zimrah felt like a great sorrow was coming for the Holy City. Without knowing why, tears blurred her vision.

Theophilus and Maarku sat and watched with wide eyes. Zimrah and Sanya were one, like it was not the first time they had danced and played together. The two rode the swells of form and sound, leaping with the highs only to drop low and leap again. There was no past, no future, just the here and now. How long this went on, Zimrah could not have said.

When it was over, Sanya was the first to speak.

"A war is coming. It has already begun."

Chapter 19

DIFFICULT FAREWELLS

Zimrah stepped out onto the sundrenched Upper City street with Sanya and Maarku. He followed close behind them, not liking to let them go anywhere alone.

"Shalom." A young woman selling prized cloth beamed at Sanya and Zimrah as they walked by.

"Shalom." Zimrah returned the greeting and gripped the woman's hand.

"I enjoyed last evening's song." The woman held on to Zimrah's hand with both of hers. "Will you be on the roof again this evening?"

Zimrah's heart filled with the warmth of gratefulness. Two months had passed since she arrived in Jerusalem. Maarku's was not the only heart Yahweh had touched through her singing.

"Perhaps. We will see how the day progresses." Zimrah smiled before they walked on. The next two stalls they passed were the same, and they were stopped by the third.

"Mama, the Pandyan Sisters!" A boy of perhaps ten years called to his mother.

"They are not the Pandyan Sisters." The boy's mother came shuffling, waving with one hand and holding a full belly with the other. "Forgive him, he's just repeating what he's heard."

It was not the first time Zimrah heard the name. Many in the city were saying the Pandyan Sisters had returned to Jerusalem. It bothered Zimrah not in the least to be confused with her mother.

"It is good to see you, Sarah." Sanya rubbed the shorter woman's shoulder. "It will not be long now. Have you decided on a name?"

As Sanya and Sarah spoke of women's things, Zimrah nudged Maarku, but his eyes were on the street around them. His guard was up today.

"Are you alright?" Zimrah stood next to him and looked out on the street as he did, trying to see what he saw.

His gaze fell on her, and his brow furrowed before he let his shoulders drop. "I spent so many years protecting my precious Sasha...I suppose old habits are hard to break."

"Are we in need of protection?" The group of women around Sanya had increased, and their laughter made Zimrah smile.

Maarku went back to scanning the street. "I cannot yet see why, but I've learned to trust my instincts. Not everyone is pleased with your evening performances. This city is home to many priests and Pharisees. They are intent on preserving, and often enforcing, their interpretations of the Torah and fiercely reject anything or anyone they deem a threat to traditional Jewish ways."

"Like my father." Zimrah had not forgotten what Sanya said happened to Jaaziel.

"They especially reject anything to do with Greeks and Romans and all their Hellenistic influences." Maarku shrugged his large shoulders. "Not that I blame them. I'm not particularly fond of Greeks or Romans either. But I'll quickly add Pharisees to the list of those I dislike if they try to do harm to the women I love."

As he was speaking, his gaze was halted by a pair of black robes across the narrow street. One of them stared at Zimrah with narrow eyes. Maarku stepped between Zimrah and the man, blocking his unpleasant glare with one of his own.

***

"Have you heard of these women, these supposed Pandyan Sisters who have been displaying themselves so boldly on the rooftops of the Upper City recently?" Saul held the door of the inn for his new friend, Amos, and shook off the glare of the large, dark-skinned man across the street.

Amos's father was a well-respected member of the Sanhedrin, and Saul's ambition gave him great cause to befriend the younger man.

"Yes, friend, I have." Amos chose a comfortable corner table and sat down. "I do not know how the women you are accustomed to in Tarsus behave, but here in Jerusalem, they are usually much less vocal."

"They were outside on the street just now, and I believe I saw one of them this past fortnight when I traveled north to inspect the teaching of the heretic John the Baptizer." Saul leaned over the table to turn two cups right side up. "Once one has caught sight of her, she is not easily forgotten."

"Was it the older or the younger one that you saw?" Amos poured himself some wine from the large pitcher in the center of the table.

"The younger. She and that Roman she travels with must have been on their way here when I saw them."

"I have not heard her myself, but they say she sings from the Torah. You do know that only Levites may sing thus?" Amos took a sip from his cup.

Saul took a deep breath to calm himself and then poured too much wine into his own cup. "This is true even in Tarsus, my friend."

Did Amos ask because he thought Saul truly did not already know—like all Pharisees, he prided himself on knowing the law quite well. Saul's face grew hot with indignation, both at Amos's tone and for the knowledge he had given. He decided to let the former go and champion the latter.

"Pah! What could this gentile *woman* know of our scrolls or our laws? This evening I will go and hear for myself. Trust in this, Amos. If what you've heard is true, she will learn our laws and what comes to those who break them. Come with me if you wish. We will search this matter out together."

Saul sat back in his chair and steepled his fingers. It was clear that no one had yet taken on the matter. He would be pleased to see to these women himself. He hoped the Sanhedrin would be as well.

***

While in the Holy City, Zimrah and Theophilus visited the temple every Sabbath to stand and hear the reading of the scrolls. Zimrah never ventured any further up to the Court of Women. She had the right, since her mother was a follower of Yahweh and, after marrying Zimrah's father, followed Jewish practices. One could petition that therefore, she would have been considered Jewish as well. Not to mention the fact that she was just formally adopted by the house of Jesse. By law, she was a Jew. But by outward appearance, she was looked at like any other Gentile, an outsider. The disapproving looks of the Pharisees kept her content to stay below with Theophilus.

It mattered little. She could hear the scrolls read just as well from the lower Court of Gentiles. And she could hear the Levites. In truth, one could hear them from any distance around the temple mount. Every day, twelve singers would stand on the steps leading to the holiest and highest part of the temple. They would sing, mostly from the songs of King David. Zimrah stood and listened with her eyes closed and her heart soaring with the voices.

The Word of the Lord always brought peace to her heart, even if the temple itself did not. From a distance its beauty was incomparable. Inside it festered with corruption.

Merchants and moneychangers set up tables each morning in the outer courts and cheated those who came to offer the sacrifices required by the law of Moses. Women and widows were treated worst of all. Without a man to speak for them, most were charged more than the normal rate for the animals they bought to give as offerings to the Lord.

The poor had to wait in long lines all day with no shelter from the sun while the rich were offered refreshment and ushered inside to do business privately. Greeks and Romans were charged double or shunned altogether if they could not, or were unwilling to, pay the higher fees given them.

After witnessing all they had, Zimrah was convinced it must have been only the favor of God that allowed them to submit Zimrah's adoption document so quickly the day they arrived.

She could not help but feel sad. The injustice and lack of mercy must have grieved Yahweh's heart as well. Perhaps it was the reason for the tears both she and Sanya often shed as they danced and sang in the shadow of the temple walls.

***

The rainy season had arrived, causing the hills around Jerusalem to come alive in green. The days grew cold, and the month of Kislev saw the streets of Jerusalem overwhelmed with people from every nation arriving for the Festival of Lights.

Zimrah and Theophilus accompanied Sanya and Maarku along with the throng of others who filled the Court of Gentiles each evening at sundown. The festival lasted eight days, and each night a ceremonial candle was lit with much joy and singing. The candle was a reminder to all of how the Maccabees successfully reclaimed the temple in battle against the blasphemous Greek king Antiochus Epiphanes.

The Festival was both beautiful and meaningful for Zimrah. At the lighting of each candle, she was enchanted by the symbolism. Yahweh brought His light to overcome the darkness of the world. He had done the same in hers.

After the festival, although winter meant rain and was not the best time to travel, both Theophilus and Zimrah felt it was time to return home.

"Stay until spring," Sanya said. "The weather will be more favorable then. What if it rains on the mountains and the roads are flooded?"

"I'm sorry, Sanya, but we cannot stay. Jesse and Nina miss us. It is time for us to return to Chasah." The bond Zimrah was forging with her new family and her longing to be at home with her old family pulled her in opposing directions.

She had grown to love Sanya and Maarku dearly, which made leaving them all the more difficult. They had filled holes in her heart she thought would never be filled. But she missed home. She missed Jesse and Nina. She could not wait to sit with her father under the almond tree at home and share all she had learned about herself and her first parents. She missed Nina's face, her voice, and her cooking.

She missed the peace and tranquility of the mountains and the gentle Leontes River. She missed her room where, on a clear day, she could see past the rolling farmlands all the way to the blue of the Mediterranean. Above all, she missed playing her lyre alone in her room, with no one watching. She missed walking along the river in her imagination with Father Yahweh. Zimrah was homesick.

Jerusalem was full of too many people. The blind and crippled begged in rags on the streets while the rich passed by in disdain. As wonderful as it was to worship Yahweh every evening in the shadow of the temple, He did not dwell there as in the days of old. Yahweh was not confined to a city or to a temple. He was everywhere.

"We will come back and visit again." Zimrah tried to comfort the sadness in Sanya's eyes. "We could come for Passover, if not this year, then the next."

"It will give Maarku and me something to look forward to." Sanya wiped her cheeks with the hem of her headscarf. "And you can write. I will have one of my clients read it to us and write you our reply." As former slaves, Sanya and Maarku had never learned to read or write themselves.

"Oh, that reminds me." Sanya turned to a wooden chest and lifted a scroll from inside with great solemnity. "Jaaziel would have wanted you to have it."

The hairs on Zimrah's arms stood on end as she opened the scroll. "Is it..."

"Yes, it is."

Tears slid down Zimrah's cheeks. "This is a gift greater than any I have ever received." She gazed at the words—having to blink repeatedly to see them. They were written in Hebrew and Greek, by a strong, confident hand. Her father's hand. It was all Jaaziel had researched concerning the Messiah.

"Thank you, Sanya." Zimrah embraced her aunt again, holding on for a long time as Theophilus and Maarku said their goodbyes.

***

Theophilus had enjoyed Jerusalem, but he was eager to have the city at his back.

Maarku clasped Theophilus's hand and held on. "Take care of her…" There was something he wanted to say, and Theophilus allowed his new friend time to gather his thoughts.

"I lost my father to a Roman sword when I was just a boy," Maarku began.

The bigger man's grip was firm on his arm, and Theophilus worried for a moment that the old rage had returned. Until he continued.

"I did not think I would ever be rid of the anger I carried. I hated Romans. I felt my past justified the hatred. And I had never met a Roman who did not look back at me with the same hatred in his eyes. Until the day you arrived."

Theophilus's eyebrow went up as he searched for a remark to lighten the heaviness of the moment. The weight of the big man's heart felt like a burden Theophilus was not worthy to carry. He then thought better of it and held his tongue. What Maarku had to say needed to be expressed, for his sake, not Theophilus's comfort.

"You are different, Theophilus. In the face of my anger, you had none. You do not think you are better than any of us, although you have a right too. We have all been slaves. You are the son of a merchant and a patrician. You have never been subject to anyone."

"I am subject to the law of God, Maarku. His law is higher than the laws of Rome or the horrible things men do to each other. I have done many of those horrible things, but I am learning that Yahweh still accepts me." Theophilus did not know where the response came from. He only knew he could not keep silent. "The only law Yahweh requires is that we love as He does. I am trying, and I know you are as well. Love leaves no room for anger or fear."

With this, Maarku took Theophilus in his big arms, pounded his back affectionately, and then released him.

When Theophilus recovered from Maarku's embrace, he turned to Zimrah and took her hand.

"You are a favored man, Theophilus." Maarku put his arm around Sanya's shoulder as she came to stand by his side.

"As are you, my friend." Theophilus clasped hands with the older man once more. He had enjoyed the time with them, for more than the fact that, like Nina, Sanya was an amazing cook.

He looked at Maarku. On the outside, they looked nothing alike. They were conqueror and conquered, but he couldn't tell the difference. They were complete opposites in a society that said they should be enemies. But they weren't. They were men who knew great suffering and loss. They had chosen to love instead, and that love had changed them. It brought them together.

"Until we meet again, *Mwana*." As he embraced Zimrah—much more gently than he had Theophilus—he rested his cheek on the top of her head. There was moisture in his eyes and a smile on his face. "It means sister's daughter in my native language."

"I am glad that you came." He pulled away to hold her at arm's length. "For Sanya's sake and for mine. You have been given a gift. There is something in you that brings peace. When you sing, your voice reaches into deep places and leaves something that was not there before. I don't know how you did it, but I am a changed man."

***

Zimrah could only shed joyful tears as she clung to her uncle. The something for which he spoke was the fingerprint of God. She reached for Sanya and brought her into their embrace, silently thanking the Almighty for His goodness. He had done wonders in bringing them together. Where she once felt so alone, she was no longer. She now had two places to call home, two groups of people to call family.

Words from the prophet Isaiah came to her mind, and she sang them out, a fitting end to her time in Jerusalem.

> "Sing for joy, O heavens!
> Rejoice, O earth!
> Burst into song, O mountains!
> For the Lord has comforted His people
> And has compassion on them in their suffering.
> He is good and His love endures forever."

Chapter 20

THE PLANS OF GOD AND MEN

Zimrah left Sanya and Maarku's house, still wiping tears with her headscarf. Almost as soon as she and Theophilus left the upper city toward the temple, they heard something happening within its walls. There was much more jostling than usual on the streets, and a noise like the shouting of many voices was coming from the temple mount. People were either pressing toward the commotion or hurrying away from it.

"What is it?" Theophilus stopped a young scribe to ask about the shouting. "What is all the commotion in the city? What is that terrible noise coming from the temple?"

"There is a man armed with a whip!" the scribe said breathlessly.

He tried to hurry on, but Theophilus held a fistful of his mantle. "What? What do you mean?"

"He's overturning the tables of the moneychangers and traders, whipping the sellers of sacrificial animals! He was bellowing something about his father's house and a den of robbers. He has no authority! A carpenter from Nazareth! He is mad!" The scribe spat the last words over his shoulder in disgust as he tried to hurry away again. Theophilus let him, but he could only move as quickly as the crowd permitted.

Theophilus's eyebrow was raised, and Zimrah could tell he was wondering the same thing she was. Should they continue out of the city? Or should they go up to stand as witness to whoever was clearing the temple? Many times during their stay, they had lamented the cheating of the poor, the injustice—it saddened them both. This Nazarene may not have the authority, but Zimrah was glad someone was doing what needed to be done.

"Nazareth?" she asked.

"Ho! Scribe!" Theophilus called to the man whose back they could still see among those on busy Tyropoeon Street. "What is the carpenter's name?"

"I heard someone say it was Yeshua!" the scribe shouted back to them before disappearing into the mass of bodies.

The coincidence was too great. The man they had met by the river, Yeshua, was also from Nazareth, the one who helped them when they thought Theophilus was wounded by bandits. "Could it be?"

The couple smiled at each other and continued into the crowd themselves.

"It is not an uncommon name. There could be more than one Yeshua from Nazareth." Zimrah said.

Theophilus nodded. "It is possible."

Zimrah had still not grown accustomed to the crush of people within the city walls. When they passed through the Damascus Gate, she was glad to be free of them. "I'm so glad to be out into the open air of the road once again."

"I'm glad to have feeling back in my arm." Theophilus shook his arm and wrinkled his nose at her. She wrinkled hers and gave him a swat in return.

They decided to stay on Roman roads this time which made their journey safer as well as easier. The terrain was not nearly as steep. Although they missed the beauty and serenity of the Jordan River Valley. The Roman Road was almost as crowded as the streets of Jerusalem, at least until they passed the Hippodrome.

Zimrah tilted her head up at the massive walls. They were built by Herod with the same scale and grandeur he had used in building the Temple. "So this is where that sound was coming from."

On Circus days, they could hear the sound washing over Jerusalem like an evil tide, reaching in to flood even the high ground of the Temple Mount.

"The roar of the mob." Theophilus moved her to walk on his right, putting himself between her and the walls. "The Hippodrome is a monument to the god Rome venerates more than any others—Mammon. It was built to house the horse and chariot races, but it also serves as a gathering place for gamblers, drunkards, the prostituting of women and children, and hosts of other horrible practices."

"I see why some wore sackcloth on circus days. It's an insult to traditional Jews." Zimrah looked away from the walls to the pavestones beneath her feet. "The sands of the Hippodrome soak up not only the blood of those sacrificed under chariot wheels, but also judgment against the land."

"Some say Herod positioned it on purpose on the road leading to and from Jerusalem so all would be reminded of Rome's dominion. It angers me. Jerusalem, in all her splendor, is not free. She's a slave." He looked back toward the city, a scowl on his face.

"I know what that feels like." Zimrah was relieved when both the Hippodrome and the crowds fell behind them and the road opened to the peaceful Judean plains.

They had not travelled far before, to her surprise, she began to miss the crowds. They did have their benefits. They made less of the spectacle that was she and Theophilus.

While in Jerusalem, she had almost forgotten how people responded to Theophilus's height and stature and the foreignness of her features. She had spent so much time with Sanya, whose eastern eyes and skin tone were even more pronounced than her own, and Maarku who was just as tall and robust as Theophilus.

Jerusalem held together within her walls people of all tribes, tongues, shapes, colors, sizes, and ethnicities. There were Arabs, Greeks, Egyptians, Lybians, and God-fearing Jews from every nation in the Empire. Especially at feast times, Jerusalem gathered under her wings every people group under heaven.

Out here though, on the roads that led north, they were once again objects of unwanted attention. Theophilus seemed either oblivious or almost to revel in his differentness. He did not seem to mind the attention in the slightest.

Upon their first meeting, Zimrah had called him free-spirited. In a way, she envied his easy confidence. Nothing seemed to shake him. The knowledge she now carried of where she came from helped her feel more comfortable within her own skin. Although, she wasn't yet as confident as her husband, she prayed that one day she might share Theophilus's ease with the attention.

They journeyed for many days from first light until the sun was only a slip on the horizon. When the huddled buildings of Capernaum finally became distinguishable from the sky reflected in the waters of the Sea of Galilee, they shared a smile. It was hours past noon, and what little warmth the winter sun had to offer was almost gone. It was the coldest day they had yet. The wind off the sea grew keen and biting.

The couple was glad for Domitian's open invitation to stay at his home when they returned. Theophilus tossed a copper coin to a boy kicking stones along the road, to run ahead to the centurion's house and herald their arrival.

By the time they entered the city gate, Caius was waiting for them. He was wrapped in a thick woolen mantle. In his arms were two additional wool coverings, one for each of them.

"Thank you, Caius." Zimrah was grateful for the wool and Caius's thoughtfulness as he helped her wrap it around her cold ears and neck. As she looked into his face though, alarm replaced her gratitude.

In the months since they had seen him, Caius's once young and robust form had wasted away. There were dark circles under his eyes, his skin had lost all color, and a slight tremor shook his hands.

"Oh, Caius, are you not well?"

"Do not concern yourself, my lady. I'm well enough to perform my duties. For that I'm thankful." He continued to speak as he led them through the tree-lined streets of Capernaum, which were quickly emptying due to the lateness of the hour and the cold. "Domitian has been away north since last you were here. He returned only this morning from Tyre."

"Tyre?" Zimrah asked.

"What business had he there?" Theophilus spoke at the same time.

"I'm sure he has much to tell you himself. I know he'll be pleased to see you. He asked if you had yet come through Capernaum when he returned this morning." Caius gave in to a fit of coughing.

The task of walking and speaking at the same time appeared difficult for him. He had to stop more than once to catch his breath. When he stumbled on a loose stone in the road, he did not refuse Theophilus's arm of support.

"What ails you, Caius? We have been gone only these three months." She cut short what came to her mind to say. Instead she finished with, "Forgive me. You need not be reminded of your illness."

"Do not apologize, my lady. Domitian has sent for physicians from as far away as Egypt. None have found a name for what ails me, much less a remedy. My declining health continues no matter what foul brews they concoct." Caius gave them a half smile to show that his illness had not affected his humor.

***

Theophilus's brow knotted in consternation. Vivid memories filled his mind of watching his mother fade from the tireless and vibrant woman he had known to one whose every breath was an effort. Eventually death came for all men, in battle or old age. This Theophilus understood. Illness however, was a cowardly thief that stalked its victims without cause or mercy. Why sickness took the undeserving before their time was a question he would one day like answered.

They arrived to find the brazier burning in the front room of Domitian's home.

"It feels good in here." Theophilus rubbed his hands in front of the fire and watched his wife unravel the wool from around her neck.

Felix brought a tray filled with hot chamomile tea and freshly baked sweet breads. "Here now. This should warm you."

"Thank you, Felix. You are a welcome sight on this cold day."

"Are you happy to see me or the food?" Felix exchanged a knowing look with Zimrah.

Theophilus stopped with a sweet bread halfway to his mouth. "Can I say both?"

The food and drink warmed him on the inside just as well as the coals warmed him on the outside. When the master of the house joined them, they were thoroughly refreshed and comfortable.

"Theophilus and Zimrah! As always, Yahweh's timing is perfect." Domitian's greeting held all the warmth of a father welcoming his children home.

Theophilus clasped the forearm of his old commander. His grip was tighter than normal, and his shoulders were stiff. He was worried about something. Was it his trip to Tyre?

Theophilus raised an eyebrow in his direction, but Domitian waved him off. He embraced Zimrah instead, giving her a kiss on both cheeks before directing her to sit beside him. "How was Jerusalem? Tell me everything."

Remembering his fondness for stories, they took their time reporting all they had experienced in the Holy City. Beginning with the chance meeting with Sanya and ending with the commotion in the temple at their departure, they praised Yahweh for his favor at every turn.

"Ah, yes. You see Zimrah? Did I not say one or both of your parents were Eastern? It was your mother!" Domitian clapped his hands and sat back in his chair, very pleased with himself. "I know my peoples of the world! At least the ones we have knowledge of."

"Caius said you were in Tyre." Theophilus spoke into the comfortable silence that followed the retelling of their journey. "Did you have time to stop by my father's offices while you were there? I received word from him while we were in Jerusalem that he is in Tyre again."

"Unfortunately, no. I was there in an official capacity. There has been some unrest among the Phoenicians and Sidonians that has hindered trade. I was summoned because of my familiarity with the region. However, the presence of a centurion, even a retired one, only made matters worse, I'm afraid. I am an old war horse, Theophilus, not a politician."

"My father mentioned something about the trade conflict before we left Chasah." Zimrah said.

"I am sure you did fine." Theophilus clapped Domitian on the back and then reached for another sweet bread.

"That I did not." Domitian shrugged, his shoulders stiff again. "I was not gifted with the skill of mediation. I train soldiers, Theo. I have not the patience to handhold governors and city elders. Besides, the weather in Tyre would not be good for Caius's health. And if I left him here, who would look after him? No, I'm not the man for this job. I believe I know someone who is though. The man I have in mind was born a patrician and has the strategic skill of an officer. As an added bonus, he is married to a learned beauty who speaks the languages of all the peoples involved."

"W-who, me?" Theophilus stammered, taken off guard by the abrupt turn of conversation.

"Did I not tell you Yahweh's timing was perfect? Who is better suited for the position? Tiberius would be grateful to have this nuisance so well managed." Domitian stood up from the cushions, stretched, and allowed the pleased look to return to his face. "I know you well, Theo. In your capable hands, this conflict is as good as settled."

"Wait a minute. I have not yet agreed to your proposal, sir." He looked to Zimrah for support.

"You will." Domitian grinned. "You can give me your official acceptance in the morning." With that, he retired to his room, leaving a wide eyed Theophilus to consult with his wife.

Felix removed the not yet empty tray of food and informed them that their room was prepared when they were ready. He left with a nod and upturned lips.

"Well, it does seem as though Yahweh is answering your prayer for direction," Zimrah said when they were alone.

During their walk from Jerusalem, Theophilus shared his concern over what he would do when they returned north. They had agreed that returning to Rome was not the most favorable option for either of them. Staying in Chasah and working with Jesse was a valid choice, as was assisting in Lucius's affairs from Tyre. Unfortunately, both of those options left Theophilus almost as displeased as the thought of returning to Rome. Their fathers were merchants. He was not. They had ended the conversation with Zimrah assuring him that Yahweh would reveal which path to take.

"How do you *feel* about Domitian's offer?" Zimrah's gray eyes looked almost amber in the lamplight. "Does it fill you with dread or excitement?"

Theophilus sighed and stretched his long legs in front of him. "When I reached my tenth year, my mother's brother took me to a senatorial session. He was one of the few senators whose ambition was only to see the needs of the people represented with fairness. The topic discussed that day concerned a bill for better water allocations to the insulae—overcrowded, poorly constructed buildings where the poorest of Rome's inhabitants lived. My uncle gave a speech that day with such conviction that he swayed the hearts of the whole senate body. The bill was passed."

Theophilus sat up and took her hand in his. "I was in awe. Armed with only his words, my uncle changed the lives of thousands for the better. In the army, I had only the power to take life. Senators have the power to give it. How do I feel? I am excited beyond words! I know this is not a Senatorial appointment. It is a step in the right direction though, more than I have had thus far. And if I do well, Emperor Tiberius will undoubtedly hear of it. It *does* feel like an opportunity for which I am—we are—uniquely suited."

Zimrah smiled that radiant smile of hers that melted his heart. "Then Domitian has his answer. We will go to Tyre."

***

The beast rubbed his hands together in delight. Theophilus had taken the bait. Men. Always so easily motivated by their ambition!

"Melqart!" He summoned the prince of Tyre before him.

"Yes, my lord." Melqart appeared in his favorite form, a grizzled old woman.

"There is a child of our oppressor coming to you. You will know her when she arrives." The beast seethed, letting his hatred for this particular Child of God show through. "Keep her occupied for me, will you?"

"Of course, my lord. It will be my pleasure."

Chapter 21

OLD THINGS MUST PASS

After a much-needed night's rest, Zimrah had a hard time leaving the comfortable bed in Domitian's guest room. The men were already at table breaking their fast with tea and dried dates by the time she joined them. Theophilus had waited for her to share his news.

Domitian was thrilled to hear Theophilus had decided to accept his proposal. "Excellent. Thank you, Theo. I feel as though a great weight has been lifted from my shoulders."

He handed Theophilus a scroll containing Tiberius's seal and commission. Within the scroll was all the authority Theophilus needed to serve as advocate and representative of the Empire. Zimrah was surprised to learn the position came with a house in Tyre and access to all the gold he would need to fulfill his role and station.

"Tiberius desires this matter settled. Tyre is too important for the flow of commerce in this region. He would not wish to see that flow halted in any way." Domitian urged Theophilus to appear in Tyre as quickly as possible. He sent a garrison soldier on horseback ahead of them to see to it that everything was prepared for their arrival.

Felix gave Zimrah a bag of provisions for the rest of their journey. They said their goodbyes to Caius with prayers for recovered health, and Domitian sent them on their way north to Chasah.

They walked in silence for the first hour, each lost in their own thoughts until Theophilus spoke. "Do you believe this decision to be part of Yahweh's plan? You have said it often enough. 'Yahweh has a plan for us.' Do you think this is part of it?"

Zimrah was moved by the uncertainty of his question. Worry lines on his brow revealed a troubled heart. Had the excitement he felt at the acceptance of the offer turned into fear? Perhaps Theophilus felt he was not ready. Domitian seemed to have great confidence in his abilities. Did Theophilus think Domitian's confidence in him was unfounded?

Just then, a bird swooped across their trail, reminding Zimrah of the ways of Yahweh.

She paused on the road to take his hand. "We have experienced much on this journey. From the beginning, I believed that Yahweh was guiding us toward the purposes He has designed. I felt so strongly that He would reveal my past, and He did. I am so grateful to have it. To have the truth of where I came from is a treasure beyond words. It makes me realize once more how wonderful are the ways of the Almighty. He does nothing without purpose, and not only for the one, but for the many.

"Forgive me Theophilus." She looked up into his brown eyes, taken with how handsome he was.

His chin was shaved when they first met, in the style of the Roman army. Now his beard was full, lending maturity to his almost thirty years.

She reached to rub the hairs on his chin. "When we began, I have to admit I was thinking only of myself, of what Yahweh would reveal of my past and what it meant for the future. I could not have foreseen all He has done for *you*. I see now that it was a pilgrimage for us both. You've been walking in His paths as well. You've heard His voice, felt His heart, and allowed Him to speak through you.

"Yahweh has united your past and your future together to reveal the destiny for which you were born. There was purpose in you being born into the ruling class of Rome. There was purpose in your uncle taking you to witness his speech to the Senate. Even though it was hard, losing your brothers, your mother, and experiencing the things you did in the army, there was purpose in it all. It shaped your heart for compassion, gave you understanding for those who have suffered and a desire to ease that suffering. Look at how you helped Maarku!" Zimrah put a hand on his chest.

"Yahweh has given you wisdom beyond your years, Theo. We have seen danger on this journey, yet you have kept me safe, and others as well. He has made you like a high tower, protecting all those around you. In all of this, there is purpose. I believe Yahweh is showing you, as He has me, that you are not alone. He is with you."

Words from one of the ancient pages she found hidden in the case of her lyre came back to Zimrah's memory. She sang them for only his ears to hear.

"Like the trees planted along the river,
    they bear fruit each season.
Their leaves never wither
    and they prosper in all they do.

"He has made you like a great oak tree, Theophilus. In your shade, many will find rest." The words Zimrah spoke were not her own. They were Yahweh's. Her forehead tingled as Theophilus bent to touch his forehead to hers.

Word travelled quickly through the small city of Chasah that Zimrah and Theophilus had returned. When they arrived, the gates of the house of Jesse were open wide, and Jesse and Nina were waiting for them in the entryway.

Zimrah fell into Jesse's arms and cried for joy. She was home.

"Welcome back, Yediydah." Jesse spoke into her hair with emotion threatening in his voice.

"I missed you, Abba."

When Zimrah spoke the Aramaic word for father, the emotion overflowed and ran into Jesse's beard. He held her for a long moment. "Daughter mine, is it official now?"

"Yes, Abba. I'm your daughter."

"You always were." Jesse held her at arm's length to set his gaze upon her. "You have matured while you were away. You are not Little Zimrah any longer. You are a woman now." He took Theophilus's hand and put Zimrah's into it, giving her into his care once more. The tears flowed, yet there was joy shining in his eyes.

"Come." Nina spoke for the first time. "Master Jesse, you have them standing out in the cold! I have tea and warm honey cakes in the kitchen."

"Honey cakes?" Theophilus said with obvious excitement. "We've been here for a full five minutes while those poor honey cakes lay all alone in the kitchen?"

Everyone laughed, and Zimrah embraced Nina on the way through the courtyard. Being here felt strange to her. She had not been gone that long, and it was the place she longed for most while away. Zimrah knew every stone on the pathway. Every branch of the ancient almond tree was etched in her memory, as familiar as the lines on the palms of her hands. They had always been there, a refuge and a sanctuary through all the fear, sadness, and despair of her youth. But everything was different now.

Jesse was right. She was not a little girl anymore. She was a married woman whose path lay before her wholly different from the one that lay behind. Her husband had accepted a position as emissary of Rome, and there was a new dwelling waiting for them in Tyre. The same uncertainty that had touched Theophilus now filled her belly. It made her want to cling to the familiar stones beneath her feet, to hold on to Nina like she did when she was a child and afraid in the night.

Jesse had spoken the truth. She was Little Zimrah no longer. It was time to walk in different paths, paths that Yahweh had laid out for her feet.

You are my home, Yahweh. Wherever you lead us, we will go. I know that You are with us.

Jesse and Nina were excited to hear of Theophilus's appointment in Tyre but disappointed that it meant they would have to leave again so soon.

"Well, at least you will not be very far away. It will all work for the best." Jesse took a sip of tea at their low table in the kitchen. "I've been postponing a trip to Carthage until you returned. I didn't want to leave Nina alone. It works better this way."

"How is this better?" Zimrah's stomach sank. The thought of how unhappy Nina would be alone in the house made her chest tight.

"If we are in Tyre, and you are in Carthage, Nina *will* be alone." Theophilus said.

"Naturally, she will go with you to Tyre." Jesse smiled as if he had orchestrated the entire affair himself. "You will be hosting and entertaining officials in this role Theophilus, won't you? It's why you've been provided with a house. There will be enough for Zimrah to do assisting you and managing the affairs of the household and servants that will undoubtedly come with it. That will allow Nina to do what she does best."

"Cook!" Nina clapped her hands with a broad grin on her face.

Zimrah took Nina's hand and smiled. The tightness in her chest disappeared. Yahweh be praised! There was nothing she would like more than to have Nina with her in Tyre. The final threads of uncertainty unraveled from her stomach to be replaced by excitement.

"Oh, Nina! I am so glad you will be with us!"

"Theophilus, you may take Nina and my daughter to Tyre on one condition," Jesse said as muted rays of afternoon sunlight filtered in on him through the windows.

"You have only to name it, Jesse."

"Before you leave, allow Zimrah to sing for me again." He took Zimrah's hand across the table.

She nodded and smiled into her father's eyes. Today she would be with him. She would sit with him under the almond tree and tell him everything. She would sing. Today, every moment would be a treasure.

PART TWO
TRANSFORMATION

Chapter 22

WHEN LIGHT SHINES BRIGHTEST

Zimrah had gone to bed early and alone. She lay staring up at the folded layers of canopy as the breeze from the open window blew the cloth in rippling waves.

Abba, what am I going to do?

"Trust Me."

They were the only words she heard from Father Yahweh these days. In the two years Zimrah had lived in the port city, she had come to understand why the ancient Hebrew scrolls called Astarte and Melqart, primary deities of Tyre and Sidon, detestable gods. She agreed wholeheartedly with the Almighty in His judgment. The corruption she witnessed in Jerusalem shone like white snow in comparison to the evil of Tyre.

In stark contrast to the Festival of Lights, the yearly festivals and observances of the Phoenicians kept the Mediterranean city under a layer of spiritual darkness. Temple prostitution and the sacrificing of not just animals, but infants and children,

183

were among the worst examples of the sort of worship the Phoenician gods required.

"My father was wise to keep me from this city." She whispered to Yahweh and her empty room. "I didn't understand his wisdom until now."

I'm miserable, Abba.

A tear fell to the pillow beneath her head. She swiped at the wet trail it left on the bridge of her nose and then sat up to hug her knees to her chest. *Pull it together, Zim. Is it all that bad?*

Other young women envied her. And, why not? She had a beautiful home, servants and slaves—she worked hard at treating them as her father had treated her—and a handsome, accomplished husband who adored her. Meanwhile, Theophilus was making a name for himself among the city's aristocracy. From the outside, Zimrah's life looked perfect. Within, she felt weak and wretched.

She left the bed for the window, looked out across the lights of the island city and to the dark sea beyond, too anxious to sleep.

Will she come again tonight, my Lord?

At least one night in seven days, she battled a dark force in her dreams. They were always the same. She would awaken to the presence of a grizzled old woman, dressed in rags, standing at the foot of her bed and looking down on them. Zimrah would then rise and wrestle with this woman through the rooms of the house, trying to force her out of the front gates. The dreams felt so real, she would awaken afterward and search the rooms for signs of their conflict.

Worse, she was losing Yahweh's voice. Night after night, He became harder and harder to hear. She didn't think Yahweh had stopped speaking. It was just all the activity was distracting her from Him, all except for the ever constant, *"Trust Me."*

Zimrah was accustomed to awakening every morning to the tingling feeling of Father Yahweh's presence on her head. Now she awoke to the kind of despair and loneliness she had not experienced in years. Her despair only deepened because she believed these struggles had been left behind with her youth. She longed for the quiet serenity of her home in Chasah. Once again, she found herself homesick.

Zimrah heard the door open behind her.

"You're still awake?" Theophilus crossed the room to stand behind her. His hands massaged her shoulders. "You should rest. We have a busy day tomorrow."

"Don't remind me." She turned from the window to bury her face in his chest.

Her misery came not only from her dreams. She was drowning in all the activity. In the daytime hours, there was a constant stream of governmental meetings, where she served as companion, interpreter, and silent advisor to her husband. The evenings were filled with dinner parties here in their lavish seaside home. She was losing herself in all the commotion of her daily life.

She had only Nina to talk to, if she could catch her in a quiet moment amidst the swirl of busy servants in the kitchen. Her father came to visit whenever he could, which had made it more bearable. But in two years, she had not found a single friend. The other officials' wives seemed to have nothing more to talk about than the latest dress styles coming out of Rome. They complained incessantly about their husbands, their household slaves, or any other list of mundane topics they found to bemoan. It was driving Zimrah absolutely mad.

Theophilus kissed the top of her head and bent to nuzzle her ear. "Come to bed."

She followed him and settled in his arms.

"Theo?"

"Hmm?"

Should she tell him what was on her mind? No comfort was to be found in him either. He and Nina were completely happy in their elements. Her father had hired another servant to care for him and his house, and Nina—needed in Tyre more than in Chasah—was running a kitchen, feeding the myriad guests that came through their doors. And Theophilus was negotiating with words instead of his sword. He was changing people's lives for the better.

"Goodnight, my love." Zimrah did not want to dampen his joy with her woes. The only light shining in the darkness was the ever-increasing news from Galilee of Yeshua of Nazareth.

The next day, Appius and his wife Annia came by to share the evening meal. Both couples were enjoying the view of the sea on the upper terrace. It was a beautiful day in early spring. The sun sparkled to ever deepening shades of blue all the way to the horizon, and not a cloud darkened its reflection on the water. The couples entertained themselves with conversation and food as they watched the seabirds swoop to splash in foamy ripples after an unseen school of fish.

"There seems to be no end to the fantasies concocted by this man's followers," Appius, the Roman governor of Tyre said.

"I have heard he is doing many amazing things, healing the sick, cleansing lepers. They say he can even raise the dead." Annia spoke rather excitedly.

Annia was a woman prone to gossip with heights of excitement over subjects Zimrah usually found uninteresting. This time though, she gave Annia her full attention.

"He raises the dead?" Zimrah patted her knee to encourage her to share more of the story.

"So they say. I heard he raised the daughter of a synagogue ruler named Jairus. When Yeshua arrived at Jairus's house, there were already mourners present, wailing for the girl."

"She was probably not dead at all. They only thought she was." Appius plucked a piece of goat cheese from a tray.

"It is curious that you should mention that, my love." Annia gazed with mock sweetness at her husband. "That is almost exactly what Yeshua said when he came upon the house. 'The child is not dead but asleep.' The wailers reportedly laughed at him. Their laughter was cut short when Yeshua came out of the house a short time later with the girl alive and well."

"It was a trick!" Appius guffawed, almost spewing bits of cheese all over the table. "Yeshua said it himself. The girl was only sleeping. You excite yourself needlessly, Annia. You must not believe everything you hear."

"Mourners do not usually wail over the sleeping, dearest." Annia's eyes narrowed defensively. "I believe even Galileans know how to recognize the dead. There was another story I heard about him raising a widow's son from his coffin during his funeral procession. Were they on their way to bury someone who was also merely sleeping? It would appear Galilee has suddenly been overcome by a heavy sleeping sickness."

Appius waved her off and turned to Theophilus on some manner of business. When her husband dismissed her, Annia looked out to the ocean with tears in her eyes. Zimrah had never seen anything affect her like this.

She rested a hand on her knee again. "It's important to you, Annia. I'm listening if you'd like to talk to me."

"Oh, Zimrah. I so desperately want the stories to be true." Annia leaned in close and spoke in a low voice so the men could not hear. "It's my daughter, Persephone. She nearly died of a fever last year. Do you remember? I was so desperate. None of the doctors' remedies were working. So, I took her to the temple of Astarte for help."

"Oh, Annia." Zimrah's reaction was involuntary.

"After spending the night in the temple, she came home, and the fever left her. I was beside myself with joy. I paid so many gifts of thanksgiving to those priests. I would be ashamed to tell you how much. My joy was short-lived though. My beloved Persephone was never the same. My sweet child has become so despondent. She's given to fits of rage so intense I fear for her safety and that of my household. It can only be an evil spirit that could create such a change in my daughter. If Yeshua can raise the dead, surely he can handle an evil spirit. I want my daughter back."

Despite Annia's attempts to speak to Zimrah privately, the men had stopped their conversation to listen. "What do you think of this trickster from Nazareth, Theophilus? You are always full of wise advice. What words of wisdom do you have for my wife? Should she believe these claims?" Appius's eyebrows raised over his glass of wine. "Did you not say you met this Yeshua while you were passing through Galilee? What kind of man did you take him for? Did he perform any illusions or sorcery while you were with him?"

"No." Theophilus hesitated. His hand went to where the slash of a bandit's sword had injured his side. Or had it?

Zimrah's eyes rested on the spot as well until she looked up, and their eyes met. His brow furrowed, and he shook his head as if to push aside the idea they both knew to be true—that he *had* indeed been wounded and that somehow Yeshua had knit his flesh back together with a single touch.

He rubbed his side. "We met *a* Yeshua from Nazareth, although he was nothing like the man the stories portray. I am not sure he is even the same man. The man we met by the Jordan was humble and unassuming. There was no lie in his eyes."

The conversation soon turned to other topics. Appius and Annia stayed to watch the sun set in vibrant orange and red into the Mediterranean. The governor thanked them for a lovely afternoon and left with promises to return the hospitality later the following week.

Zimrah could not shake Annia's story about Yeshua. Was is true? Had he truly raised the dead? She went over the encounter by the river over and over again in her mind. Had he indeed closed the wound in Theophilus's side with a touch and then went on like nothing out of the ordinary had happened? Could he be the same man from Annia's story?

Sleep did not come easy to her that night.

***

Zimrah was alone in a dank room with no windows. She lay on a raised slab of cold stone, and there were candles burning at her head and at her feet. By the light of the candles, she could see why she could not move her arms and legs. They were bound. But the pale limbs were not her own. Zimrah was seeing through someone else's eyes. There was no sound except for a low droning chant coming from the throats of many men behind her. An overwhelming stench was covered by the thick smell of frankincense.

Her vision blurred. When it cleared again, there was a hooded man standing at her feet. He was dressed in white—a priest of Melqart, the patron god of Tyre. She had seen similarly dressed men near Melqart's temple. It was hard to breathe. Her heart raced and her arms and legs were weak. She struggled against her bonds to no avail. The man clambered up onto the slab, pulled the cloth around her legs up to her waist with rough hands, and climbed on top of her, his heaviness unbearable. She couldn't breathe! Her ears were filled with the screams of many other young women in the room.

Zimrah shut her eyes tight against the horror and tried to call out for Yahweh to save her. No sound came. She struggled against the hands that held her. The wails of dying newborn babies rang in her ears right before she awoke with a start.

"Zimrah! Wake up! You're safe. You're safe now."

The hands that held her belonged to Theophilus. She was in her own bed. It was just a dream.

Theophilus held her as she sobbed into his bare shoulder.

"Oh Theophilus." She sobbed through ragged breaths. "They killed the babies! They sacrificed them on the same altars they were conceived on!" Mustering her courage, she told him everything she had seen in the dream.

***

Theophilus was at a loss. He did not know what to do to ease his wife's suffering. It both surprised and disturbed him that she had seen these things. She could not have known they actually happened! Only the priests themselves and a handful of city officials knew.

Theophilus's heart beat wildly in his chest. He could only hope that what she had seen had been images from Tyre's bloody past and not current day practice in the temple of Melqart. Thinking about it made the hair on his arms stand up.

Were her dreams some kind of warning from Yahweh? Or were they birthed from the evil forces that even he could sense still lingering within the walls of this ancient city?

She pushed out of his arms and sat up. "I want to go home, Theo. It's hard for me to say that out loud. It's like admitting defeat. I'm not strong enough for this kind of war. I don't know how to fight. I miss Chasah. I miss Jesse's house. I miss the Leontes and the peace of the mountains. I miss Yahweh!"

"What about your lyre? You haven't played in months." Playing the lyre always brought her peace. Why had she given it up?

"I can't reach Him!" Zimrah wailed. "Every time I try to play, it's like there is thick stone over my head. My voice falls flat back down to my own ears. I cannot reach His shelter in my mind. Every time I close my eyes, there are only the images from my dreams. I'm losing myself in the darkness here."

"Then you have to go, Zim. Go home to Jesse's house for a little while. Perhaps there you can reach Yahweh, and He will show you what to do. I can meet you there in a few days after I've finished with the delegation from Damascus, and then we'll figure it out."

Saying those words tore his heart in two. He could not bear the thought of being parted from her, but if it eased her suffering, he would endure it. Two days, three at most, and they would be together again.

***

Theophilus had fallen back to sleep, but Zimrah couldn't. The images from her dream replayed themselves over and over behind her closed eyelids. The pitiful cries of the sacrificed filled her ears.

Yahweh, please help me! I can't rest. I feel as if I will go mad. Please, Abba. Tell me what to do.

With her cry came a new image. She saw herself in the small alcove where she first played to Yahweh. It had been months since she had been there, before the darkness took hold. In the image she was playing her lyre again.

"Come to Me, sing to Me, before the day is done."

Zimrah heard the voice of Yahweh whisper so softly, she was not sure if what she heard truly was His voice. Perhaps it was only her tortured mind, pulled to the point of breaking, grasping for relief.

It did not matter. She would go.

Rising from Theophilus's sleeping side and lighting the lamp beside her bed to carry with her, she padded quietly on bare feet to the alcove. The lyre lay there in its case—dusty from months of disuse—waiting for her. Zimrah sat on the stone floor, cushioned with pillows against the cold, and prayed again before she began to play.

"Abba Yahweh, please help me. Show me what to do." She remembered what Rebecca, the red-haired lady in her dream had said, that all she had to do was call. "Rebecca, I do not know who you are. I think you may be an angel. If you are, please come. Come and help me now as I sing."

Trembling fingers produced no loveliness that night. The song that came was full of remembered truth alone. It brought little comfort to her discouraged soul.

> "You rescue me because You love me.
> You protect me. I trust in Your name.
> When I call on You, You will answer.
> For You are the God Who Saves.
>
> "There is no land too far.
> There is no night too dark.
> There is no valley too deep.
> Where You cannot recue me.

"You will rescue me because You love me.
You protect me. I trust in Your name.
When I call on You, You will answer.
For You are the God Who Saves.

"This land is too far.
This night is too dark.
This valley is too deep.
Rescue me, Lord.
Rescue me."

Zimrah put her lyre down and leaned her head back on the cushions. A single tear rolled down her cheek, and she swiped at it with cold fingers. "Abba, will you leave me here in this dark land forever? When will you come and rescue me?"

***

When Zimrah cried out with the power of the Word, her authority to command the angelic host gave them release. If she could have seen the light that poured forth from a daughter drowning in deep, dark waters who reached for truth, she would have leapt for joy.

Flashes of light exploded from swords held back for much too long. Demons of darkness, blinded by the scorching light, had no recourse. They could not even see the angels blazing with fury who dispatched them. The angels' wings flamed, and their eyes burned like coals of fire.

After the battle, when not a dark spirit was left alive, and Melqart had retreated in terror, Rebecca looked around at her companions and laughed. "That was fun!"

Not too far from where Zimrah sang by the light of a single flame, her song reached the ears of One whose hearing had been attuned by power without reckoning. Melody flowed into His dreams like a wind filled with light, sound, and love. At the rising of the sun, Yeshua's heart was drawn north, to the child who sang to Him.

Chapter 23

THE RISING SON

When morning dawned, Zimrah walked the causeway connecting Tyre to the mainland with Theophilus holding her hand, her lyre, and her small travel bag. Not one time did she look back at the city. Her feet ached for the road home. She had been back several times before in the two years since she had lived in Tyre. This time felt different, more like an escape than a visit.

"The sea is so calm this morning." Her face was set over the still water and toward the rising sun. "I wish I felt its peace."

"You will." Theophilus brought her hand to his lips. "Peace is only five miles away."

"I hate leaving you to finish with the delegation alone."

"I'll be fine. My Phoenician is getting better every day." He winked at her. "I'll meet you in Chasah as soon as it's over."

Theophilus sent a trusted soldier—waiting for her on the mainland—to accompany Zimrah on the short journey home.

It was as though she did not take a breath until the walls of Chasah were within sight.

Her childhood friend, Arisha waved to her as she passed through the market. However, Zimrah had neither the heart nor desire to stop and share pleasantries. She quickly returned the wave and continued on as if there were hounds at her heels. Nothing but the locked gate of Jesse's house would end their pursuit.

Once safely inside, she leaned for a moment to rest on the strong wooden gate and sighed her relief.

"Abba!" Her feet took her deeper into the house and out into the sun of the courtyard. "Abba, are you home?"

"Zimrah?"

His voice came from inside his study. She let her traveling bags drop to the floor when she saw him standing under the archway. The beauty of the ancient almond tree in full bloom in the middle of the courtyard did little to raise her spirits as she ran into his arms.

"I didn't know you were coming home today." Jesse was happy to see her until he saw her face. He stroked her hair to comfort her shaking.

"What is it, Yediydah? Are you alright? Did something happen?"

"I missed you." Heat rose in her cheeks, running back home like a child. "I know why you kept me from that city, Abba. You were protecting me. It's full of such terrible darkness. I was sinking deeper and deeper. I couldn't find the light." Zimrah felt like she was speaking to Yahweh as well as to her father.

He simply held her for a long moment. "I think I understand what's troubling you. Come, Zimrah." He led her across the courtyard to her room, picking up her bags along the way.

Surrounded by the familiar, in the place where she had spent so much time with Yahweh, her back straightened and her breath came easier, like the hounds had finally stopped their chasing. A bit of long lost peace inched its way back into her soul.

Her attention caught on a comb, a little ivory butterfly that Jesse had given her when she was twelve. She took it from the niche in the wall and fingered it lovingly as Jesse spoke.

"You may not know this, Daughter. We have been blessed to live in times of peace, but in times of war, this room served a much different purpose." He moved to the southeast window and looked out over the winding Leontes River and the mountains beyond. "The watchmen were assigned here. Their role was to walk the city walls, to stay up high and watch for signs of the enemy coming from afar. Once the enemy was spotted, it was the watchmen's responsibility to warn the city below. It was a heavy burden. If the watchmen fell asleep or neglected their task, the city would fall."

Jesse turned to see Zimrah by his side with the butterfly comb in her hair. "I remember that. It's the gift I gave you all those years ago. He turned fully toward her and took both her hands. "Yahweh has also given you gifts. This room was not chosen for you by chance. You are a watchman, Zimrah. Like the watchmen of old, it is a heavy burden. Know that Yahweh would not have given you such a responsibility if He did not also give you the ability to bear it."

"I've seen horrible things, Abba." She was filled again with a sense that she was speaking to Abba Yahweh as well. "I have seen things I don't understand."

Yahweh spoke back to her through Jesse. "You don't have to. Whether you feel Him or not, Yahweh is with you. You belong to Him. That will never change. Take the things you have seen before Him. He will show you what to do."

Jesse took the bag that contained the heavy case of her lyre and put it in her hands. Placing a hand to her cheek for a moment, he left her alone to be with the Almighty.

As Zimrah played, all the horror and torment of the last two years melted away like wax before a flame. The hindrance that she described as thick stone over her head dissipated, and Zimrah worshipped, basking in the light of Yahweh's love. As she poured out to Him all she had seen in her dreams, just as Jesse said, Yahweh was there to help her understand. In His presence, turmoil turned to peace and then to joy.

When Zimrah stopped singing, she leaned back on the pillows of her bed, the lyre still in her hands. She couldn't keep the smile from her face.

"It is so good to be with You again, Yahweh." She whispered to the Lord of All, sensing His presence there beside her.

"And with you. I missed you."

Joyful tears filled her eyes. Zimrah took the time to rest in the sweetness of the moment for a while before rising to put the lyre back in its case. Her thoughts drifted to Theophilus.

"What do I do now, my Lord?" She didn't have to say what was in her heart. Yahweh already knew. She didn't want to return to Tyre, yet what of Theophilus? Like Nina, he was happy there. Indeed, he was born for the position. Within months of his administration, the trade lines between Tyre and Rome had begun to open again. And now, after two years of his oversight, they were running more safely and efficiently than ever before. Just as he hoped, Tiberius himself had taken note of Theophilus's good work.

Zimrah was proud of her husband and pleased he had found the path to his heart's desire. She knew, though, that his happiness was diminished by her misery. The dilemma had stood like a wall growing taller and taller between them for months. It felt strange admitting the wall existed, even before God and her empty room.

Yahweh, what do I do? If His answer was for her to return to Tyre, she would obey. Yahweh would give her the strength to endure.

"Go to the river."

"My Lord?" It was not at all the response she expected to hear. Nor did it seem to contain an answer to the question she had asked. She would have doubted the words were His at all if she were not still feeling the tingling on her forehead.

"Go. Go to the river."

His words were followed by a sense of urgency and an image of the waters of the Leontes sparkling in the sunlight.

"Go now."

"Yes, my Lord."

Zimrah snatched her headscarf from the end of her bed, hurried down the steps to the courtyard, past the flowering almond tree, through the kitchen, and down the back steps that led to the gentle waters of the Leontes.

"I'm here, Yahweh. What now?"

The sound of the water flowing over the rocks and the wind blowing the leaves of the trees was the only response. Remembering the morning in Capernaum when Yahweh awakened her to watch the sun rise, Zimrah turned her face to the west and closed her eyes. She let the warmth of the sun fill her with an awareness of Yahweh's presence just as her singing had done only minutes before. He was everywhere.

With her eyes still closed, she began to hear a male voice humming a melody. It was coming from the east and grew slightly louder as if the singer were walking in her direction. Zimrah almost turned to see who it was but stood still. She listened instead. The melody reached her ears and gave her pause. Both the song and the beautiful voice were familiar. It was hummed without words, so she added them without turning.

"Daughter mine,
fair and fine,
Light in the morning sun.
Come to me,
sing to me,
before the day is done."

Then Zimrah did turn and open her eyes. A man dressed in tan robes was walking toward her, still humming the melody to the song she knew so well. She knew his face and the name that went with it.

Yeshua of Nazareth.

"Hello, Zimrah." Yeshua had a smile on his bearded face. "I was hoping to find you here."

Zimrah could only stare at him in open-mouthed awe and confusion. "You were hoping to find *me?*"

She was amazed both at his presence and his words. This was the man about which she had been hearing so much, even from Tyre! This was the man who was healing the sick and raising the dead, if the stories were to be believed. Why would he would be looking for *her?*

"Yes. I came here to find *you.* Theophilus said when we met by the river that day that you were from Chasah. You are very special to my Father, Zimrah."

So many questions went through her mind at once. She couldn't hold on to one in particular to ask first. Her mouth dropped open again, making Yeshua chuckle.

"Come, let us sit here and talk awhile." Yeshua led her to a couple of large rocks beside the river, and they sat together.

A question finally settled in her mind and made its way out of her mouth. "How did you know that melody?"

"Since the day I first met you, Zimrah, I have seen you in my dreams. There is always that melody. I didn't remember that it had words until I heard you singing them just now."

"I heard it first in a dream as well." Zimrah was amazed. "It was sung by a young man walking beside a river just like this." Zimrah gestured to the water flowing merrily beneath their feet. "I have seen him often in my dreams. I never really understood who he was though."

"That was me!" Yeshua stated it easily, like it wasn't the most amazing thing she'd ever heard.

He must have seen the confusion in her eyes. "You've known my Father for a long time, Zimrah. I saw you as you sat in the watchtower and sang to Him. You have worshipped in Spirit and in truth. You've seen my Father, so you've seen me. I and the Father are One. I'm the Son He has been showing you was coming. The S-o-n of God."

Zimrah's mind was flooded with memories of her time with Yahweh. In almost every song, every dream, every vision, there was imagery of the sun, whose light never burned her eyes.

"John tried to tell us. We didn't understand."

"Jaaziel knew the truth, too."

"How do you know about my father?" The hairs on her arms and neck began to rise. Her mind still fought against the truth her heart already accepted. "How can you know all these things about me?"

"Because I AM, Zimrah. I am who Jaaziel believed I am."

"The Messiah."

Zimrah's words came out in a whisper, barely audible.

"I Am He."

Tears began to flow onto Zimrah's cheeks. Her skin tingled, and her ears buzzed. It had to be true. It was the only way He could know what He knew, that He could be doing all the wonders people were saying He was doing.

"Have you really raised the dead?"

"I have." Yeshua's eyes shone with joy.

His word was enough. Zimrah believed. The Messiah had come. Nothing would ever be the same again.

"Come, follow me." Yeshua's grin was wide and wonderful.

Zimrah's heart leapt with joy. There was nothing she would love more. She felt her heart would race itself right out of her chest until she remembered Theophilus.

"My husband—"

"I know. All will be well. He is here now." Yeshua gestured to the house above them. "Go and tell him all you have seen and heard from me. I'll be waiting for you in Capernaum."

Chapter 24

WITH THE EYES OF FAITH

Zimrah awoke with a start. She was lying against the pillows on her bed in her room in Chasah. The lyre was still in her hands. She had fallen asleep. Meeting Yeshua by the river had been a dream! Yet every inch of her body tingled. It may have been a dream, but she knew what she had to do.

She rushed downstairs. Theophilus was sitting with Jesse just as Yeshua said he would be.

"There you are, Zim!" Theophilus said before she could catch her breath enough to speak. "The delegation from Damascus ended sooner than expected," was all he managed before she interrupted.

"I have seen him!"

"What? Who?"

Zimrah took the seat beside him. "I have seen the Lord! Yeshua of Nazareth!"

She told him and Jesse about her dream.

"He told me you would be here." Zimrah grasped Theophilus's arm, as if the force of her touch alone would help him understand.

His brow furrowed. "You were sleeping. You probably heard me come in, and your mind translated it into your dream."

"No, Theophilus. It's true. Just as Jaaziel believed. He is the Messiah we have been waiting for. *Yeshua* is the Son of God! John tried to tell us that night by the river. I understand it now. All of it. He invited me to follow him and said he would be waiting for us in Capernaum. We have to go!"

Deep silence filled the room.

"Well." Jesse sighed and rose to excuse himself. "It appears you two have much to discuss."

Theophilus didn't speak until Jesse's retreating steps could no longer be heard on the stone floor. "Zimrah, I know our time in Tyre has been hard for you."

"This doesn't have anything to do with that."

"No? Are you sure?" Theophilus's tone was calm, his words measured. "Because this is madness. I have heard these tales all my life. Yeshua is the son of god? Like Achilles? Like Hercules? They were said to perform mighty feats as well. You can't believe everything you hear, Zimrah!" His words were coming faster now, harsher. "You want to go to Capernaum because you saw Yeshua in a dream? You think it was real?"

"You sound like Appius." Zimrah's voice remained quiet, even though Theophilus's had risen as he spoke.

He sighed deeply to calm himself. "Forgive me. I know you've seen things in your dreams before, and you want me to understand, but I can't. This? This is not the same! In all our time at the temple in Jerusalem, we heard it over and over. 'The Lord our God is One God.' He is a jealous God, but Yeshua told you he and the Father are one? It makes no sense!"

It was Zimrah's turn to sigh. "I don't have all the answers, Theophilus. I only know that we must go. We went all the way to Jerusalem following my dreams, and look what happened! We have to follow this path. It *does* make sense if you look with eyes of faith."

He ran his hand through his hair. "It makes little sense to *me*."

Abba? How do I help him see? Zimrah sat back, closed her eyes, and rubbed her face with her hands.

"Come follow me." Yeshua's smiling face filled her vision.

She would go, even if she had to go alone.

***

Theophilus wanted so much to understand, to share the joy he could see shining in Zimrah's eyes. In the two years they had been married, there was nothing about which they had truly disagreed until now.

"You must trust me. You must trust Yahweh." Zimrah gripped his arm again, her voice choked with emotion.

"I do." Theophilus slumped his shoulders in resignation.

Even in the beginning, there were things about her he didn't understand. It was part of what caused him to fall in love with her. He had never met anyone like Zimrah. As her husband, he could command her to stay. Yet, if he did, it would be the end of her trust in him and their relationship would never be the same. It would be a loss too great for him to bear. A man couldn't control those he loved and expect his love to be returned. His father had taught him that. Intense love filled him even as he gazed into her gray eyes.

"I won't try to stop you, but... Be careful, Zim." His voice was a whisper again. "If there is trouble, I won't be there to protect you." The face of the bowman and the arrow that had nearly taken her away forever came into his mind.

"Come with me." Tears filled her eyes and dropped onto her cheeks. "Please, Theo."

His heart was breaking. He would rather face an army than her tears. Perhaps she would stay, change her mind, come to her senses. "You know I can't. I haven't been released from my commission in Tyre."

Zimrah wiped her tears with both hands. After a moment, she reached up to stroke the hairs on his chin and smiled. "Yahweh showed me something wonderful in the heavenly court. Whatever may come, we will be together. We'll grow old together. All will be well. Yahweh is with us. I'll stay on the Roman road. I'll stay with Domitian. I'll write as soon as I arrive and every day until we're together again."

She wouldn't change her mind. She seemed soft and impressionable on the outside, but inside was a core of stone. Theophilus lifted her into his arms to carry her to their bed. They had this night. He would use it to help her remember his love. Perhaps it would serve to return her all the more quickly to him.

***

When the huddled buildings of Capernaum came into view, Zimrah wanted to dance, and would have if there weren't so many other people on the road. The Sea of Galilee reflected the sky like a looking glass. From where she stood, she could make out little dots on the water—fishing boats. She breathed the sea air and smiled.

The walk from Chasah had been easy and beautiful. The sun was bright in a blue sky, and she could not remember the last time she felt so light and free. She didn't feel in the least bit alone. Theophilus—and her father as well—had tried to persuade her to wait at least a day. Theophilus would send the soldier to accompany her again.

She had refused. She was following the will of the Almighty and His Son. Who could hurt her or stand in her way? "Yahweh will protect me."

He was not happy, but he finally acquiesced. She had spent the first day looking over her shoulder and listening for hoofbeats. Knowing Theophilus, he had sent the soldier anyway with instructions not to let himself be seen.

As she drew closer to the city gates, a crowd of perhaps thirty people leaving the city walked toward her on the road. They turned off to sit in an open space nearby and listen to the man who separated himself from the rest.

The crowd grew in size with each passing moment, and by the time Zimrah reached where they were, it had swelled to what looked like almost a hundred. She thought the man was John the Baptizer, until she was close enough. Her height allowed her to see over most of their heads. It was Yeshua! He looked just as He had the day before in her dream.

When He had finished speaking, some left the crowd for the road, but many more remained. Three large men were trying to keep those who stayed from trampling Yeshua in their eagerness to reach Him, but a petite young woman was able to slip past their defenses. She held a child of about three years in her arms.

"Teacher! Please, my boy. It's his ears, Rabbi. He cannot hear. I know you can make him well."

Zimrah could tell by the woman's clothing that she didn't have much. She held onto her son as if he were the only treasure she had in the world.

The people grew quiet as Yeshua, compassion shining in His brown eyes, drew closer to the boy. He smiled and ruffled his hair gently to put the frightened child at ease. "What is his name?"

"It's Benjamin." Tears were already falling from her chin.

Yeshua placed His hands on the boy's head and then brought his lips close and whispered into little ears. The One, born to be Savior of the world, spoke a word into that which was dead and created new life.

"Benjamin."

The boy jumped at the sound.

"Benjamin?" His mother stared at him in stunned amazement.

Benjamin turned in her direction with surprise on his face. When it turned into a smile, his mother let out a joyous cry and cradled his little body close to her heart. She laughed and cried at the same time. The crowd erupted into thunderous praise.

Benjamin's mother bounced him in her arms as the people cheered. Zimrah was overwhelmed and couldn't stop the flow that wet her cheeks and the front of her tunic. She shouted and clapped right along with all the rest.

Benjamin reached for Yeshua. He held the boy, speaking his name and throwing him high in the air only to catch him again. Benjamin squealed in delight.

Zimrah was in awe of what she had just witnessed. Yeshua's miracles weren't just stories any longer. She had seen Him perform the miraculous right before her eyes. He opened a child's deaf ears, with joy and with no pretense, asking nothing in return. There was no more doubt in her mind that Yeshua had healed the wound in Theophilus's side that day by the Jordan River.

When some of the excitement died away and many of the crowd remained, Yeshua walked awhile along the road, still holding Benjamin. His mother and the crowds followed. He came to the side of a hill, climbed it, and sat down in the cool grass. As He began to teach, Benjamin fell asleep in His arms.

"God blesses those who are poor in spirit and realize their need for Him, for the kingdom of heaven is theirs. God blesses those who mourn, for they will be comforted. God blesses those who are humble, for they will inherit the whole earth. God blesses those who hunger and thirst for righteousness, for they will be satisfied."

When Benjamin began to stir, Yeshua gave him back to his mother. She played with him in her lap, tickling him and clapping his hands together just to delight in his response to the sound.

Yeshua's teaching was so different from the other teachers Zimrah had heard in the temple in Jerusalem. They droned on and on about the slightest nuance of the law. Yeshua spoke with simple authority, in a way that was understandable to those who were listening. She drank every word like one who had found water in the desert.

"You are the light of the world, like a city on a hillside that can't be hidden." He gestured to the city that lay high on the mountain above them. "No one lights a lamp and then puts it under a basket. Instead, a lamp is placed on a stand, where it gives light to everyone in the house. In the same way, let your good deeds shine out for all to see, so that everyone will praise your heavenly Father."

Zimrah's tears continued to flow. Yeshua seemed to be speaking to her alone, explaining the ordeal she had just gone through in Tyre and why Yahweh had allowed it. He went on to teach His followers about many things needed for living. He spoke about loving, not just their neighbors, but also their enemies. He taught about true righteousness and how to live without worry or fear for tomorrow. He taught them about forgiveness and how to pray. Like a stream running through all he spoke, there was the Kingdom of God and the Father. Yahweh.

When Yeshua finished teaching, He made His way back down to the city of Capernaum. Zimrah and the crowds followed Him. Before they reached the city, a heavily cloaked man approached Yeshua on the road.

"Leper, leper!" The people in the crowd shouted, keeping their distance from him as the law commanded.

The law was not written without reason. Leprosy was a horrible and contagious disease that ate at its victims' flesh.

Yeshua, payed heed neither to the customs of the law or the crowd behind Him. He kneeled, face to face with the afflicted man.

Those watching gasped. According to Jewish law, Yeshua had just defiled Himself. He was now just as unclean as the leprous man.

"Lord," the man with leprosy said, "If you are willing, you can heal me and make me clean."

"I am willing." Yeshua ignored the response of the people. He had eyes only for the man in front of him. "Be healed!"

The man's skin changed from white to brown before Zimrah's eyes. He held out his hands, and everyone present saw fingers grow where there were none only moments before. No one shouted their praise as loudly as the man himself. Yeshua helped him to stand in front of them all.

Before the crowd drew in closer, Yeshua spoke to him. "Do not tell anyone about this. Instead, go to the priest and let him examine you. Take along the offering required in the Law of Moses for those who have been healed of leprosy. This will be a public testimony that you have been cleansed."

He hugged Yeshua fiercely then disappeared within the mass of people. Many of them went with Him to the city gates.

When the rest of the crowd began to disperse, Zimrah stood alone drumming her fingers against her thighs. What should she do now? Should she try to speak with Yeshua—with the Son of *God*—face to face? Would the men around Him even allow her near Him? And if so, what would she say? What did one say to a man who had just done the impossible before her eyes? Would He remember her? Would He know who she was like He did in the dream? Would He know about the dream? Would He know why she had come?

As she stood frozen in indecision, her gaze fell from Yeshua to the ground. A great weight seemed to crash down upon her, destroying all the joy and lightness she had felt while watching His miracles. What had she done? Had she really just left her husband to follow a man she only knew from her dreams? She'd left the safety of her husband *and* her father's house, and here she was, standing by the side of the road *alone*.

What would people say? No one would understand what she'd done. She was a woman, thinking about going up to a man, surrounded by a group of other men, none of whom she knew, to say what? She had no idea! She didn't really know why she was here. If it truly was Yeshua in her dream, why had He sent for her?

The weight of all the questions seemed to crush her to the rocks beneath her feet. Maybe she could crawl back to Chasah. She raised her eyes a little when a pair of sandaled feet appeared in front of her.

"Zimrah of Chasah." Yeshua smiled at her.

She opened her mouth to speak, but before she could get anything out, He spoke first.

"I know you from the river."

"Yes, my Lord," was all she could manage. She wanted to ask which river, the Jordan, or the one from her dreams, but her beating heart was in her throat, blocking the words.

"I knew we would meet again. I'm glad you've come." He looked around. Was He looking for Theophilus? "Do you have friends here in this city?"

"Yes, my Lord. A friend of my husband lives here in Capernaum. The centurion. But it's improper for me to stay there alone." Her words came out in a heap now. "I left Tyre in such a hurry that I didn't have time to bring anyone with me."

"It is well. There's a woman here, without children or family. Her husband divorced her when she became my follower. I'll send her word. You'll be a great blessing to each other."

"Thank you, my Lord, but please? Can you tell me why I'm here? I dreamt that You bade me to come, but I don't know why. What am I to do?"

Yeshua let out a merry laugh and took both her hands in His.

"Not to do, Zimrah, to *be*. Remember? Oh, Little Bird! You can only be who you were made to be. All you must do is be who you are."

He squeezed her hands and then was gone. She stood where she was and watched until He too disappeared beyond the city gates with His followers.

Zimrah had nothing left but to enter through the gates herself, her mind awash with equal parts relief, joy, and confusion.

***

The beast stood in the heavenly court. He could do nothing but shake in anger and frustration as the proceedings took place around him. He was too flustered to pay attention.

Look at the so-called Almighty, sitting so smugly in that big ugly chair he calls a throne. Pah! *So Zimrah had commanded her angels. Big deal! The beast glanced over at Rebecca, Garbar, and Phanuel. So they had their swords and armor back. Only because Rebecca had cheated and told Zimrah she could call her!*

I would like to take that diamond sword of Rebecca's and shove it down her throat!

Well, he was the beast, wasn't he? He'd been doing this a long time, hadn't he? Sometimes old tricks were the best. Zimrah had always been weak. He only had to remind her of her weakness. He would send her old Tormentors after her.

Except she was now in Capernaum, where he had no prince. So what? The Son was there. Big deal! He could get to her anytime he pleased. What did he need with a prince when he had the hearts of men? And like he said before, men were so easily manipulated by their ambition.

Chapter 25

MORE FUEL FOR THE FIRES OF

FAITH

When Zimrah reached the steps leading to Domitian's house—she hadn't sent him word and hoped her unannounced arrival would be well received—she found a woman sitting on the bottom step waiting for her.

"You must be Zimrah." Joy made her face shine. "I'm Hannah, a follower of Yeshua. He sent word that you were in need of a chaperone. It would please me greatly to serve as your maidservant if you would allow me." Hannah's words were spoken humbly.

When she stood, her back was straight and her brown eyes unwavering. Her clothing, though worn, was clean and tidy. She was older than Zimrah, with a light complexion and brown hair that fell in waves beneath her headscarf. She carried a single bag with her.

Zimrah had still not grown accustomed to having servants. Marrying Theophilus had changed her status in ways she could not have imagined. He lavished her with gifts and saw to it that her every need was met in abundance. He had sent her to Capernaum carrying a coin purse large enough to support an entire household for more than a year. Zimrah smiled at the chance to use what she had been given to benefit another.

"It's good to meet you, Hannah. I'm Zimrah of Chasah, also a follower of Yeshua. I could use a friend more than a maidservant, though."

Hannah's smile was radiant. "Yes, my lady."

"Just Zimrah is fine between us." She winked at her, missing Theophilus. It was something he would have done. "It hasn't been that many years since *I* was a slave."

"Yes, my lady." Hannah's eyes grew wide, and her mouth dropped open. "You were someone's slave, my lady?" Hannah looked Zimrah up and down, and then her cheeks went red for doing so. "Forgive me."

Zimrah smiled and gestured for them to sit where Hannah had been sitting before. "No need. Yahweh has blessed me more than I can say. My life changed after I married."

"As did mine, but not for the better. I will never forget the day my husband discovered I'd become a follower of Yeshua. He came into the house, his face purple with rage, and screamed at me. 'You were seen in the synagogue! Listening to that false prophet. What do you think the other Pharisees will say when they find out my wife has been listening so attentively to this man? I'll be ruined!'"

"It took every ounce of courage I had, but I stood straight and looked him in the eye and said, 'I'm not only listening,'" I believe he speaks the truth. I believe He is the Messiah, Eli!'

"'Do you know what I believe?' he asked me. 'I believe I can find a wife more faithful to her husband's concerns.' Then he grabbed me by the hair and dragged me to the door. 'You, out. Now!'"

Hannah hung her head and pulled her headscarf more tightly around her face. "He drove me from our home with nothing but the clothes I was wearing. I went to Yeshua in despair. I had nowhere else to go. He told me not to worry, that His Father loved me and would provide for me."

Zimrah put a hand on her knee as they sat together in the shade of Domitian's house.

"I would like to say that my faith was strong, that I didn't falter. It would be a lie. Life with my husband was not easy. He was a hard man to love, but I had shelter and a home. After he divorced me, I had nothing but my splintered faith." She looked at Zimrah with moisture in her eyes.

"When I received Yeshua's message today that the wife of a Roman official had left Tyre to follow Him and was in need of a companion, I didn't hesitate. I hurried here as fast as I could."

Zimrah's heart was bursting, and her hand went from Hannah's knee to her arm. "I'm so glad you did. I believe Yeshua was right. We will be a great blessing to each other." She stood. "Come. Let's see if the centurion is home."

Taking one of the packs Zimrah carried off her shoulder, Hannah walked with her up the stairs.

"Lady Zimrah! It's good to see you." Felix ushered them into the entryway. "My master will be happy to see you have arrived safely. Master Theophilus sent a carrier to tell us you were coming."

He took their bags with the welcoming smile Zimrah remembered from her last visit.

"Greetings, Felix!" She should have known Theophilus would not have overlooked sending word on her behalf. Zimrah introduced Hannah. "Is Domitian home?"

"Capernaum is a small city. We are acquainted." Felix smiled at Hannah. "Yes, Master Domitian is home. He's not left Caius's bedside in days."

Felix led them through the house to Caius's chamber. "His illness has worsened since you were here last. He is near the end. Some elders have come from the synagogue and are in with them now. Please, give me a moment."

They reached Caius's door, and Zimrah recognized the Hebrew prayers and blessings being spoken from the elders within.

Felix whispered in Domitian's ear, and he quickly came out and embraced her.

"Zimrah! What a wonderful surprise." Domitian managed a smile for her benefit, although his face showed the evidence of his grief. "Shalom, Hannah. I've heard how cruelly your husband treated you. You didn't deserve to be put aside, but I'm not surprised you and Zimrah have found each other. Theophilus asked in his message if I could see to a companion for you. I would not have chosen anyone better than Hannah.

You are both welcome to stay as long as you wish." Domitian put a hand on each of their shoulders.

"What brings you Zimrah, other than to grace my home with your loveliness?" He appeared to catch himself. He looked back in at Caius lying on his bed and spoke again without waiting for her answer. "I'm glad you've come. We've not had anything to smile about for much too long. There is nothing more the physicians can do. Caius is near death."

"I'm so sorry, Domitian. I know how much he means to you." Zimrah looked at Caius—a much too thin, wasted figure under the covers—and was filled with sadness. Her emotions quickly changed from despair to hope as an idea began to form in her mind. She glanced at Hannah and, by the look in her eyes, thought she may have had the same idea.

"Domitian, I've come because of Yeshua the Nazarene. You must have heard how he is healing the sick." She was excited, and her words came quickly. "I've witnessed his power myself. He opened the ears of a deaf boy and cleansed a man with leprosy just this morning, right before my eyes! He is here in Capernaum now. I know if you asked, he would come and heal Caius. He's so young. It cannot be Yahweh's will for him to die!"

Domitian didn't hesitate. He turned and walked back into the room, with Zimrah and Hannah trailing behind him. "Please, my friends," he said to the elders, interrupting their prayers. "I have just received word that Yeshua, the Healer, has returned to Capernaum. I'm a Gentile and would not want to offend the Teacher by going to him myself. Would you please find him and ask if he would come?"

After only a little discussion, the elders agreed. Within moments, two of them hurried onto the streets of Capernaum in search of Yeshua. Zimrah and Hannah replaced them at Caius's bedside.

"I had desired to bring him to Yeshua months ago." Domitian took Caius's skeletal hand. "But I waited too long. He was much too sick to leave his bed. I hadn't thought of the possibility of Yeshua coming to us." He bent to whispered in Caius's ear. "No fear, Caius. I've asked the Healer to come."

Domitian wiped his feverish brow with a cool cloth. "Lady Zimrah is here to see you."

Caius turned his head to see Zimrah. "It is wonderful to see you, my lady." His voice was only a hoarse whisper, and his lips were cracked. Speaking was an effort. Tears slipped from dark circled eyes down gaunt cheeks, red and dry from fever.

Zimrah retrieved a small cask from her pack and began to smooth almond oil over his skin. She mixed lavender with the oil and dabbed the mixture gently onto his lips.

"Ah, a woman's touch." He reached for her hand and managed to give Domitian a wry look.

"You see, Zimrah." Domitian grinned through his tears. "Already you've improved his humor."

Caius turned back to Zimrah. "Play for me?"

"Of course. There's nothing I'd like more." She let go of his hand to remove the lyre from its bag and case.

What should I sing, Abba Yahweh? Only one song came to mind. The melody was as familiar and lovely to her as the waters of the Leontes. Focusing her attention on Caius alone,

Zimrah sang with all the love and compassion that welled in her heart for him.

"The Lord is my light
and my salvation.
So why should I fear?

"The Lord is my fortress,
protecting me from danger.
So why should I fear?

"For I am confident,
I'll see Your goodness, Lord,
here in the land of the living.

"For He will hide me in His sanctuary.
He will place me out of reach.
Then I will hold my head up
high above my enemies,
Who surround me on every side.

"For I am confident,
I'll see Your goodness, Lord,
Here in the land of the living,
Here in the land of the living."

As Zimrah sang, a change came over Domitian's face. He whispered to another of the elders who stood beside him, and within moments, two more elders hurriedly left the room.

Not long after they left, the change appeared first in Caius's eyes. Where he could barely keep them open before, they opened wide. It was like he was awakening from a deep sleep that had lasted too long. He put a hand to his head, and his hair began to grow, full and brown.

"I'm beginning to feel better." His hand and face grew pink and plumped with life. The dryness disappeared around his mouth. Caius smiled as everyone else in the room cried.

When the elders returned, he was sitting up in bed—completely whole and in good health. His eyes were bright. His skin was ruddy in color. Even his hands had lost their skeletal form and were filled again with strength and life. Nothing of the illness that had bound him to death only minutes before remained.

"You found Yeshua!" Zimrah said as all of the elders returned to crowd Caius's room. Only Yeshua could have caused the transformation she had just watched come over Caius.

"Yes, we found him." One of the elders bobbed up and down in excitement. "We gave him Domitian's message just as he gave it to us. 'Lord, I am not worthy to have you come into my home. Just say the word from where you are, and my servant will be healed.'"

"That was about twenty minutes ago," another elder with a silver beard said. "When did Caius begin to show improvement?"

"At the same time." Domitian's eyes were big. Was that a little fear replacing the joy in his eyes?

"Lord Domitian, how did you know what you asked of Yeshua would be enough to heal Caius?" Hannah asked.

"I remembered my time in the army." Domitian stared off to the right, seeing another place and time. "Just as I was subject to the authority of my superiors, others were subject to me. I told them to 'Go,' and they went, or 'Come,' and they came. I realized Yeshua must carry even greater authority to perform the miracles he does. He must represent the highest authority, even that of Yahweh Himself."

"Yeshua was pleased." The silver bearded elder looked to his companions, and they nodded their affirmation. "He said he had not seen such faith in all Israel! He proclaimed in the face of many of the Pharisees who were present that many Gentiles will come from all over the world to sit with Abraham, Isaac, and Jacob at the feast of the Kingdom of Heaven and that many Israelites will be left out. Oh, how the Pharisees fumed. You should've seen them! He declared this just after speaking of *your* faith, Domitian."

Domitian was a barrel of a man, tall and robust. His years had only hardened the muscular frame needed for the duties of his station. But at the retelling of Yeshua's words, he sat and wept into his hands.

Caius left his bed for the first time in months. He wrapped his arms around his master and added his joyous tears. "Master, you rescued me from the streets of Ephesus and cared for me since I was a child. Your faith has made me well."

Chapter 26

TO QUESTION THE IMPOSSIBLE

L ater that evening, Caius saw to the women's needs while Zimrah fretted over him.

"I'm fine, my lady. I cannot say how good it feels to be free of that bed." He showed them to their room and, at Zimrah's request, brought her a beautifully carved bone pen, a full pottery inkpot, and a sheet of papyrus to write a letter to Theophilus.

Zimrah and Hannah unpacked their bags, chatting while they did so, like they had known each other for years instead of less than a day. When Zimrah sat down to begin her letter to Theophilus, Hannah stared at her.

"You write, my lady?" Hanna sat on the cushion next to Zimrah at the low table and peeked over her shoulder at the words that emerged from Zimrah's practiced hand.

"Scandalous, I know." Zimrah chuckled, sliding the papyrus over so Hannah could have a closer look. "I learned when I was very young."

"Didn't you say you were a slave?" Hannah's brow wrinkled. "I've never heard of any woman who could write, much less one who was once a slave."

"My father, Jesse of Chasah, is a righteous man. Before he adopted me, he was my master. He's a merchant and had no sons to help him with his bookkeeping, so he taught me instead. He never treated me as a slave." Zimrah's heart ached for her father. "He even saw to my betrothal while I was still a slave. He spoke to my husband's father Lucius, also a merchant and an old friend, about me."

"Lucius Servillian? The merchant from Rome? Does he have an office in Tyre? My husband, who had business with a few merchants, spoke of him." Hannah sat back, her eyes flitting from the letter to Zimrah's face. "I've also heard that Lucius Servillian has a handsome son. He brought peace to the trade disputes between Rome and the Phoenicians."

Zimrah smiled as Hannah's expression went blank for a moment. "Wait. So, you are the wife of Theophilus Servillian?"

"Yes." Zimrah smiled at Hannah's reaction and missed her husband all the more.

Hannah's eyes were huge. "A slave learning to read and write and marrying a Servillian? What kind of crazy world have I just stepped into?" She gazed at Zimrah and then looked down. Her voice was a whisper. "You've given up so much to come here. Why did you leave? If it's not painful for me to ask."

"Not at all." Zimrah told Hannah about what it was like for her in Tyre. It felt good to finally have someone to talk to, someone she could call a friend. She spoke freely about the dream that had led her there and about meeting Yeshua outside the city when she first arrived.

"Do you think the Teacher knew what you saw in your dream?" Hannah sat up with great interest.

"I don't know." Zimrah felt with Hannah the same warm camaraderie of faith she felt with John the Baptizer and his followers. "He did know me, though, and seemed to know why I had come to Capernaum. He said it was for me to be myself. I have no idea what that means."

Hannah put a hand on Zimrah's shoulder and nodded. "Yeshua often speaks in stories and riddles that not many understand."

"You know what worries me the most though? Is what Lucius, and everyone else for that matter, will say when they hear I have left Theophilus. Who does that? What kind of woman leaves the man she loves to come to a city alone to be— to be whatever I'm supposed to be here?"

Zimrah's cheeks flushed slightly, thinking of Lucius. *Abba, Yahweh, please do not let him judge my actions too harshly.*

"Does he love you?" Hannah eyed Zimrah's letter again. "Your husband, I mean."

"He does, shamefully. And I miss him dearly. I wish that he were here with us, witnessing what we have of Yeshua. I can only pray he will understand who Yeshua really is. I believe one day he will. After what we have seen today, I *know* Yeshua is the Son of God, and no heart is too hard for Him to reach."

"I wonder what that would be like, to have a husband who loves you and that you can love." There was moisture in Hannah's eyes. "Do you know what worries *me* the most, my lady? It is that maybe God never gave me any children because I did not love my husband."

"No, Hannah. I don't think that." She put down the pen so she could take Hannah's hand. "I think He knows what He has planned for you. It will be good. You'll see."

"Hearing of your faith strengthens mine. Yahweh is good. He took a slave girl, taught her to read and to write, and gave her in love to a Roman prince!" Hannah rubbed her face, letting her hands linger against her cheeks for a moment.

"Now the Messiah has come, and we are among his followers, witnesses to the Kingdom of Heaven on earth. God has done so much for you. Has He done any less for me? He rescued me from the house of a horrid man who beat me for no other reason but to see me cringe when he walked in the room." Hannah looked out the window and toward the city. "When I had nothing, He gave me purpose."

Zimrah locked eyes with her new friend, and they shared a teary smile, breaking the tension of the moment. "Yahweh is merciful and *good*. We're walking the path He has laid out for us. We've seen His glory."

***

Theophilus walked the distance from his home to Lucius's office near the Harbor of Sidon, Zimrah's letter in his hand. Gulls circled noisily overhead as he pushed his way through narrow, pedestrian-clogged streets. The bustle, clamor, and noxious smell of fish and unwashed dockworkers in the harbor district, usually a passing annoyance, did not even wrinkle his nose. Theophilus's mind was elsewhere.

When he arrived at his father's offices, he mounted the stairs to the working space on the upper floor and found his father deep in conversation with a man well acquainted with the Servillian family. When their eyes met, Lucius beckoned him with a raised finger and continued in conversation as though he couldn't hear.

"My son looks troubled." Lucius gestured to Theophilus's furrowed brow. "Tell me, Luke. What remedies would you prescribe to ease an overanxious mind?"

"Besides a fair draught of wine?" The young physician chuckled and greeted Theophilus with a quick shake of his forearm. Then he stepped back and looked him over. "What ails him? He looks fine to me. Is all well with his wife? I am very fond of him, you know. His humility and compassion, they are rare motivators for a patrician's son."

Theophilus smirked and pounded Luke's shoulder. "I am fond of you as well, my friend."

"Yes, his wife is well in the sense of her health, but she is away." Lucius ignored Theophilus as if he hadn't spoken. "That fact alone is problem enough, although he does not see it. I believe it is Yeshua, the Nazarene, whom Zimrah has left to follow, which concerns him more."

"Ah, yes, the Miracle Worker," Luke replied. "He greatly interests me as well."

"Enough." Theophilus chuckled. "As much as I am pleased to see you Luke, and entertained by the two of you speaking as if I'm not here, I need to speak to my Father if you don't mind."

"Absolutely, I was just leaving." Luke grasped his forearm and then his father's. "Until we meet again."

"Give me a moment, Theo. Make yourself comfortable." As Lucius walked Luke out, Theophilus took one of the two chairs on the balcony overlooking the harbor full of ships below. As he waited, he re-read Zimrah's letter.

Ave Theophilus. Si vales, bene est,

It is the evening of the second day of Aprilis, and I am writing to you from the home of our most treasured of friends, the Centurion of Capernaum.

Beloved Theophilus, I have not been away from you for long. With all that has happened since I last saw you though, it feels like an eternity. Domitian has granted me leave to stay here whenever and for however long I may need. (Thank you for sending news of my arrival and asking Domitian to see to a companion.) I pray this news brings you peace. I am completely secure and well looked after. Domitian has declared much pleasure in having women about to grace his home.

Before Domitian had a chance to see to it, Yeshua sent to me the most wonderful of blessings. Her name is Hannah, and she is well known to Domitian's household as a woman of both impeccable character and unordinary loveliness. (I have seen the way Domitian looks at her, and I believe him to be quite taken with her. She has recently been divorced by an abusive husband for following Yeshua, and it will be no small wonder to me if Yahweh has not further plans for the two of them. I will keep you appraised.) I have great expectation that Hannah and I will be the blessing to each other that Yeshua believed when He sent her to me.

I am happy, Theophilus, though I miss you terribly. I am most grateful for your leave to follow Yeshua as I wished. I have seen amazing things today, things that have left me with no doubt that He can only be who He says He is. The deaf hear, the leper is cleansed, and dear Caius, who was near death when I arrived, is well! Yeshua healed him with a word. He was not even present, Theophilus! He had only to speak the word from afar, and Caius was whole again!

I am now sure that it was He who healed your wound the day we first encountered him. There is no longer any question in my mind. He is the Messiah! Come and see for yourself, Theophilus. Please. I know that if you can only but see what I have, you will understand.

May the Almighty be with you, my love, until we are together again.

Zimrah.

Theophilus was indeed very pleased that Zimrah was with the centurion. There was no one else he would entrust with her safety more than his old general and trusted friend. It was not that which troubled him enough to seek his father's counsel. It was the last paragraph of her letter. Zimrah was content. Her happiness was what he desired, especially after the misery she recently endured in Tyre. What baffled him was the reason behind the heaviness he felt. Zimrah was happy, but he was not.

"A woman with child will not stray far from home." Lucius joined Theophilus, sitting in the chair opposite him on the small alcove balcony.

"Father, please." Theophilus sighed, his eyes squinting to block some of the glare off the sea. His attention was caught by a war ship, galley full of chained rowers, pulling out of harbor.

"It's not a terribly bad solution, Theo. Have you tried? My son needs his wife, and I need a grandchild to bounce on these old knees."

"Sometimes these things take time. It's only been two years since—"

"Long enough."

Theophilus sighed again. "Be at ease, father. Not everything is under my control. If my wife is not yet with child, it's not for lack of trying."

"And I do not blame you, Theo. Zimrah is a beautiful wom—"

"Father!" He was finally exasperated enough to shift his attention from the ship to his father's teasing eyes.

"Come then, tell me. I know my son." The question reached his eyes. "Something troubles you, more than the ails of a lonely husband."

"I don't know." Theophilus's gaze fell to the harbor again. "She wrote to me and is faring well in the home of Domitian in Capernaum."

"I know you worry for Zimrah's safety. But hearing where she has found herself should put your mind at rest."

"She is safe with the centurion."

"Good. All is well then." His father, brushed his hands together.

"No, all is not well father! She's following a man who claims to be the Son of God, of Yahweh! What is there to be done of that? It is ludicrous. Madness! How can a man such as that be trusted? Yet Zimrah does! The things that he is said to be doing—miracles, healings, even raising the dead. They are impossible! She wrote that she had witnessed some of these miracles herself and is sure he is who he says. Yet how can that be true?"

Theophilus had struggled to keep his voice low without success. Everyone had turned from their work to stare at him. Many of them had known him since his youth. With a wave of his hand, the elder Servillian sent them back to their business.

"Have you met this man?" His father exaggerated the stillness in his voice, as if hoping his demeanor would calm Theophilus.

"Yes, once." He raked a hand through his hair, ashamed of his previous outburst.

"Did he seem mad to you?"

"No sir, not at all."

"Or a speaker of untruths?"

"No."

"And what of Zimrah? Has she ever been known to be a poor judge of character or prone to indiscretion in the company she keeps?"

"Of course not! In fact, I have relied on her good judgment many times during negotiations. Her intuition has always proved true."

"You trust her then?" His father wouldn't let it go.

"Yes. Without question."

"Think of the matter logically. If this man is not mad, or untruthful, and if you trust Zimrah's judgment, then you must believe what she has seen with her own eyes. Or go and search out the truth for yourself."

"Oh!" The exclamation tore from Theophilus as the truth hit him like a physical blow. Here was the heart of the matter. "Zimrah said as much in her letter."

"What concerns me is that you're more concerned with *why* she has gone, instead of the fact that she has gone away in the first place." His father was voicing his opinion for the first time and put a hand on his shoulder to soften his words. "It is not right, Theo. A young woman should be with her husband. Has she given you word in that letter as to when she will return?"

"No sir, she has not."

"Do you truly have no problem with this?"

Theophilus turned his gaze to the harbor again. "Of course I do, Father. I want her with me, but I will not command her to stay."

"And why not? It seems a perfectly respectable thing to do."

"Because if I did, she would obey. She is not like Mother. Mother would agree with everything you said, pat your hand, and then do as she wished regardless of your commands. Zimrah would obey me. She would come home, but eventually she would resent me for it. It would always be between us."

"Nonsense! You are her husband. If you know she will obey, then write her back this instant. Tell her to come home."

"I cannot, Father. I will not."

"Then be prepared, my son." He rose to return to his work. "Mine will not be the only voice of opposition you, or she, will endure."

Later, Theophilus could not recall if he had bid his father farewell, or how crowded the streets of Tyre had been on his walk home. His thoughts swirled like a storm trapped inside his head. He had gone to his father for sound advice and perhaps some comfort. He left with little of either.

His father had been right on one account though. Theophilus feared seeing for himself the truth that a part of him already knew. If he dared to go and see the things Yeshua was doing, if he saw the miracles for himself—after hearing Sanya tell Jaaziel's tale of Yeshua's birth and the testimony of John the Baptizer—then Theophilus would have to accept that Yeshua truly was the Son of God, virgin birth and all.

Everything he believed about the world would have to change. Was it possible that the Almighty would bear a son? The realm of the eternal, mixing with the mortal, miracles and magic, it shook him to the core.

Could it all be true? Theophilus had always planted his feet in what he could touch and see. His mind fought against fables or legends or any such fanciful thinking. True, he believed Zimrah's Tormentors were real. And he had put his faith in Yahweh, an unseen God. He had made the decision to serve Him. Yet, where would that decision lead?

His father's opinion about Zimrah leaving home aside, the turmoil in his soul swirled around this one question. Was he willing to believe? Was he willing to give up his truths for a greater one?

Theophilus sat at the low kitchen table in the house in Tyre and let his head fall into his hands.

Nina walked into the room. She took the cushion next to him and rubbed his back. "Oh, Master Theophilus. I hate to see you this way. I don't know why Zimrah left. Is all well between you?"

"How do you do it, Nina?" Theophilus didn't look up. "How do you remain so true, so constant? Has believing in Yahweh never been hard for you?"

"Oh." Nina put a hand to her heart. "That's what's bothering you? An issue of faith?" She took a moment. "Well, yes, it has. The time after Master Jesse's wife and baby daughter died was very, very hard. I must admit that I questioned His goodness."

"How do you continue to serve him?" Theophilus turned so he could search her eyes for the answer.

"I don't serve Him as one serves a tyrant master. I serve Him as I have Master Jesse, and now you. I love Him. He is my Lord, and He loves me. Now that I'm older and a little wiser, I know He is good. Even if I don't understand His ways, I know His love. The kind of love He gives is like my honey cakes." She chuckled. "Once tasted, it can never be replaced with any other."

"Well, I know that's the truth." Theophilus didn't understand all of what Nina had said. But her hand on his back, her faith, and her humor gave him the comfort he was seeking, at least for a little while.

Chapter 27

THE RING OF COVENANT

After finishing the letter to Theophilus, Zimrah couldn't sleep. Hannah's breathing was even and rhythmic. She was sleeping soundly. Zimrah longed for such peace. Her mind, so full of joy and wonder after witnessing the miracles of the day, had slowly tumbled into turmoil.

The room Caius prepared was lovely. It was the same one she and Theophilus had stayed in. It reminded her of him. The night was still, and Zimrah missed the comfort of his arms around her.

Soon the barrage of questions from earlier in the day returned, whispering accusingly in her thoughts. With them came a deep, dark sense of fear and shame.

"What have you done?"

"What kind of woman leaves her husband like you did?"

"No one will understand."

"Remember what it felt like to be alone?"

"They will reject you again."

"Jesse, Theophilus, Nina, Lucius."

"They all hate you for what you've done."

"What if Theophilus decides not to have you back?"

"You had it so good."

"Every woman in Tyre envied you."

"You have ruined everything!"

"You must leave this place."

"Leave now! Go back to Tyre!"

"You must leave now before it's too late!"

The Tormentors. Their presence made Zimrah feel small and weak, like when she was a child. Well, she wasn't a child anymore. She could lay there listening to their accusations, or she could get up and do what Yahweh had taught her.

She rose from the bed, donned her outer tunic, took her lyre, and padded from the room. They were in the hallway too, a thick fog of shame surrounding her. She ached to escape, to run away, but it would do no good. They would only follow. There was only one way to silence their voices.

In Tyre she had her little alcove. This was someplace new. Where could she go to play? She found herself in the small clematis covered atrium before thinking to ask.

"Where should I go Abba Yahweh?" The sound of her voice was in itself a relief against the barrage of doubt.

"Look up."

Zimrah heard the response right away and obeyed it. By the light of the moon, she saw a thin stair rising to the rooftop behind a wooden post grown thick with vines. She smiled. Within moments she was making herself comfortable on a low couch strewn with many pillows. The city lay dark and quiet beneath her, and the Sea of Galilee twinkled in the moonlight beyond. The full moon and the host of stars above were the only canopy.

"This is perfect, Abba! Thank you."

Already her head was clearing. The night breeze and the beautiful view did much to lift the fog from her mind. She strummed the lyre with the cool wood against her heart and imagined herself walking in a field of green. Before long the young man whose face she could not see was there in the distance. She knew His name now, and as He came nearer, His face came into view. It was Yeshua of Nazareth.

She wanted to reach His side, but something held her back.

"Did I do the right thing?" Zimrah raised her voice to cover the distance between them. "Am I where I'm supposed to be? Did I do the right thing leaving Theophilus to follow you? What am I to do here in Capernaum? I know You said it was not to do, but to be, but I don't know what that means! Please, will you speak to me clearly?"

Her chest heaved, and tears rolled down her cheeks as the questions within strained against the anxiety that had been building through the day. The melody produced by her fingers changed, and she began to sing a new song.

"I've been told to hide my eyes.
Stay low, disguise, don't reach too high.
I've been told get used to shame,
things will never change.
It's always been this way.
Then You came and You say."

Then Yeshua sang:

"Look up, Child.
Don't you know who you are?
Look up, Child.
And reach, reach for the stars.
From dust you were made, but not for shame,
for glory.
Look into My face. I'll teach you the way
to glory.
Child, look up.

"No fear in Me.
No shame in Me.
No doubt in Me.
No hiding in Me."

Zimrah repeated this part, and it rang out like an anthem, exploding from her heart.

"No fear in me!
No shame in me!
No doubt in me!
No hiding in me!

"I look up, God.
I know who I am.

I look up, God.
And reach, reach for the stars.
From dust I was made, but not for shame,
for glory.
I look into Your face. You are the way
to glory.
God, I look up.
I look up."

When Zimrah finished her song, she was no longer in the field of green, and Yeshua was no longer far away. He was right beside her, holding her hand. They walked through a desert place.

They didn't walk long though, before an oasis came into view.

The oasis was not large, but lush. Huge, green leaved trees surrounded a spring fed pond. Thick grass, soft and cool, was barely disturbed by their treading feet.

Yeshua led her to a large stone beside the pond of water. "Sit with me, Zimrah."

His voice flowed into her heart like liquid love. They sat beneath the shade trees and bathed their bare feet. Dust from the desert washed off Zimrah's heels and disappeared in swirling circles into the deep water. Her tears started to flow again, and she rested her head on Yeshua's chest when His arm came across her shoulder.

"Tell me, Beloved." His voice was a whisper.

"I don't know, my Lord. I only know that I don't want to leave here. I want to stay with You." She gestured to the oasis around her. "It's so hard, battling the doubt that comes at every turn. There is no doubt here, no fear. Can't I stay?"

"Yes, you can, and you must learn to." Yeshua chuckled and held her closer. "The desert is no place for you to live. You've found this place before. You must learn to remain. But don't let your heart be troubled. Soon, the Comforter will come, and He will guide you."

Zimrah didn't know who the Comforter was, but it didn't matter. Her heart gained more strength at His every word.

"I have something for you, if you will accept it." Yeshua pulled a small object from a fold in His robe. He held his palm out to her, and there was a signet ring, similar to the one Theophilus wore, resting in the middle of it. This one was much more delicate and beautiful. "I want to make covenant with you. I promise to always be with you. Here in this place."

"And what must I do?" Zimrah asked as He slipped the ring on her finger.

His smile was patient, and he held her close again.

"Come back here. Be who you are, and do what you've always done. *Sing.*"

The word dropped into her soul like a pebble in a pond and rippled through her heart in waves.

She awoke with a start, still on the roof of Domitian's house. Her lyre rested against her chest, and the morning sun was rising over the sea.

***

The next day was Sabbath, and the beast stood on the wall of Capernaum overlooking the marketplace. He had instigation demons working the crowd, and by midday, there was talk of two things in the city—Yeshua had performed another miracle on the Sabbath, and singing was heard by most in the middle of the night. That the singer was female was a point of contention he delighted in stirring up among the religious leaders.

"Tell them that the singing came from the direction of the centurion's house."

Brows furrowed, and hand gestures grew sharper and more pronounced. Oh, how he loved raising the ire of the religious. They had not forgotten how Yeshua had dishonored them before the people concerning the centurion's faith when his servant was healed.

When the singing continued night after night for more than a week—and word spread that the centurion had a Gentile woman staying with him—the religious leaders had had enough. A runner was sent to the Sanhedrin in Jerusalem, and one man returned to investigate, the man the beast had handpicked for this job.

Saul of Tarsus.

***

Zimrah had no idea of the windstorm swirling around her until she and Hannah were stopped by a stranger in the marketplace.

"Pardon me, if you do not mind me asking. But do you have a relative in Jerusalem? An aunt perhaps?"

Zimrah turned to see a bearded young man in a black robe with a tasseled scarf over his head. A Pharisee. The top of his head came to only about the bridge of her nose. He smiled and handed her the basket of dates she had just been reaching for.

"Yes, I do." Zimrah took the basket from him and offered a smile of her own in return.

"Yes, of course. You look just like her. Especially when you smile. I have met her you know. Sanya is her name, isn't it? A former—well, let us say, entertainer in the court of King Herod?"

"Yes." Zimrah narrowed her eyes.

"And you visited with her perhaps two and a half years ago, didn't you?"

"Yes, I did." Her stomach dropped.

"And you sang on rooftops there as well, is that right?"

The stranger's friendliness disappeared, and everything seemed to stop for a moment, including Zimrah's heart. He stood on his toes to put a wagging finger in her face. "You will stop this immediately!"

His shouting drew the attention of everyone in the marketplace. Hannah held on to her to give her some support as the man continued his tirade.

"Who do you think you are? Singing from *our* holy scrolls? Have you no shame? The psalms of King David are sung only by the Levitical priests!" His face turned bright red. "This is not some backwater, Gentile village like Chasah! There is a synagogue here in Capernaum, and that is where *our* priests will do the singing! This is a Jewish city, and you—you, a *Gentile woman*—have no right or authority to sing in this, or any other, Jewish city! You will stop immediately, or there will be dire consequences. Do I make myself understood?"

Zimrah didn't reply, and the stranger left no time for one. He turned on his heel with his robes aflutter and left her to the stares of everyone around them.

Zimrah could not stop herself from shaking on their way through the market and back to Domitian's house.

"Who was that?" Hannah whispered.

"I don't know."

"You were afraid, my lady, but it didn't show." Hannah tried to console her. "I know what it is like to be yelled at by an angry man."

Zimrah's heart felt like it would race right out of her chest. "It wasn't my first time."

"Really?"

"When I was a slave, I was struck and shamed in public all the time by the people of Chasah. They hated me. It has been a long time though."

"Oh yes. I forgot. I'm still having a hard time imagining you as a slave. Well, you did well, my lady. I would have crumpled into a heap of tears."

"I wanted to."

They held on to each other. Then the tears *did* come. Being humiliated like that reminded Zimrah of days she hoped to never see again. All the pain came flooding back, pain that had long been forgotten. She was very grateful to have a friend by her side. As a slave, she had no one.

"What will you do now?" Hannah asked after the flood of Zimrah's tears subsided. "Are you going to keep singing?"

"I don't know." She wiped her face with her headscarf. "I wish Theophilus were here."

"That man knew you'd been in Jerusalem! And that you're from Chasah."

Hannah was right.

"I wonder if he really met Sanya. I hope she is not in any trouble because of me." Zimrah said.

"She probably would have sent word."

"I hope so." A heavy weight descended on Zimrah's chest, and her ears began to ring. What *was* she going to do? How was she to be who she was created to be if she was not allowed to sing? It was what Yeshua asked her to do! Suddenly, the Tormentors were on her again like a flood.

"Was it really Yeshua who asked you to sing?"

"It was just a dream!"

"You are mad if you believe it was real."

"This has been nothing but your imagination!"

"Why would the Nazarene waste time with you?"

"A woman."

"A Gentile."

"You have not seen him since you arrived."

"Your dreams mean nothing!"

"Go home, Zimrah!"

"Go back to Tyre before there is even more trouble!"

Domitian took one look at the women when they arrived and rushed over to them. "What's happened?"

Zimrah remained quiet, still battling both shame and doubt.

"Hannah? Tell me."

Zimrah was still shaking.

"We met a man," Hannah explained. "A Pharisee. He shouted at Zimrah in front of everyone in the market! He told her she must stop her singing."

"I was afraid they might do something like this." He led the women to the atrium and sat Zimrah down with a cup of watered wine to calm her. "I've heard from the elders that the leaders of religious law are not pleased with her singing. Who was it, Hannah? A Galilean? Did you know him?"

"No," Hannah shook her head and accepted a cup of wine as well. "I've never seen him before, and his accent was strange. He mentioned Zimrah's aunt in Jerusalem. I had a feeling he had just come from there."

"It must have been Saul."

"Saul?" Zimrah raised her eyes from the floor for the first time.

"My friends in the city said there was a man named Saul who came from Jerusalem asking about you."

"He seemed to know a lot about her," Hannah said.

"I'll have words with him." Domitian stood with both anger and determination shining in his eyes.

"No Domitian." Zimrah was horrified and hurried to block his path to the entryway.

"You are under my roof, Zimrah!" Domitian gripped her shoulders to move her out of his way. "And under my protection. This man is a coward. He knows full well that you are here but had not the courage to do what was proper and come and speak to me first. He chose to waylay you alone in the market!"

"Please, Domitian." Zimrah wiped the tears that had come again. The heat of shame enflamed her cheeks. "It'll only make it worse. He's right! I have no authority to sing the words of God. I *am* just a Gentile woman from Chasah."

"That is not true! Remember who you are, Zimrah." It was Caius now who spoke. "If he knows about you, then he should know you have been adopted into a Jewish house. And you are the daughter of a priest. A Levite! Are you not? Your mother believed in Yahweh. By Hebrew law alone, that makes you one of them."

"Yes, but they don't know that." Zimrah gestured toward the city.

"Yahweh does," Caius said. "And so does the Nazarene. He is the one who has given you authority to sing!"

After Yeshua healed Caius, he had gone many times to hear his teaching. He believed with his very life that Yeshua was the Messiah. Because of his faith, Zimrah trusted Caius with her dreams. Every morning he waited expectantly to hear what she had seen while singing on the roof the evening before.

"That only happened in a dream, Caius! What if they are just that—only dreams?" Zimrah let the tears flow unchecked as everyone looked on in compassion. They had no answer for her fears.

"Lady Zimrah," Felix interrupted. "You have a visitor."

A woman followed Felix into the muted light of the atrium. She was very small in stature, slender, and was about middle age. Her robes were light and flowing, and her eyes were bright.

"Shalom. Please excuse my interruption. I am Mary of Magdala, and I have come with a message for Zimrah. It is from the Teacher."

"Shalom, shalom. Please join us." Domitian pointed her to a seat on the couch.

Mary settled herself at his invitation, and Caius filled a cup for her from the pitcher of watered wine.

"You have a message from Yeshua?" Excitement replaced the shaking in Zimrah's middle.

"Yes, my lady. It is this." Mary held out her hand, and everyone drew near to see what rested there.

When Zimrah saw what was in Mary's hand, she gasped and burst into tears again. No one else could have known what it meant. Zimrah had told no one of it, and by the shocked look on her face at Zimrah's response, it seemed that not even Mary knew.

What Mary had brought from Yeshua was a small, delicate, and beautiful signet ring.

It was the ring of covenant He had given her in the dream.

Chapter 28

DIRE CONSEQUENCES

Theophilus fought against every instinct raging within him. He wanted to ride to Capernaum that very moment. He imagined covering the miles that stood between them, finding Zimrah, snatching her up in the saddle, and taking her away from there. He would leave only dust in his wake.

Domitian's message had arrived via carrier only moments ago, folded and strapped to the pigeon's leg. Theophilus held up the slip of parchment and read his friend's familiar handwriting again.

TROUBLE WITH A PHARISEE FROM JERUSALEM.

Zimrah had not mentioned it in her latest letter. Perhaps whatever the trouble was had not yet occurred. Or perhaps she was trying to prevent the very thing his instinct encouraged him to do—ride like mad through the gates of Capernaum and bring her home.

And why did he not? If he were honest with himself—or more mature in the ways of the Yahweh—he might have seen the truth. The forked tongue of jealousy that had taken root in Jerusalem was bearing fruit. In the basest part of his personality, Theophilus was jealous of Zimrah's faith and hurt that she had left him because of it. Deep down, he wanted her to realize her error, apologize, and come home on her own.

"Oh, my sweet, gentle Zimrah." He sighed into his empty bedchamber. "What am I going to do with you?"

Theophilus walked to the window, pulled the drapes open, and let his gaze follow his heart south.

***

It was true. All of it. Zimrah knew that now. She wore her betrothal rings on her left hand and Yeshua's covenant ring on her right. Looking down at it now, her throat closed, and her chest grew tight.

It was just as she had seen it in the dream, silver bands intertwined around a circular plate with a *tav* written in ancient Hebrew script in its center. The letter was etched and encircled with tiny flowers and vines. She had told no one of the ring, not even Caius. There was no other way for Yeshua to have known about it unless he was really there with her in her dreams.

"It *is* all true." She spoke it out loud so her ears could hear the words. "I know who I am and what I must do."

Despite Saul's command and threat of dire consequences, Zimrah took up her lyre and climbed the narrow stairs to the roof. The stars twinkled above her, and the Sea of Galilee rippled below. She sat on the couch, arranged the pillows, leaned back, and began to strum, then to sing.

Soon she was in the oasis, leaning her head on Yeshua's chest.

"I am here, my Lord. I have come."

"Yes, my brave Little Bird."

"What should I sing?"

"Whatever is in your heart."

So, she sang. She sang, and she soared higher and higher. She soared above the city, above the sea, above the mountains in the distance, above the accusations against her. She soared until she could see nothing but stars above and sea below.

Yeshua was there with her, shining in splendor, shining in glory. She sang of His beauty. She sang of His love and His faithfulness.

The next day, she dared not leave Domitian's house, and no one came to arrest her, so she continued the following evening. Night after night she sang. She sang from the heavenly Court. She sang from the oasis, and from the desert, and from the field of green. She sang the words of King David, of Joel, and Isaiah the prophet. And always, with her in her dreams was Yeshua.

One evening He reminded her of the dream of the battlefield she had while in Jerusalem.

Once again, she was flying above the battle. Rebecca, the red-haired lady she had seen in the heavenly court, dressed in armor and wielding a bright sword, flew by her side. Zimrah soared as she sang, destroying the enemy below with her song.

Then she remembered Jaaziel's scroll. She sang about Yeshua's birth, about the star that heralded His coming, and about the angels who told shepherds to go and give Him praise.

Months went by with no sight or sound of Saul.

"Maybe he returned to Jerusalem." Hannah spooned diced tomatoes into her hummus. It was late for a morning meal, but Zimrah had stayed up on the roof later than usual the night before.

"Maybe it was nothing but a threat." Caius poured hot water into a large ceramic bowl lined with fresh mint leaves. Their soothing aroma filled the room, reminding her of Nina's herb garden.

Domitian took the cup of tea Caius offered. "Perhaps he's admitted to himself that he truly is a coward and is simply waiting for you to leave my house."

"Well, I cannot stay inside forever." The walls of the house were closing in around her.

Mary Magdala—who had quickly become a good friend and a regular at Domitian's table—followed Felix into the atrium and took the cushion beside Zimrah.

"Shalom Mary." Zimrah welcomed her with a hug and a bowl of hummus. "We were just discussing whether or not it's safe for me to go and see Yeshua today."

"Has Saul been seen in the city recently?" Domitian's nose flared when he spoke the name.

"No one has seen him since the day he threatened Zimrah in the market." Mary stirred the olive oil she had drizzled over her hummus. "In Jerusalem either. He's disappeared."

"Well, we're glad for that." Hannah broke a circle of flatbread for herself and handed the other half to Mary.

She took it with a nod of thanks. "As are we. None of the followers wish for you to stop singing, Zimrah. We were gathered at Peter's house last night when you sang the song of Yeshua's birth, about the Magi and the star. Some were hearing it for the first time. Your songs speak truth and build faith."

"My father Jaaziel was there. The Sanhedrin commissioned him to investigate the matter of Yeshua's birth. He wrote down everything, and Sanya gave me his scrolls. He was killed for telling others what he learned."

"And now you're singing that knowledge out for all to hear." Domitian's jaw clenched. "Do you think they would not like to do the same to you? Stay here, Zimrah, where it's safe."

"I have been, for months now." She put her spoon down a little harder than she intended. "Forgive me. I'm grateful for your protection, Domitian and to you, Mary and Caius, for news of Yeshua and His teachings. But my heart is aching to see Him face to face and speak to Him of what I'm dreaming each night."

Her gaze drifted up toward the roof. "I love singing and being with Him in my dreams. But He is here in Capernaum, and I've not seen Him since the day I arrived. It brings me so much joy to hear that the followers are encouraged, but I don't really know *why* I'm doing what I'm doing. Is it to bolster the faith of others alone? If so, that is reason enough. Yet, sometimes while I'm singing, a sense of great importance overwhelms me. I believe there is much more happening than I know. I long to understand more, and Yeshua is the only one who can answer my questions. I'm determined to go. Seeing Him would be worth any risk."

***

Domitian had a sinking feeling in his gut. Something was not right. It had been less than an hour since Zimrah and Hannah left to see the Healer, and Domitian had been pacing the courtyard almost the entire time. It was probably the centurion in him, always imagining the worst, but he could not shake the feeling that something had happened. He had offered to go with them, but Zimrah refused. He should have insisted.

"Hang it all! She is not the centurion of me." He was on his way out to find them when Hannah returned, breathless and hysterical. She ran right into his arms. "Th-they took her!"

"What! Who took her?" They hadn't even been gone an hour. Who could have known she'd left? Unless they had been watching the house.

Caius and Felix rushed into the entryway at Hannah's cry.

"It—it was Saul! He was with two other m-men and they t-took her!"

Domitian passed the weak-kneed Hannah to Caius so he could don his outer cloak.

"I should not have let her talk me out of going with you." He swore under his breath and belted on his gladius. "Where did they take her, Hannah?"

"I—I don't know, my lord." Hannah only cried harder, her words coming between fits and sobs. "I only saw that th-they covered her h-head with a shroud before they p-pushed me away! I ran straight h—here! I sh-should never have left her!"

"It's not your fault. There's nothing you could have done." He shared an anxious look with the other men, the sinking feeling turning into a knot. It could mean nothing good that they covered her with a shroud before taking her. "I'll find out where she is and bring her home."

***

Night had fallen to silence when Domitian returned, stomping through the entryway and into the courtyard, frustrated and alone. He stepped into the light around the central fire in the atrium and stared into the flames like one lost.

Hannah gasped as soon as she saw Zimrah was not with him. "Where is she?"

"I do not know. I could get nothing from anyone. No one seems to know where she is except Saul, and he is nowhere to be found!" Imagining all sorts of horrors of what they might do to her, he sat down hard on a cushioned bench and hung his head in his hands.

What was he going to do? How in heaven was he going to tell Theophilus he had lost his wife?

***

On the roof of his house in Tyre, Theophilus was in good spirits. Jesse was visiting from Chasah, and Nina had outdone herself with the evening meal. Lucius had come to see his old friend Jesse and they were reminiscing and enjoying themselves—as much as possible without Zimrah—when the carrier bird arrived.

"We didn't know what to think when we saw poor Anton bruised and sprawled out on the floor." Nina laughed and her belly shook.

"At least it was just the one eye." Theophilus rose to retrieve the bird. He received messages from all over the region and sometimes from as far away as Rome.

"With only one eye though, he was walking sideways for a week!" Lucius closed his eye and tilted his head with his hands out in front of him, pretending to be blind.

Wiping his hands on the *moppa* and throwing it at his father, Theophilus laughed as he lifted the pigeon from its perch, giving it a bit of bread from the table at the same time. When he brought the slip of paper over to the lamplight, the laughter died within him. His heart seemed to stop beating and then race out of his chest. He stood still for only a second, then sprung for the stairs like a madman, knocking over the table and their meal in his haste.

"What is it, Theo?" Lucius called after him.

"Domitian sends word." Theophilus had no time to stop. His mind reeled as a list of possible scenarios jumbled with all he would need to bring with him. What would they do? Imprison her, yes, but would they cane her? Whip her? The worst they might do was too much to think of.

Everyone followed him to the stairs and tried to keep up so they could hear what the matter was.

"Zimrah's been arrested!"

Theophilus shouted commands to the servants as he tore through the house like a whirlwind.

"Saddle and water my horse!" he said to one.

"Pack my carrier with provisions!" he said to another.

"I'll need my gladius and cloak!" he said to a third.

All these things he did without much conscious thought. Only one thing drove his heart and limbs. "I must get to her."

He bid farewell to Lucius, Jesse, and Nina and kept his eyes fixed toward Capernaum as they disappeared into the dust behind him.

Yahweh please! Help me reach her in time.

***

Zimrah awoke in the cold darkness. Her head ached, and her hands were bound behind her back. With arms tingling and aching horribly, she groaned as feeling came back into them.

Was the shroud still over her face? No, a lamp flickered somewhere off to her right. Even that little bit of light hurt her head. She was in a large, stone chamber with no windows. The stone was very dark. *Abba, let it be basalt. Let me still be in Capernaum.* She lay on a rough wooden cot with clean smelling blankets folded under her and tried not to panic.

"Ah, awake?"

Zimrah startled at the deep voice that echoed in the chamber. She couldn't tell from which direction the voice had come.

"Here, let me help you with those. They aren't needed. You won't try to escape, will you?"

She flinched and held in a scream when a form appeared out of the dark to lay hands on her. The hot fire of fear burned in her middle.

"Shh, shh. I'm only removing your bonds. Honestly, I forgot they tied you."

Her hands were cut free. Keeping her eyes on the man as he moved away from her again, she rubbed her arms. They were stiff and sore, but it felt good to move them freely. Zimrah breathed deep and tried to calm herself. Allowing the fear access would do her no good.

She reached for Father Yahweh in her mind, sat up, and found the reason for her aching head. A lump throbbed just above her neck in the back under her hair. Both the lump and the hair around it were sticky with what must be blood.

"Ah yes. Necessary unfortunately. I could not have you screaming and struggling the whole way here."

"Where am I?"

The man moved a chair closer to her cot and sat down. The light was dim, but she recognized him. It was Saul.

"Somewhere safe, secret, and blessedly soundproof. You could sing all you wanted in here, and no one would ever hear you. You have been a horrible thorn in my side, Zimrah. Do you know that? I didn't want to have to resort to this, but you left me little choice. We've had enough trouble floating about. First with John the Baptizer, who is dead in case you haven't heard. Herod solved that little problem for us. The man finally did something right. Then with this Nazarene! Pah! As if anything good could come out of Nazareth."

"John is dead?" Zimrah could not help the tears that flowed. The information frightened her all the more for the situation she was now in.

"Yes, yes, but let us not get distracted from the point. You, young lady! I warned you, but you continued to defy me! I stayed hidden, hoping to lure you out. My plan worked, though it took you much longer than I hoped. I can't have you singing your lies every night for all to hear."

"They are not lies." She was afraid, but not *that* much.

"Yes, they are!" His shout was loud and unexpected, resounding in the chamber and making her ears ring.

When she spoke again, her voice remained quiet and confident. "It is the truth. Yeshua *is* the Messiah."

Saul leapt from his chair to strike her but checked his hand at the last moment. His arm slowly moved back to his side. He took a deep breath and smiled instead.

"I'd rather not resort to physical chastisement. It is Sabbath after all." He sighed and returned to his seat. "Such a little thorn, but oh, the pain of it! How does your husband put up with you? Maybe he does not? Eh? Maybe that's why you are in Capernaum and he is in Tyre. Why is that? Is it because he knows you are hopelessly deceived? That this Yeshua has fooled you like he has so many others?"

Zimrah would not allow herself to be rattled by his outbursts or taunts. He was just trying to frighten her, cause her to doubt.

"You know of my husband? Then you must know who he is. You can't keep me here. Is that why you waited to take me on the road, when no one was watching?" Zimrah sat up and leaned toward him with narrow eyes.

"Hmm. I've heard that you're no fool. You understand more than I would like. Well, we all must work within the confines of our station. And there lies my dilemma."

Saul stood and began to pace back and forth with his hands clasped behind his back. "The blessing is that no one knows for sure that you're in my custody. It is a question of proof. There's only *one* who saw me take you, and she is a woman. By the testimony of two or three witnesses is a thing established—two or three *men*, my dear. The law is clear. Your Roman would have no case against me that will hold in court."

"Perhaps no earthly court, but what of the Court of Heaven? Nothing goes unseen."

This time Saul did strike her. "What do you know of it?"

Zimrah's ears rang, and her head felt like it would burst. Nausea threatened to empty her already empty stomach. Saul went on yelling at her for a while, but she understood none of what he said until the ringing subsided. When it did, she interrupted his tirade to speak again. "There is a place where heaven and earth meet, Saul. In that place there is no pain, no fear. There is only love. There is only Yahweh, and Yeshua is there! He shines in light and glory, and nothing you do can stop the knowledge of who He is from spreading. It will cover the earth!"

Her voice grew louder and louder until it filled the chamber, and for a moment, it sounded like it came from someone else, even to her own ears.

Saul stood over her, shaking in anger for more than a minute. There was something else, under his anger.

Fear.

He turned on his heel, his footfalls retreating through a creaking door she couldn't see from where she sat. He took the lamp with him.

Zimrah was left alone with nothing but the darkness.

***

Saul climbed the stairs and returned to the light, emotions bubbling within him like water in a pot. Sunshine still streamed in through the windows above. The light was all yellows and oranges like after noon and before twilight. He had been with the woman for longer than he imagined. He stood in one of the rays of the sun with his eyes closed, taking deep breaths.

The woman. He could not remember being more agitated, angry... remorseful—he was sorry he had struck her, especially on the Sabbath—and just plain irritated in all his life.

That woman! What was he going to do with her? She wouldn't stop. Her conviction was too strong. And such words she spoke! Pah! Courts of Heaven! Things unseen!

"What could she possibly know of such things? Eh?" He swallowed back the fear he had felt while below.

Perhaps Herod had the right idea about how to solve these kinds of problems. It wouldn't be hard. She couldn't survive another day or two in his little hideaway. He had left her no water. The Sanhedrin would be pleased, and his name would be honored among the highest council in Jerusalem!

If he let her die though, he ran the risk of turning a small problem into an even bigger one. He had to admit, the woman had friends in extremely high places. And she was a *married* woman! Married to a Servillian, no less! The name alone brought to mind images of vast villas along the Tiber in Rome—of power and prestige Saul could only dream of.

He had looked into her past. She'd been a *slave*. How she had pulled off a union like that was beyond his reasoning. By all evidence he could find, this Servillian *loved* her. Madly! This changed the game altogether, and not in his favor. He cringed thinking of the giant Roman—heart full of revenge and murder in his eyes—stalking him in the night.

Proof or no proof. There would be no honor if he woke up dead with the business end of a gladius in his gut. Then what would become of all his ambition? Eh?

"Ugh!" Saul shoved the lamp he was still holding into a nearby shelf, too hard. The lamp broke in his hand, and a bit of blood trickled from his palm.

He must speak with the others. Yes. Wise counsel. That was what he needed in this situation. They would help him solve this problem. Whatever the Sanhedrin decided, they must do it quickly. Time was running short.

Chapter 29

LIGHT IN DARK PLACES

Zimrah dared not move for more time than she could recount. She sat in the dark and waited, hoping and listening to the blood pound in her ears. Perhaps Saul would return. Did she want him to? If he would only bring her some water. She was so thirsty. He could have at least left the lamp. The dark silence pressed like a weight all around her.

After what could have been an hour or five minutes, she had an idea. Could she find the door that Saul used to leave the chamber? Perhaps he had left it unlocked. She stood, waited for the nausea to settle and the room to stop its spinning, took two steps, then promptly fell over the chair beside her cot.

A bruised hip, skinned knee, and another bump to her head were the only rewards for her trouble. It was so black! She couldn't tell if her eyes were open or closed! Lying where she fell, Zimrah fought the panic that tightened its cold grip on her heart. The Tormentors were not far behind.

"You will die here."

"Saul isn't coming back."

"Ever."

"Death will keep you quiet. Will it not?"

"No one knows where you are."

"Domitian will not come."

"You'll never see Theophilus again."

"No one will ever find you."

"And why should they?"

"You were warned!"

"You should have listened!"

"This is your fault!"

"You deserve this!"

"You brought it upon yourself!"

She could almost feel their clawing fingers in the darkness closing in all around her. She rolled painfully onto her back, placed her hands flat against the numbing stone, closed her eyes, and took a deep breath.

"Abba Yahweh, if ever I needed you, I need you now." The sound of her voice silenced the voices in her mind.

Instead of their cold accusations, there was the warmth of Yahweh's voice.

"Remember your training."

She did remember. Her throat was horribly dry and her voice hoarse, but Zimrah could still sing.

> "The Lord is my light
> and my salvation.
> So why should I fear?

"The Lord is my fortress,
protecting me from danger.
So why should I fear?

"Send out Your light, Lord.
Guide me to Your holy mountain.
Send out Your light, Lord
and Your truth.
Guide me to You."

She sang the truth until the Tormentors' lies were pushed far away. When she stopped, she was still locked in the chamber, still in complete darkness, but she no longer felt alone.

The stone floor was hard and cold, so she slowly rose to her feet. Lightheaded and dizzy, she managed to find the cot—after first going in the wrong direction and running into the stone wall—and lay back down on it. She thanked Yahweh for even that little bit of comfort. Her body had begun to shake uncontrollably. There were folded blankets on the cot, and she covered herself.

She should have been miserable. The back of her head hurt. Her legs were cramping. She was tired. Her cheek was bruised where Saul had struck her. Hunger and thirst clawed at her insides. She had no idea how long she had been in this room or if she would ever leave it again. She didn't know where she was or if anyone would come for her. But she smiled in the dark.

"I'm not alone. Abba, You are with me." Her voice echoed in the chamber, sounding stronger than she felt. "You love me, and You have a plan for my life. I remember what You showed me through the window in heaven. I grow old with Theophilus in the house of my father. I will not die in this room. Thank You for this cot. Thank You for this blanket, and thank You that You will never leave me."

***

The Father sat before the court in both joy and sorrow. His daughter was suffering, yet the lessons she was learning about Him and about herself because of it brought Him great joy.

Her suffering was not over. The worst was still to come. Darkness was so hard for the beings He created to dance in the Light. He closed His eyes and entered into the pain with her, pain that others of His children had caused. Deceived thinking. It was the root of so much evil.

Darkness. Hunger. Fear. Thirst. A tear fell from His eyes.

"Rebecca." He summoned the warrior before Him.

In an instant she was there, dressed not in her armor but in the flowing blue gown.

"I am here, my King."

He smiled, knowing she had been waiting expectantly for His call.

"Will you go and comfort My daughter Zimrah?"

Rebecca's smile in return was radiant. "Oh King, it would be my great pleasure."

***

Zimrah was surprised that she could see. A grayish kind of light illuminated the room. There was the ceiling above her, the chair she had fallen over to her right, and a small table in the corner behind the chair. She saw the door. It was indeed bolted tight. The cold was terrible, seeping through the blanket and into her bones.

Then there was a sound, a whispering, screeching, familiar kind of sound. The Tormentors.

Their black, writhing shapes hovered in the corners, climbed the walls, and hung from the ceiling. They were everywhere. As soon as she became aware of them, they attacked.

Flying at her with wings, teeth, and claws, they came from every direction, tearing at her mouth and throat. The onslaught lasted for more than a minute. She tried to scream but produced only a gurgle. Her throat was ripped and torn. There was nothing left for her to scream with.

Zimrah startled awake, mewling and trying to protect herself with her arms. Opening her eyes made no difference. There was only blackness again. She put a frantic hand to her mouth and throat and found them whole. It was just a dream.

But was it? The Tormentors were here. She could still feel their cold presence all around her, hiding in the dark.

Only a hoarse whisper came out when she opened her mouth to sing. Her lips were dry and cracked. Her tongue felt swollen to twice its normal size, and there was a horrible cramping in her middle. Her arms and legs were heavy and hard to move. Her body was in agony.

Water. She needed water, but there was none. The Tormentors had done their job after all. She couldn't sing. They were there to gloat and watch her die.

"You are not going to die, Little Bird."

A sweet feminine voice spoke out of the darkness.

Someone sat down next to her on the cot. Zimrah felt no fear, which surprised her. A warm hand touched her brow, and the heat of it spread to warm her whole body.

"Wh-who are you?"

"Shh. I know it hurts to speak. I'm a friend. Don't you recognize my voice?"

A picture flashed in Zimrah's mind of a lady in blue flowing robes with a long red braid lying over her shoulder. Could it be? Perhaps she was still dreaming.

"Rebecca?" Zimrah's voice was barely a whisper.

"Yes, it is I."

"Dream?"

"No, this is not a dream. I'm here," Rebecca said with a smile in her voice.

But the door was bolted.

"How did you—?" Zimrah was struggling so badly with what was reality and what was not. Rebecca? Wasn't she an angel? But how could that be if she were really here? With some effort, Zimrah lifted her hand to her forehead, trying to rub away the fog from her mind. The movement made the room spin.

"How did I get in here?" Rebecca laughed her little bell laugh. "Walls and doors mean nothing to me. Worry no more about such things, Zimrah. Know only that I'm here, and you're safe. The Almighty sent me."

"Tormentors?"

They had been there—all over the room—only moments before.

"The demons are here—huddled together in a corner now, hiding from the Light. Look, you can see them too."

Zimrah turned slowly to look behind her. She blinked twice and rubbed her eyes. A mass of dark shapes, like a nest of snakes writhed in the corner. The Tormentors. There they were. She had sensed them all her life but had never seen them before.

One of the forms—like a lizard with a large head and wings—flew from the mass toward the wall at the same time as a man rose through the floor.

"Who's that?" Zimrah asked.

"Oh, that's Garbar."

The man was huge, with arms and legs like tree trunks. He grabbed the reptilian creature out of the air and smashed it against the wall. Light rose from his chest through his arm and into the Tormentor, who disintegrated in the flash of light.

"Garbar?"

"Yes. He's another warrior. He's quite skilled at dispatching demons, but don't tell him I said so. His ego can get away from him sometimes."

Garbar disintegrated the rest in a blur of arms and flashing light.

"Your Tormentors are gone now. And they won't return."

Zimrah breathed deeply, and peace filled her heart as the air filled her lungs. There was not a shadow left, and even their cold presence was gone. All that was left was the warmth of Rebecca's hand. The heat of it washed over her in waves, reminding her of Yahweh's love. The feeling made her think of another.

"Theo."

Rebecca's hand rested on her cheek. "You know, there was a time when I was not so sure about that big Roman. He's changed my mind though and proved himself true. Rest Zimrah, all will be well."

Neither of them spoke for a few minutes as Rebecca continued to stroke her head. Zimrah dozed off again...for a few minutes. Or was it an hour? A day? When she awoke, Rebecca was still there. So was the thirst.

"Water?"

"I know you're thirsty. I'm so sorry I can't help with that. I'm charged to bring you only comfort. It will be over soon. Even now the decision has been made, and Saul is on his way. I can't stay with you like this for much longer."

"Please, don't leave me." Zimrah reached for Rebecca's hand. Her chest heaved with emotion that couldn't flow from her eyes.

"I'm with you Zimrah, more than you know. I have been with you since the day you were conceived. You can't always see me, but know that I'm here. You only have to call, remember?"

Rebecca moved her hand to Zimrah's cheek. "The Father is very proud of you, Little Bird. You bring Him great joy. You're learning and growing, and as you continue to sing, much more will be revealed. You must go to Jerusalem and take Theophilus with you. You will lead him to places he would never go on his own."

Rebecca's voice seemed to reach in and clear Zimrah's head, bringing clarity into her mind so she wouldn't forget. "Go to Jerusalem. You'll be needed there."

In the next instant, Rebecca was gone. Zimrah's hand held only air, and the weight lifted from the cot beside her.

The chamber door unbolted and creaked as it opened. She squinted at the light that poured into the room.

Saul had returned.

Chapter 30

EQUAL PARTS JOY AND REGRET

Zimrah was in and out of consciousness, but she knew three things. The shroud was pulled over her head again, she was lifted off the cot and carried out of the chamber by rough hands, and Saul was speaking to her. She tried to concentrate on what he was saying.

"The others helped me decide what to do with you, my dear..."

She was jostled and missed a few words in the pain that flared.

"...Wise counsel is so important, you know..."

Stairs going up.

"...The bigger problem will be solved soon, whether you stop your singing now or not will no longer matter..."

Birds singing, like they did in the morning, right before dawn.

"...the weed will be pulled by the root. Then all the deceived will come back to the fold...and all these false claims, raising a man from the dead after four days! Pah! His lies will die with him..."

Zimrah felt herself laid on hard ground. The shroud was removed, and Saul's face came into focus above her.

"...hope we'll never meet again..."

Then he was gone.

All was quiet except for the birds. There was no sound of people. The sky was just beginning to brighten, and the air was cold. Zimrah used the trunk of a nearby tree to pull herself up. Relief flooded her heart. She knew where she was. Capernaum, on the quiet street leading to Domitian's house. It was not that far away!

Thank you, Abba.

She took a step. Her head pounded, and her legs shook, but she continued, holding on to anything she could find to stay upright. A bit of wall, a tree, a shrub. She was almost there! Just a little more—one foot, then the other.

Breathe.

Pray.

Step.

Breathe.

Pray.

Step.

Her progress was painfully slow. What would have normally taken only a minute or two seemed to take an hour. She continued this way until finally, there was Domitian's door. She made it!

To her wonder and surprise, the door opened, and Theophilus and Domitian came out of it. At the sight of her husband, what remained of her strength gave way to pain, and she fell.

***

"Zimrah!" Theophilus vaulted the stairs and caught her before she hit the ground.

She was alive! Yahweh be praised! Looking at the state she was in though, made him want to cry then murder whoever had done this. Murder them slowly.

Her face was gaunt and pale. There was a bruise on her cheek, and her lips were cracked and bleeding. Her wrists were cut and bruised where she had obviously been bound. Theophilus cradled her head, and his fingers brushed a large lump in the back, just above her neck. Her hair was matted with dried blood, and she felt too light and frail in his arms.

"Dear God, Zimrah!" His heart was mixed with equal parts horror and guilt.

He should have followed his instincts and ridden to Capernaum before *this*. He should have stayed with her, come when she asked him in her letters. Regret stabbed like a sword. He should have abandoned everything to come with her when she first left Chasah. What a prideful fool he had been! His anger and jealousy seemed so meaningless now.

Domitian was at his side. "What have they done to her? Bring her inside! Quickly."

Theophilus carried her to her bed. She tried to smile at all the faces, but her cracked lips began to bleed. Theophilus didn't know where she had been or what had happened to her, but he wanted to reassure her. "We're all here, Zimrah. You're safe now." He focused on his wife to keep the murderous thoughts at bay.

"She needs water." Hannah brought Theophilus a wet towel, and he pressed the cloth to her lips. "Not too much. Slowly so her body has time to take it in."

Hannah hovered, as if she wanted to say or do more, but Theophilus was not leaving Zimrah's side. He needed time with her, and Zimrah needed him.

Zimrah lifted a trembling hand to rub the hairs on his cheek. Theophilus brushed a tangled lock of hair from her forehead and whispered his love to her.

***

"Theo." Was it really him? Was she dreaming again? Zimrah let the warmth of his body ground her.

"I'm so sorry," he whispered. "I should have been with you. I never should have let you come here alone."

"Not your fault." Her voice was barely above a whisper and still hoarse, but Theophilus was close enough to hear her.

"Who did this, Zimrah? Was it Saul?"

Zimrah only shook her head. She would not answer. It would do Theophilus no good if she did. He would want revenge. He might even kill Saul, but what would that bring except something else for him to regret?

She held no blame or malice in her heart. There was only joy that she was safe and back in Theophilus's arms. She lay on her own bed with the warmth of the morning sun streaming in through the windows. The handsome face of her husband was before her.

He offered the cloth, and blessed moisture rolled onto her swollen tongue. She swallowed. It was the sweetest water she had ever tasted. Zimrah nodded her thankfulness before all was black again.

***

"She's out." Theophilus turned to Hannah. "What does she need?"

"Honey and wine, please my lord," she said to Domitian who nodded gravely and hurried off.

"Set water to boil, will you please, Felix?"

"Yes, of course." He bowed and disappeared down the hall.

"Caius, we will need clean linen we can cut into strips for bandages."

"I'll get a sheet from the storage chamber."

Theophilus was impressed and rose from the bed so Hannah could take his place. She felt Zimrah's forehead and the pulse at her wrist. "She's been days without water. Probably food too."

"How do you know what to do?" Theophilus asked as Hannah pressed the wet cloth to Zimrah's lips.

"My husband was a hard man." Hannah adjusted herself on the bed so she could turn and look up at him while still holding onto Zimrah's wrist. "I've been beaten too many times to count. It was probably why I was so afraid of you when you first arrived. I had to nurse myself or allow myself to be nursed after the beatings. It taught me much. I never thought I'd be grateful for the knowledge until now."

Theophilus put a hand on her shoulder, thinking of the last few days from her perspective. He must have seemed like a

madman storming through the city, threatening every Pharisee he could get his hands on. When that proved unfruitful, he had paced the house, pestering her and Domitian with the same questions over and over again.

"What time was she taken? Where did it happen? Show me! How many were with Saul? What did they look like? Which direction did they go after they took her? Where in the city might they have taken her?"

Domitian had come to Hannah's rescue more than once. *"Leave her alone, Theo! She's told you all she knows!"*

Theophilus scrubbed his face with his hand. "I'm sorry I frightened you. I was just—"

"I know." Hannah looked down at Zimrah and pressed the cloth again. "You were worried for her. Now that I've seen you together, I understand. You were angry and frustrated. I felt the same way and wanted to help. I just didn't have any answers. It all happened so fast!"

"I was pretty intense, wasn't I?" Theophilus chuckled at himself and was grateful that Hannah did the same.

"Yes, you were! I thought, 'Is this the same Theophilus Servillian I've heard so much about? The one who *peacefully* negotiated the trade agreement in Tyre?'" Hannah laughed outright, and Theophilus joined her.

Now that Zimrah was out of danger, it felt good to laugh.

"I see why Zimrah loves you." His hand went to her shoulder again.

Hannah smiled. "I see why she loves *you* too."

Chapter 31

TO PLACES HE WOULD NEVER GO

No! Absolutely not!" Theophilus followed her into their
room in Domitian's house. "How can you even think of
going there now? After what you've just been through?"

A week had passed, and Zimrah finally seemed to be acting
like herself again. Under Hannah's care, her wounds were
almost completely healed, and the lump on the back of her
head had gone down. She pulled out their traveling bags from
beneath the bed.

"This is madness!" Theophilus cursed under his breath and
raked a hand through his hair. "You will be in danger again!
Jerusalem is a political firestorm waiting to happen, Zimrah.
Wait until after Passover at least, please! You know what the
city is like during feast times. Especially this feast and
especially this year!"

Theophilus had gotten word that Emperor Tiberius had
sent Pontius Pilate to see to all the rumors of rebellion coming
out of Jerusalem. He knew Pilate, knew what kind of man he

was and what kind of methods he preferred—the harsh and brutal kind.

Negotiations had concluded in Tyre. Commerce out of the port city was sailing smoothly again, and Emperor Tiberius had rewarded Theophilus for his good work by suggesting he go to Jerusalem to assist Pilate. He was not looking forward to the assignment. In fact, he was thinking extremely hard about how to politely decline, until Saul of Tarsus arrested Zimrah.

Even though Zimrah refused to say, Hannah had seen Saul take her. By all indications, he had been acting on authority from the Sanhedrin and had probably returned to Jerusalem after leaving Capernaum. Theophilus harbored ideas of following Saul to share a few *words* with him and the Sanhedrin. He would let his gladius do the talking.

Theophilus knew his wife. She would beg mercy for her captors. It was why she remained silent. So, he was more than a little surprised when she awoke after her ordeal insisting they return to the Holy City, together. In none of his daydreaming of the slow and painful demise of Saul of Tarsus was Zimrah there as witness.

Taking her by the hands—she was already packing for their trip—Theophilus brought her to sit on the bed with him. "Please Zim, you can't come with me." He sighed again to calm himself. "Tell me why you want to come."

"I don't know my purpose yet, just that we both have to be there. I have a feeling it's not for any reason either of us could imagine right now. I know only that she said we must go together."

"Wait. What? Who said?"

"There was a woman named Rebecca. She was there with me in the chamber at the end. She said we must go to Jerusalem. Both of us. I think she's an angel. I've seen her many times in my dreams, but she *was* there. Unless I was dreaming again when I saw her. It's all so jumbled in my mind."

Theophilus could only stare at his wife.

Perhaps the days without food or water, the fever combined with the blow she had taken to the head, had pushed her over the edge. Was she truly going mad this time?

"I know it doesn't make any sense to you, but—"

"I know." He sighed. "I have to trust you. Trust Yahweh. But you said yourself that you may be confused. How do you know Rebecca was real?"

"I don't know for sure. But I do know that Yahweh is leading us." Zimrah rubbed the worry lines on his forehead. "He knows the plans He has, Theo. Following Yahweh has always led us to good."

"Except when you were almost killed."

"*Almost.*" Zimrah smiled. "I'm still here."

Her smile was radiant. There was nothing he could do against it. Arguing any further was pointless. Confused or not, she would convince him. In truth, she already had.

"Alright. We'll go together, but you must stay by my side at all times. You are my shadow! Do you hear? No venturing about the city without me. Promise me."

"Yes, my lord. I promise."

In the end, Domitian's entire household was convinced. Everyone except Felix made the journey south. Everyone had at least one good reason to come along, besides seeing to

Zimrah's safety. Hannah would not leave her mistress's side. Domitian went along because if there was trouble on the road, two swords were better than one. Caius heard from the other followers that Yeshua had gone to Jerusalem for Passover, and so he went as well.

"I wonder why we'll be needed in Jerusalem." Zimrah walked beside Theophilus through the city gates of Capernaum. "I'm glad Yeshua will be there. I never did get to see Him the day I was taken. Perhaps in Jerusalem, I'll have the opportunity to speak to Him."

"I'm glad for the size of our company. It increases the number of eyes on you." He took her left hand and squeezed it, feeling the ring Yeshua had given her.

He had been upset when he first saw it, and the jealousy had risen again. But after hearing what it meant to her—and being assured by Domitian that she never saw Yeshua except in her dreams—his jealousy subsided. He agreed with her that something bigger must be happening, even if he didn't yet understand what. "I pray that this time, Yahweh's *good* won't lead you to more trouble."

***

Zimrah was impressed that Pontius Pilate had seen to a house for them in the Upper City, but it was barely used. Domitian felt right at home staying in Antonia Fortress, and Caius lodged with his master. Pilate kept Theophilus fairly busy, and Zimrah and Hannah spent most of their time with Sanya and Maarku.

They had gathered there for the Passover meal the night before, all except Theophilus, who had left earlier that day for Bethlehem on some errand for Pilate. Before he left though, he made Zimrah promise to stay inside Sanya's house until he returned.

After the Passover meal, Domitian and Caius said their goodnights and returned to the fortress. The night was quiet, and Zimrah fell asleep hoping when Theophilus returned in the morning he would come with her to find Yeshua.

Before the morning sun rose to shine its light on the Holy City, desperate pounding awakened the household. Zimrah followed Maarku—all his muscles tense—to the front gate.

"I am seeking Lady Zimrah," a cloaked woman panted breathlessly as he opened the front gate.

Maarku growled under his breath to have been so rudely awoken at this hour, but his shoulders relaxed slightly that it was no one more threatening than a lone woman at the gate.

Zimrah didn't know who it was until she spoke again. "Please, my lord. There is not much time!"

"Mary! What's happened?" Zimrah brushed past Maarku and ushered Mary of Magdala in, offering her a seat. Her friend hastily waved off the gesture. Sanya and Hannah entered the room as well.

"Forgive me, Zimrah. I have been searching for you. We didn't know where you were staying." Mary breathed with tears in her eyes. "It was Judas. He led the priests straight to the Teacher. There were Roman soldiers and Temple guards. Zimrah, they beat him in the night and took him before Caiaphas and the Sanhedrin. He is there now!"

Zimrah brushed away the tears that had fallen unbidden on her cheeks. She reached for her outer cloak and turned to find Hannah, Sanya, and Maarku standing nearby. "I know I promised Theophilus to stay here, but I must go to Yeshua." Zimrah expected them to protest her decision. Instead, they too pulled on cloaks and hoods.

Maarku held his staff. "I don't think Theophilus will mind as long as you are not alone. We will go with you, *Mwana*."

***

Theophilus's gallop slowed to a maddening canter and then a sickening trot as he neared Jerusalem. He had to admit, the road leading to the Holy City from the north was not as crowded as he had expected. At least Pilate had lent him a horse and he had not had to walk the five miles to and from Bethlehem. It was bad enough he had to miss the Passover meal with the others at Sanya and Maarku's. The lighter traffic leading into the city was most likely due to the fact that most had spent the night within its walls.

Now that the massive walls were in sight, the crowd was headed in the other direction, away from the city. He had to slow the horse before entering the gates, but there were not as many people as he would have thought. When he finally rode the stallion into Antonia Fortress, Domitian was there to greet him.

"Yeshua of Nazareth was taken in the night by the Sanhedrin." Domitian held the horse's head and looked up at Theophilus with furrowed brows.

"Where is she?" Theophilus slid from the horse like a force of nature. He was dressed in the garments of his station, as an emissary of Rome, and his mantle billowed behind him.

"She is safe, Theo." Domitian moved from the horse to Theophilus, struggling to hold him long enough to answer his question. "Amazingly, none of Yeshua's followers were arrested with him."

This finally slowed Theophilus's headlong rush. "Well, where *is* she? Is she at Sanya's? I need to see her."

"Theo, wait!" Domitian stopped him again with a hand to his chest. "She went down with them—to Golgotha."

"The Nazarene is being *crucified?*" Horror plastered on Theophilus's face like a mask.

Was there something he had missed? What had Yeshua done? How could they be crucifying him like some—some notorious criminal? He expected they would kill him, with a spear or a sword. But Crucifixion? Oh dear, sweet Zimrah! And she was there witnessing that atrocity?

"When?" Theophilus gritted his teeth, his jaw and fists clenched.

"They should be there now."

Theophilus started in that direction before his friend had finished speaking.

"Through the Damascus Gate!" Domitian called after him.

"You're not going with him?" Caius asked Domitian before Theophilus was too far away to hear.

Domitian's voice was flat and lifeless. "I have witnessed my fill of death."

Chapter 32

THE WAY OF SUFFERING

"Crucify him! Crucify him!" The crowd sounded like a pack of barking dogs around a corpse.

Zimrah's legs weakened beneath her at the sound. If Mary, mother of Yeshua, were not there with them, Zimrah might have given in to her panic. She must be strong for Mary. Instead of panicking, she held onto Sanya and Maarku for strength and prayed.

Abba Yahweh, is this truly happening? How can this be? Why? He is Your Son. He has done so much good, healed so many! Where are they now? Where are the blind men that now see? Where are the demon-possessed that He delivered? How can it be that so many scream for His death? He did nothing wrong!

A vast mob had gathered in the court of Pontius Pilate, the Roman governor. He was arguing with the crowd, saying he could find nothing this man had done that was worth a death sentence. Yet the crowd would not listen.

"Give us Barabbas!" a group of Pharisees at the front demanded.

Surely, Pilot will not listen. It was customary for a prisoner of the people's choosing to be released during Passover, but Barabbas? He was a notorious insurrectionist and murderer, rightly being held in prison for his crimes. Pilot would know this. *Release Yeshua instead.*

"Kill Yeshua, and release Barabbas to us!"

No!

"Why?" Pilate asked. "What crime has he committed? I have found no reason to sentence him to death. I will release him."

"No! No! Crucify Him!" the crowd insisted.

Only a few in the crowd protested for His release.

"No! Let him live!"

"Mercy!"

Their voices were overpowered in the roar of those who called for blood.

After this, Zimrah ignored the angry mob and the scorching of her heart because of them. Instead, she fixed her gaze on Yeshua. He stood there silent before them, beaten beyond recognition, His life-blood pouring into a pool at His feet. *Precious, gentle Yeshua.* Yet even now, in spite of how much pain He must have been suffering, there was peace resting upon Him.

She closed her eyes and saw the lamb from her vision at the Jordan River. The lamb's neck was wounded in sacrifice.

"Worthy is the Lamb who was slain—
to receive power and riches,
and wisdom and strength,
and honor and glory and blessing."

Zimrah sang quietly and took a deep breath to stifle the wail that rose in her throat. If she let it forth, it would never stop.

"Yahweh?" She sobbed, holding her head in her hands against the pressure that was building there.

"This must be."

Zimrah heard His still voice whisper, as if from right beside her, like a comforting arm around her shoulders.

"Do not be troubled or afraid. He is the Passover Lamb. He is fulfilling My purpose. With His blood, I am purchasing a people for Myself. This is not the end. It is the just beginning."

Understanding broke upon her, and her limbs trembled. It had all led to this! Since before her journey to Jerusalem began, Yahweh had been preparing her heart and mind for this truth. All the dreams and songs, the words of John the Baptizer, the visions, they were all for a specific purpose. Yeshua was the man of light who had died on the battlefield in her dream.

Even wrestling with the old woman spirit in Tyre was teaching her to leave the natural, fallen world behind and look to a higher place. All the writings of the patriarchs and the prophets for thousands of years had been about this day! Yeshua's eyes found her in the crowd and rested upon her just before he was led away to die.

Yeshua and two other convicted men were forced to take up the *patibulum*, a heavy wooden crossbar, upon their shoulders and walk the tight packed streets of Jerusalem. Roman soldiers tried to keep the people back, to clear the way, yet their arms and shields could not hold back the insults and jeers hurled by the crowd.

The other two men who had not been scourged with a whip of leather laced with rocks and broken glass, had an easier time carrying their load. Yeshua had little strength left, here at the beginning of this death march. What strength He had continued to flow out of Him with the blood that dripped from His back and head onto the wooden beam and Jerusalem's stone streets. He could not continue very far. By the third time He fell to the stone pavers, the soldiers had had enough.

"You!" One of the soldiers called to a dark-skinned man from the crowd. "Come here! Today you have been blessed by the gods to serve Rome!" The soldier sneered as the others laughed.

The legionnaire pulled the man from his wife and children.

"No! No!" His wife's cries mingled with those of the women who followed Yeshua.

With a grunt the soldier lifted the beam that had fallen on top of Yeshua. Another soldier helped him heave it onto the man's shoulders as his children screamed for him. He carried the wooden beam with Yeshua stumbling behind. Zimrah wanted to run up to Him, to help Him walk, to ease His suffering somehow, but she was locked in by the crowd.

Yeshua dragged His feet, His arms at His sides, His head and back stooped low as if still carrying the heavy beam.

Zimrah tried not to look at the trail of blood He left on the pavers. She kept her focus on Him. He seemed to be concentrating on staying upright, every step a portrait of pain and determination.

The condemned were herded through the gate in Jerusalem's wall to Golgotha, the place called skull. It was the place outside of the city where the enemies of Rome were crucified, near a crossing of many roads so all could see and fear.

Zimrah squeezed her eyes tight and covered her ears with her hands. She could still hear the screams of the other two condemned men. She had heard they were thieves, slaves as she'd once been. A soldier was assigned to each of them as a mounted centurion oversaw their execution. They were stripped naked, their hands and feet nailed to the hard wood, and their bodies lifted up for the scorn and contempt of the on-lookers.

Yeshua, with hardly the strength left to stand, waited as two other soldiers prepared His cross. The bottom of the *stipes*, the vertical bar of the cross, was bolted to the ground with a hinge-like mechanism. The soldiers took the *patibulum* from the man who'd been pulled from the crowd and attached the beam horizontally. One of the soldiers completed the task while the other busied himself with something Zimrah couldn't see.

"It is said this man is a king!" The soldier walked toward Yeshua with a crown fashioned from thorn-wood. Yeshua screamed as the soldier, with mock solemnity, mercilessly crowned Him and then dragged Him to the waiting cross.

Zimrah's head felt light. Her vision blurred with black spots, and her lungs screamed for air. Could this truly be happening?

Abba! Her mind reeled with images of Yeshua from her dreams—smiling, laughing, singing. His love had opened her understanding of Father Yahweh all the more. He had transformed her thinking. When she was with Him in the heavenlies, nothing was impossible.

Zimrah tried to remember all she had seen. The man made of light on the battlefield, the lamb that was slain. Yahweh had been warning her. Yet as the soldier lifted the hammer to strike iron into Yeshua's flesh, wails of sorrow tore from her throat. They mingled with the other women who were there with her and Yeshua's own screams.

She was not alone in her grief. To her right and left were others who mourned. Mary, mother of Yeshua, Mary of Magdala, Suzanna, and many of the other women were there to stand as witness. John, the only one of the twelve who had braved the fear of arrest, was also there to witness and to mourn. They had all known Him.

Zimrah opened her eyes as Yeshua's naked, bloodied, and disfigured body was lifted up for all to see. Taking hold of the hands of Hannah and Sanya beside her, Zimrah began to sing.

"Glory to the One who was and is and is to come.
Blessing to the One who reigns forever and ever.
Honor and power to the Lamb who is slain.

"Worthy is the Lamb—
to receive power and riches
and wisdom and strength
And honor and glory and blessing!

"Blessing to the One who reigns forever and ever.
Honor, glory, blessing, and strength!"

The song was taken up by all of the followers. They held hands, trading their wails for melody and strength. The song echoed and bounced off the close stone walls, causing a hush to fall over the hateful, jeering crowd. They sang until a bitter voice rang out above them all.

"Stop that!" one of the soldiers shouted.

When the singing continued, he took hold of a nearby *pilum* and advanced toward them.

"I said *stop!*"

The voices of the crowd joined in with the soldier's, calling for them to be silent. The others obeyed the soldier's command, yet Zimrah held her voice steadfast, ignoring the tightening grips of the hands she still held.

Sensing the soldier's advancement, Zimrah opened her eyes to see him marching toward her, spear in hand. She focused not on him or his *pilum*, but on the dark forces that swirled around and through him. This was their day, the day they held dominion, but not over her. She would die singing praise if that was what the Father desired of her.

Chapter 33

SALVATION HAS COME

I said *stop!*" The soldier's command rang out again.

All of the other voices hushed, except Zimrah. Her sweet voice rose above the raucous din. Theophilus could not quite distinguish the words, but the melody was familiar. It was amplified by the limestone walls that were Golgotha.

"Zimrah." He breathed her name.

Gathering his linen cloak with his left hand and drawing his gladius with his right, Theophilus ran for the source of the command in a mad sprint.

"Yahweh, please!" He prayed under his strained breath. "Help me reach her in time."

As the crowd and soldiers came into view, he saw that the one advancing on Zimrah had a *pilum* in his hand. *Almighty God! A pilum?* Death would be sure if he failed to reach her.

Theophilus had been riding all morning, but he forced his weary muscles to respond and ran even faster. Just as the soldier lifted the spear, Theophilus blocked his thrust with his own sword before it could silence her beautiful voice forever.

"I am Theophilus Servillian of Rome, Tiberius Caesar's ambassador from Tyre, and you will not touch these people!" Theophilus spoke with every bit of authority given to him by birth, experience, and station.

The soldier was so taken by surprise that he dropped the *pilum*. His face said it all. From where had this giant come? His gaze went from Theophilus's full height to the gladius in his hand to the signet ring upon his finger. He glanced at Zimrah behind him and then to his centurion. The centurion nodded, and the soldier quickly picked up the spear he had dropped and returned his attention to his work.

Theophilus didn't move an inch until the soldier's and centurion's attention turned elsewhere. He sheathed his sword and spun upon his wife.

"Zimrah! You are the bravest, most exasperating woman I have ever known!" He crushed her in a firm embrace and whispered in her ear. "Yahweh be praised! You're safe. How many times am I going to have to save your life, woman?"

"Theophilus! How? How did you know?" Zimrah stammered, her heart pounding against his broad chest.

"I saw Domitian. He told me what happened and that you were here." He took Hannah's and Sanya's outstretched hands to reassure them as well and nodded a greeting to Maarku.

A cry from one of the dying men brought their attention back to the reason they were all here.

Theophilus turned and took in the horror of the scene. "Was there nothing we could have done to stop this?"

Theophilus had witnessed far too many crucifixions. Yet none could have prepared him for this. Yeshua the Nazarene— whom others had called Teacher, Rabbi, Healer—was hanging from the middle cross.

Theophilus had not gone to see him, even when he had come to Tyre, the very city where he lived. Appius's wife Annia had gone and brought her daughter to be healed. Yeshua delivered her from an evil spirit, just as he had healed the gash in Theophilus's side. After hearing Annia's story, Theophilus had still not believed.

The Healer hung by his nailed hands and feet. One of his shoulders looked out of joint, and blood dripped from open wounds on his back and sides. Yeshua had been scourged before they nailed him to the cross.

The muscles in his legs quivered with exhaustion as they struggled to lift his body enough to breathe. His face, below a wicked looking crown fashioned from thorns, was a swollen mass of blood and bruised flesh. He'd been badly beaten. Patches of his beard had been pulled out.

Above his head there was a sign that read in Latin, Greek, and Hebrew, *Yeshua of Nazareth, the King of the Jews.* Yeshua had little time. He would not survive much longer.

"What happened?" Theophilus shook his head, his eyes fixed on the cross. "What did he do to deserve this?"

"Nothing. He did nothing but love," Zimrah said.

"Father, forgive them," Yeshua called out in a strangled voice. "For they know not what they do."

At this, the mob erupted with insults again.

"Listen to him," they scoffed.

"He saved so many others. Let him save himself!"

"Save yourself if you are truly the Messiah!"

"Or if not the Messiah, perhaps the Son of God can take himself down from that cross!"

"Perhaps he has not the *tools* to save himself?"

At this particular jeer, the crowd laughed and pointed at his nakedness. Some began to leave, heading back to the city. They patted each other on the back, proud of their wit and content to leave the insults to others.

One of the thieves dying beside Yeshua joined in the mockery. "Yes, save yourself and us too! Are you not the Christ?"

Part of Theophilus agreed with him. Could Yeshua not come down from the cross and prove to all those who scoffed, himself included, that he was indeed the Son of God?

"Have you no fear even of God?" the other thief said. "We deserve this punishment for our crimes, but he has done nothing to deserve this fate!"

Yeshua turned his head with great effort to look at the man who had spoken.

The man returned Yeshua's gaze. "Remember me when You come into Your kingdom."

"Truly, I say to you. This very day you will be with me in Paradise," Yeshua said.

The man broke into sobs of joyous tears.

Theophilus's heart raced, and his breath was tight in his chest. This man, this condemned criminal had more understanding in his final moments than Theophilus had in the past three years.

What was it all for? All of the miracles, all of the teachings that Zimrah had written to him about, was it all for this horrible, meaningless end? Could there be more? There *must* be.

The exchange he had just witnessed between Yeshua and the criminal burned in Theophilus's mind like a live coal among the ashes. He could see the peace and joy on the criminal's face even now. Obviously, there was some missing truth that he understood.

"When you come into your kingdom," he had said.

What kingdom could he be referring to? The teacher was on the verge of death. Yet, had not Yeshua answered him? Paradise. A paradise that would be his after death, that he would see *this very day.* Could that be it? Could there be a kingdom beyond this world where Yeshua truly was King? Was this kingdom what Zimrah saw in her dreams?

"Help me understand, Zim. What am I missing? Why does Yeshua have to die? Why like this?"

"He is dying for us." Zimrah placed a hand on his arm. "He is the Passover Lamb. He's being slain for us, for our sins, taking the punishment *we* deserve. His death is purchasing our freedom, Theophilus. He's making us right with God, now and forever, for those who have the courage to believe."

Courage.

Theophilus looked down at the tear-streaked face of his wife. Behind the sorrow, he saw the same peace the criminal shared, the peace that had always surrounded Zimrah like a light in the darkness.

Yahweh? Is it true?

"This is My beloved Son, in whom I am well pleased."

Theophilus recognized the voice of the Almighty for the first time, as if the Father himself were standing beside him.

"As I am pleased with you, my son, Theophilus Servillian."

With the voice came a sound like thunder, and the ground shook beneath their feet.

"Eli eli lama sabachthani," Yeshua cried out in a loud voice.

In the midst of a cloudless sky, darkness fell on the land, throwing the earth into shadow. Earthquake. Darkness. It was too much for the raucous mob. They screamed and ran for their lives until only the followers and the soldiers remained.

"It...is...finished." Yeshua struggled for His final breath.

Theophilus could remain standing no longer. He dropped to his knees and sobbed into his hands, his whole body quaking with the earth. "Forgive me, Yahweh! I've been so full of foolish pride! How wrong I've been!"

In that moment, Theophilus could feel Yahweh's acceptance, His pleasure. He was not angry. He was not withholding His love until Theophilus could prove his worth and commitment to Him. Theophilus was forgiven, his unbelief forgotten as if it had never been. Just as the criminal who hung beside Yeshua, Theophilus had found paradise.

When the earth stopped its shaking, Zimrah's gentle hand on his shoulder caused him to look up. Yeshua breathed no more.

"It's over. He's gone," Theophilus said.

"No, my love." Zimrah smiled through her tears. "This is not the end. It is just the beginning."

THE END.

Epilogue

The beast stood atop the hill of Golgotha with an overwhelming sense of doom curdling his stomach.

The Son was dead. His lifeless body hung limply from the wooden beams. He should be elated! He had finally won. Hadn't he? Around the time when the first nail was hammered home though, the beast began to think twice. Something just didn't feel right.

Now that he thought about it—it had been too easy. Had he played this all wrong? How had things spun out of his control so quickly? The beast looked down at the little mewling singer girl, standing at the foot of the cross.

Zimrah!

Even in her sorrow, she had been singing heaven songs! Ugh! He had almost silenced her once and for all, but again, that accursed Roman ruined it! He had appeared out of nowhere and blocked the spear with his sword! *Who does that? Who walks in front of a pilum with just a short sword?* And the worthless, little dung of a soldier had backed down! The centurion too!

"Grraahh!"

Where had he gone wrong? With narrow eyes, the beast looked at Zimrah again, beginning to analyze the last three years in his mind. He *had* missed something. Something big. Was it her songs? Was that why he had not seen this situation more clearly? Was it her? Had it been her incessant singing that had blinded him? No! Could it be?

The beast turned his gaze to the One, now dead by his hand. He hoped the grizzly sight would boost his spirits, but he only felt the sinking feeling in his stomach again. Something was definitely wrong with this whole thing.

When the earth had quaked and the darkness fell, it startled him. The ridiculous underlings around the cross began to salute, cheering his praise. Until he silenced them with a blast of fire from his mouth.

"This is not my doing, you *idiots!*" he roared.

Three of his princes swooped down from the sky in a panic.

"Excuse our interruption, my lord." Astarte was already bowing and cringing at their breach of protocol.

"We know you didn't summon us, oh Despicable One." Baal was laying it on thick. Perhaps it had been the sight of the beast blasting a few of his underlings with fire that put the tremor in his voice. "But we thought you would want to know."

"Want to know what?" Usually, he would be less irritated by their groveling, but the disappearance of the sun at midday was distracting him.

"Heaven is celebrating, my lord!" Melqart blurted as the others glared at him.

"What? Why?" How could they be celebrating at a time like this? "Look! Don't you see? I just killed the Son!" Something was not copasetic, but could that something be big enough to make heaven rejoice? Now? It made no sense!

"Yes, lord, but He's not returned to heaven as you thought." Baal gestured to the middle cross for emphasis. "He's come to us! The veil in the temple just split in two, and He's kicked down the gates!"

"What? Which gates?" the beast asked.

"Death!" Astarte cried.

"And The Grave!" Melqart howled.

"They're gone, my lord!" Baal hollered.

"Who?" The beast's stomach was really bubbling now.

"The captives, sir!" Baal said.

"How many?" The beast's face turned red with shame. He knew exactly which captives Baal was referring to.

"All of them." The princes answered in unison.

It was then that the beast remembered the Son's final words.

"It is finished," He had said.

Indeed. It was.

Author's Conclusion

Courage. The Lamb has been slain. It is finished. The price has been paid, for you and for me, Beloved. Every day can be a new beginning, the beginning of a journey into ever deeper places with Yeshua, our King. There is so much more to be experienced with Him.

I know this is true because I have been where Zimrah has been. I have seen what she has seen. Her journey of intimacy with Yeshua, the Nazarene is mine, and if it has stirred your heart in the slightest, it can be yours for the asking. *Knock and the door will be opened. Seek and you will find.* The King has revealed much of Himself to you already. He appears in many forms to those who have learned to see.

I am so honored that you have taken this journey with me, Beloved. If this story has been your first introduction to the One called Christ, I am honored all the more. Accepting the gift He died to give you is as easy as the man who died beside Him discovered. If you long for a new beginning, pray this prayer with me.

Yeshua, Jesus, thank you for the price that You paid for my freedom. You bore the punishment I deserved for my sin. I see my need of You. I don't want to live my life alone any longer. I want to live it with You. I accept You as my Lord, and Savior and ask You into my heart and into my life. I understand that You are the way, the truth and the life. I desire to follow where You lead me, to live a life of faith from this day forward.

Thank you for giving me Your Holy Spirit and for making me new. In You, Jesus, I am free from the power of sin and death now and forever. Hallelujah, amen!

Glory to God in the highest heights! The person this story reveals, and to whom you just prayed, will change your life. You will never be the same.

If you are already walking with Him, I pray this story encourages you to even deeper intimacy. Living with Yeshua is such an adventure, isn't it? One that puts us on the road we were born to walk. Let's live every day in expectancy to see and be with Him as we remain in His love. He is our guide to discovering the unfailing love of the Father's heart.

Love to you always,
Susan Valles

Coming Soon!

Prologue

The Spirit breathed deep, recalling the sensation like cool water flowing into a dry desert place. He closed His eyes. Heaven. Earth. Time. Breath. A single day, four thousand years. Any amount of time was too long a wait for the marriage of the created with the Uncreated One.

Oh, how He had missed the Bride, but the wait was over. The time had finally come again, if not yet in fullness. Even in measure, some was better than none.

The stone was cold under His feet and the sealed chamber was silent and dark. A sparkle flared in His eye, lighting His face and the chamber like the rising sun. His vocal chords stirred and vibrated the earth around Him. The resulting sound rumbled like thunder in the rocks and summoned a host of harmonious accompanying voices.

Darkness trembles in the light,
When the Sons of God arise.

Arise, arise, arise,
Sons of God arise.

Mountains melt like wax,
When the Sons of God arise.

Arise, arise, arise,
Sons of God arise.

The dead come alive,
When the Sons of God arise.

Arise, arise, arise,
Sons of God arise.

Hallelujah.
Sons of God arise.

The Spirit danced in the light to the rhythm of the song and His rapidly beating heart, throwing sparks of lightning and color with every move. He couldn't help Himself, the joy was just too great.

He knelt beside the raised stone and spoke the Name above all other names.

"Yeshua."

Space and time in the stone chamber bent outward. The reality between heaven earth stretched just short of breaking as the breath from His mouth washed over the still, linen covered form. The Spirit watched as living creatures in His breath merged with flesh. Love, joy, peace, and the rest all found their home in the body of the Son.

What was wrapped in the chords of death a moment before, exploded in a flash of light brighter than any that had ever been. The Spirit did not blink, but if He had, He would have missed it. Eternity in the blink of an eye.

The Son breathed in the breath the Spirit breathed and His body transformed in the light into something new, the first of many.

Reunited with the Son, the Spirit danced with Him in fire and light through the rough stone tomb. The fire within illuminated the rocks and trees, the grass and the wide eyes of the soldiers. That is before they fell to the ground and hid their faces. They were unable to take the weight of glory.

"Soon," whispered the Son.

The Spirit's skin tingled as He nodded His agreement. *"This is the day. The glorious birth of the people that will."*

For more information on the latest releases, music, podcasts, videos, books, and more visit www.susanvalles.com and subscribe!